VICTOR
IN
TROUBLE

VICTOR

IN

TROUBLE

A SATIRE BY
ALEX FINLEY

Smiling Hippo Press

For information about this title or to order other books and/or electronic media, contact the publisher:
Smiling Hippo Press
SmilingHippoPress.com

ISBNs:
softcover: 978-0-9972510-4-3
eBook: 978-0-9972510-5-0

Printed in the United States of America
Cover and Interior design: 1106 Design

For John, the other John, Ben, Tom, George, Alex, and James

Also by Alex Finley
Victor in the Rubble
Victor in the Jungle

"Not intelligence collection, but subversion; active measures to weaken the West, to drive wedges in the Western community alliances of all sorts, particularly NATO, to sow discord among allies . . ."

—Oleg Kalugin, former head of Foreign Counter-intelligence, KGB, explaining Russian Active Measures

---

"America first!"

—Donald Trump

"It is our conclusion . . . that the Russian intelligence services' assault on the integrity of the 2016 US electoral process[,] and Trump and his associates' participation in and enabling of this Russian activity, represents one of the single most grave counterintelligence threats to American national security in the modern era."

—US Senate Select Committee on Intelligence bipartisan report on Russian Active Measures Campaigns and Interference in the 2016 US Election, Volume 5, p. 948

"Italians first!"

—Matteo Salvini, head of Italy's League party

"A close aide to Italy's deputy prime minister Matteo Salvini held covert talks to pump Russian oil money to his far-right party."

—BuzzFeed News, July 10, 2019

PROLOGUE

Valeriy Chekhov dusted off his Academy Award. *"Moy dorogoy Oskar,"* he said, as he caressed his dear golden statue. He displayed his most prized possession on a shelf above his desk at Lubyanka, the headquarters of the Russian Federal Security Service, or FSB, one of Russia's intelligence agencies. He laughed, placing the Oscar back in its prominent position. None of his predecessors at the KGB had managed to win an Academy Award from America. They had released several films over the years, but their propaganda had appealed more to a domestic audience. An American film award had been elusive.

The 1956 film *A Cabbage Utopia* had been a triumph, of course. Even in the heady days of perestroika, when Valeriy had first seen it as a high schooler thirty years after its release, its message reverberated among him and his comrades. It followed a hard-working crop laborer named Aleksei, who joyously tilled the soil in the name of the proletarian revolution. His beautiful wife, Katya, spent the film concocting an array of delicious cabbage-based dishes, which she would deliver with a smile to her rugged, dirt-smudged husband as he returned from a productive day in the field. As she pranced out to greet him, she sang a moving rendition of the title song—"Cabbages from our motherland's womb, protect us from a capitalist doom," Valeriy sang, remembering—and twirled her skirt as her red hair cascaded out from under her kerchief. The film, and the red-haired Katya specifically, had stirred yearnings in Valeriy's teenage mind years ago, compelling him to protect the revolution and ultimately setting him on his path up through the ranks of his beloved country's spy service.

But the film had not excelled internationally. The United States and its allies—"the West," Valeriy sneered—was deep in its red scare at the time, fearful of any notion of Bolsheviks, revolution, and dependence on cabbage. Other leftist revolutionary groups around the world, who, Valeriy was sure, would have loved *A Cabbage Utopia*, were unable to enjoy its message of perseverance, as they most often found themselves without access to a functioning film projector or a reliable supply of electricity. Such was the struggle in those days.

Another film, *Spy Me Up, Spy Me Down*, had deeply affected Valeriy. The movie was a tribute to the KGB, the omnipotent and omniscient spy service of the USSR. Two intrepid Soviet spies, Georgy Markov and Peter Averin, foil an American spy who has crossed the Finnish border through the forest. The American attempts to steal information about Soviet military bases in the area and tries to romance the daughter of a top Soviet general. The two Soviet spies utilize advanced technical equipment—including a shoe with a heat sensor that allows them to pursue the American as he tries to hide in the forest, and a walking cane that strapped onto the spy's back, allowing him to fly—to track the American.

The film's climax featured a heart-stopping car chase through Leningrad; the American in a stolen taxi, the Soviets in a sexy black Volga with a silver racing stripe down the side. Years later, when Valeriy discovered Western cinema, he realized the car chase scene in *Spy Me Up, Spy Me Down* looked remarkably like that in the James Bond film *Goldfinger*, although Bond's Aston Martin looked gauche, in Valeriy's mind, compared to Markov and Averin's Volga. He determined the Western moviemakers had stolen the car chase scene from *Spy Me Up, Spy Me Down*, conveniently overlooking the fact that *Goldfinger* had been made two years before *Spy Me Up, Spy Me Down*.

Many other Soviet propaganda films had flopped altogether. *The Five-Year Engagement* was meant to be a love letter to the Communist Party's centralized economic plans, each of which was to push development in particular sectors over a five-year period. *The Five-Year Engagement* was to be about the Party's sixth five-year plan. Anatoly Ilyushin, a dashing actor with a Stalinesque mustache, played the lead role of Yevgeni, a worker in a factory producing irons. Yevgeni falls in love with Eva, a girl-next-door-type who counts out the tiny screws Yevgeni needs to assemble his irons. The two agree to hold off their wedding until after the factory meets its five-year production quota. The moment of their engagement was to be a touching scene, with Yevgeni promising Eva her very own iron as a wedding gift and the two of them sealing the deal with a handshake under a portrait of Joseph Stalin holding an iron in the air triumphantly, encouraging his workers to seize the means of production. But the Party abandoned the five-year economic plan two years in, then adopted a new seven-year economic plan, throwing production of *The Five-Year Engagement* into chaos.

When Ilyushin got sent to Siberia for shaving off his mustache, the production of the film never recovered.

Crush the West was a romance-slash-thriller in which the lead character, Luka Elkin, travels to a United Nations meeting in New York as an aide to the Soviet leader and promptly falls in love with a Times Square hooker, Sally Oswald, whom he proceeds to save from the decadent capitalist system that forced her into her sorry situation. During filming, the head of the props department was sent to West Berlin to purloin a Pepsi can for the movie's climactic scene: Sally—upon learning from Luka that blow jobs are supposed to be a manifestation of love, not dirty money—would crush a can of Pepsi with one sticky hand, symbolizing her decision to crush the West and return to Mother Russia with Luka. Unlike the fictional hooker, however, the actual head of the props department found that life in West Berlin sipping Pepsi suited him quite nicely. He defected. The film was never completed.

Post-Soviet Union attempts had also stalled. In the early years after the end of the USSR, many producers had tried to rewrite old scripts, but replacing reverence to socialism with the notion that capitalism was good proved a hefty task. And while investment was easier to come by—suddenly everyone wanted to spend money in Russia!—so many film crews were finding other, more lucrative, opportunities, such as opening Burger King franchises or selling off Soviet submarines for five hundred actual American dollars. Everyone was still getting a hang of capitalism, at that point, but no one much felt like concentrating on making propaganda films.

Despite these setbacks, Valeriy pursued the milieu of propaganda as he entered the FSB in the mid-1990s. But this, he thought, admiring his Oscar, was more than he could have imagined.

Winning America's top film award for a propaganda film he had shepherded from beginning to end was such a proud moment. He hadn't given a thank you speech, of course. He couldn't be present at the awards. No one knew of his involvement.

Blackhouse had taken America by storm. It was the dramatic reenactment of the life story of Lawrence Blackhouse, a young American who had worked for different US intelligence agencies and defected to Russia with millions of classified American intelligence documents, which were disseminated by the Committee for Clear and Candid Policy. CCCP, as it was known, claimed to be a transparency organization, but in reality, Valeriy and his colleagues held some sway with the group's leader. Although the actual Blackhouse liked to believe he was a hero who was informing the American public about government surveillance, in reality, Valeriy's colleagues had quietly helped lead Blackhouse to the edge of treason, nudging him to steal the documents while making him believe it was all his idea to begin with and that he would be a hero for doing it. Valeriy's colleagues had then helped build the narrative that Blackhouse was a hero, successfully getting a large group of Americans to buy into the story, including a number of Hollywood actors, who often took to social media to laud Blackhouse the man and attack anyone who questioned why he ended up in Russia (Valeriy's colleagues had also made sure Blackhouse would eventually end up in Russia, but they were fine with that part of the story being left out). As Valeriy and his comrades had hoped, Blackhouse the man became a polarizing figure in America, with half the country believing him to be a hero who blew the whistle on a heavy-handed state surveillance system, and half the country calling him a traitor for stealing secrets and absconding to Moscow.

When Valeriy first hit on the idea of making a film about Blackhouse, he sought out the famous Hollywood director Peter Oliff, who had a history of traveling often to Russia and had spoken publicly about his love of the country. He also had a history of being against the US establishment. One of his previous films, about the assassination of a US president, pinned the murder on a deep state cabal led by America's top intelligence agency, the CYA—the ultimate nemesis for Valeriy and his comrades. The director was the perfect match for Valeriy's film project.

Valeriy had approached Nikolai Surikov, a businessman who had bought the state-run gas company, RosGaz, for fifty-two dollars when the new Russia was still finding its footing. Surikov was now one of the country's richest men. Valeriy met with the oligarch and suggested he use one of his subsidiaries in the United States to pitch the concept of *Blackhouse* the movie to the American director and sweeten the offer with a large investment in production of the film. The oligarch understood—correctly—that Valeriy's suggestion was a direct order from Russian President Darko Vlastov. Vlastov was generous with businessmen like Surikov, as long as they understood their own responsibilities on behalf of the president and never forgot who allowed them to hold positions that made them powerful and rich.

The film was a masterpiece of propaganda masquerading as a cinematic interpretation of liberal ideals. Lance Whitaker, a young whippersnapper of an actor who was active in California's tyrannical vegan movement and who had vocally supported Blackhouse the man, played him in the movie. The story portrayed Blackhouse as a computer genius from a young age who was ostracized by his contemporaries, who couldn't bear being unable to match his intellectual superiority. He later joins the military. Despite having spent most of his childhood sitting in front of a computer not moving, he is on the verge of proving his physical strength and dexterity when a teammate, consumed with envy of Blackhouse's skills, trips him during an obstacle course contest, sending Blackhouse tumbling and breaking both his legs. Nevertheless, Blackhouse, the hero that he is, drags himself through the mud and across the finish line as dramatic music crescendos. Blackhouse then returns to his computer chair, this time at the CYA, where his colleagues once again spurn him because they can't endure their inferiority. He discovers a deep-state bureaucracy run amok, with the government listening in on every phone call in America, logging every keystroke on the internet, and filing away every dick pic for posterity. One of the movie's climactic scenes shows a government official jacking off while listening to Blackhouse's grandmother on the phone. Blackhouse realizes only he can save the country from itself.

Valeriy made sure certain parts of the story were left out. The film had no scenes of Valeriy's comrades meeting Blackhouse—in Geneva, in Los Angeles, in Hawaii—telling him he'd be doing his country a major service by exposing his government's hypocrisy (his comrades were never so crass they would direct him to steal top secret documents; when possible, they used a much more subtle approach). Nor were there any scenes of Blackhouse allowing himself to be represented by lawyers Valeriy's comrades had hand-picked, precisely because they were former FSB colleagues. And there certainly was no scene of Blackhouse living in an apartment in Moscow paid for by the FSB after Blackhouse had been fully debriefed and squeezed of his knowledge of America's intelligence apparatus.

Blackhouse the movie broke box office records its opening weekend and Oscar buzz began shortly after. In fact, the Oscar campaign was organic. Valeriy had not choreographed it. The ads in *Variety* and a billboard over Sunset Boulevard showing a mud-streaked Whitaker as he crossed the obstacle course finish line with his broken legs—the words "Being a patriot can be a dirty job" under the picture—were part of a very real swell of support for the film. It culminated with *Blackhouse* winning Best Picture. The real Blackhouse, the man, virtually attended the *Vanity Fair* Oscars after-party, streaming through Skype on an iPad attached to a Segway he controlled from Moscow. He did vodka shots with Lance Whitaker.

Valeriy stood back to make sure his Oscar statue was properly centered on the shelf. The sun glinted off the gold. Valeriy smiled. Blackhouse, both the film and the man, had been a major coup for Valeriy and his comrades, but the operation almost seemed quaint when he thought about what they were planning next. The divisions Blackhouse had wrought on American society would seem like minor hiccups in comparison. Valeriy and his comrades had something much bigger planned this time, an operation that would polarize not just American society to the point of political paralysis. Valeriy was about to use his propaganda machine to split the entire Western alliance—"the West," he sneered again—and bring America and her European allies to their knees.

CHAPTER ONE

"You'll finally see where your grandmother is from," Victor said to Oliver, as the wide-bodied airplane banked over the impossibly blue Mediterranean Sea. "So much history. So much culture." He was bursting with excitement as he turned from the window toward his son. The teenager looked unimpressed. Victor thought for a moment then said, "You're going to eat really well for the next two years."

"Now you have my attention," said Oliver.

Victor smiled. "Fettuccini with porcini mushrooms. Strozzapreti with zucchini flowers and bacon. The best ice cream in the world. Valpolicella wine."

"Yes, please!" said his wife, Vanessa, sitting on the other side of him.

"Amarone wine. Barolo wine." He stared off into the distance. The plane began its descent, but Victor's head was still in the clouds. "My retirement tour in Rome." He sighed with delight.

CYA case officer Victor Caro had been thrilled when he got the assignment to Rome Station. After nearly twenty years chasing terrorists, dismantling guerilla groups, and staring down dictators, he was ready for a low-key but fun tour in the Eternal City. He had been born in Italy and spent his early years there. Fluent in both the language and the culture, he was eager to immerse himself and his family in the many pleasures of his heritage and to end his career far from the politics of Washington, DC, and Director, the headquarters of the CYA. This tour in Rome was a chance to enjoy one of the world's most beautiful cities and to eat and drink his way to the finish line, when he could walk away knowing he had served his country for two decades but was still young enough to pursue a new adventure of his own, free of the bureaucracy of the US government.

"Two years to eat pici al ragù and decide if I prefer wine from the Veneto or Piedmont region," Victor said. "Then I change my mind and try another bottle and change my mind again, repeating ad infinitum. Two years in Italy coasting to retirement, then sailing on my own boat into the horizon."

Vanessa Caro looked out at the sea. "What are we going to name the boat?" An FBI special agent, she had also managed to land a job in Rome. She joked that the stars had aligned, but in reality, she had aligned them. When she learned of the job opening in Rome for Victor, she had walked approximately 132 miles over the course of two weeks through the halls of FBI headquarters in Washington, talking, arguing, and flirting with anyone who could help her line up a position at the US Embassy in Rome. She hated coffee, but in those weeks, she drank it with anyone who knew anyone who might be able to pull a few strings. It had worked. She had landed the position of legal attaché, the FBI's representative, at the embassy in Rome.

"How about Sparklepony?" Vanessa said.

Victor gave her a look and shook his head. "The boat will be named No Pants. Because that's how I plan to live in my retirement."

The plane touched down and the Caro family weaved their way through the airport. Hundreds of people were waiting in line at passport control, where only two agents were working. One got up and said to the other, "Espresso?" and walked away. Victor walked around the line to a small side aisle, over which was a sign that read, "Diplomats." The Caros marched past the waiting, disheveled hordes who seemed to give off fumes of exhaustion after their long flights from around the globe, and went straight to an agent who waved them through after a quick scan of their documents. A teenage girl in the long line sneered at Oliver. He winked at her.

They arrived at baggage claim and dropped their backpacks on the floor. They waited for the carousel to start, their bodies and minds oscillating between the fatigue of jet lag and the adrenaline rush of starting a new adventure. It had been an overnight flight from Washington, but none of them had slept.

As they waited, they stared robotically at a television above the carousel. A graphic of the United States flashed as the Italian presenter said, "We turn now to the upcoming presidential election in the United States. An anonymous child has come forward to tell her story about how US Democratic presidential hopeful Willa Bennett tried to steal her kidney at a campaign rally earlier this year. The ice cream magnate, whose catchphrase 'This kid needs an ice cream!' became a campaign sensation after her young son had a tantrum at a political rally in the spring, has been the focus of criticism from conservative political activists, as well as from the extreme vegan movement, which takes offense at her promotion of lactose products."

Victor and Vanessa each groaned. "I thought we'd gotten away from this nonsense," Victor said.

He recalled how, shortly after the infamous rally when Bennett first held up her crying son and said, "This kid needs an ice cream!" to thunderous applause, obscure blogs and social media accounts with no followers had begun to spread rumors that her ice cream products were made with slave labor. The story had worked its way through the media ecosystem, the narrative blossoming along the way, eventually birthing a conspiracy theory implying that Bennett was murdering children and making ice cream from their kidneys. "Kid needs ice cream sounds a lot like KIDNEY ice cream. Coincidence? #KidneyIceCream" was a common message, repeated—verbatim—across a number of social media platforms by users with long strings of consecutive numbers in their names. "Willa Bennett Tried to Steal My Kidney!" was a headline that screamed in enormous letters from the top of the tabloid paper *The National Inquisitor*, which lined grocery store checkout lanes across the country and was owned by a big supporter of Bennett's opponent, Republican Senator Richard Redd.

The story had passed, as well, to the conservative news media. "Is Willa Bennett cultivating children's kidneys to help her ice cream empire?" Kip Lawson, a personality on the conservative channel Facts News, whose motto was, "Truth, the Right Way," had asked on his show one night. "Are we, as a nation, prepared to simply *hand over* our offsprings' internal organs so *she* can reap the benefits?" he continued, staring into the camera and looking like an angry, quivering, congealed blob of mayonnaise come to life.

He then showed a photograph of a young Hollywood star, Amber Vanderkamp, wearing flip-flops and cut-off shorts and holding her hair back while she licked an ice cream outside one of Bennett's ice cream shops. "Amber," Lawson said, staring deep into the camera. "Why do you hate America?"

Adding to the clamor had been the Committee for Clear and Candid Policy, the same organization that had disseminated the US documents Lawrence Blackhouse—the former American intelligence officer now living in Moscow—had stolen. Just last week, as Victor and Vanessa had been knee-deep in packing boxes, the group's web site, CCCP.org, had published thousands of emails purportedly from Willa Bennett's company. The emails had been procured by Russian government hackers, Victor knew, specifically, a Russian military intelligence group known as Pickled Bear. Many of the emails were uninteresting. Some had been doctored. Together, according to the conservative media ecosystem, they painted a picture of a power-hungry woman ready to sell— literally, according to one doctored email—her grandmother's kidney for success.

Despite being in the middle of preparing for an international move and actively trying to avoid the story, Victor had nonetheless been overwhelmed by insane media reports. "Willa Bennett Accused of Killing Children, Harvesting Organs for Ice Cream," had been a typical headline, Victor recalled. It was a true headline—people had accused her of this—but the sensational nature of the headline and the reality buried in paragraph forty-two of the news article—that Bennett had not, in fact, harvested children's organs for ice cream, or for any other reason—made adherence to objective truth a whimsical fantasy.

Victor looked at the television above the baggage carousel as the Italian presenter continued with the report about the child who was allegedly a victim of Willa Bennett. "The child gave an exclusive interview last night to New Russia News. Let's go to the tape."

New Russia News, Victor knew, was a media channel funded by the Russian government. The US government suspected it received direct orders from the Kremlin about talking points and narratives to promote. For weeks now, the channel had been reporting that Bennett was trafficking humans to feed her slave-dependent ice cream factories.

The screen cut away from the news anchor to show a young girl in blond pigtails, her legs sticking straight out on the chair because she was so small. She held a stuffed bear, whose name was Pickles, according to a heart nametag around the bear's neck. The girl's face was pixelated to hide her identity. The letters NRN, the logo for New Russia News, appeared in the lower left-hand corner of the screen.

"Ms. Bennett brandished an ice cream, and I thought, what a special treat." NRN had dubbed over the little girl's voice with a man's deep tenor. Victor figured this, too, was meant to obscure the girl's identity. But the words, also, seemed disjointed, coming as they were from a toddler.

"Do four-year-olds talk like that?" Oliver asked.

"No," Victor and Vanessa said in unison. All three Caros cocked their heads to the side, looks of bemusement on their faces as the interview continued.

"As I reached for the ice cream, she snatched it away, as though teasing me, taunting me. Then she touched me here." The girl placed a tiny hand on her lower back. "You can have the ice cream only if you give me your kidney."

"She made it clear to you that you had to trade your kidney to get the ice cream?" the NRN interviewer asked.

"Yes," said the dubbed voice. "It was clear she intended to give me the treat only if I allowed the extraction of my blood-filtering organ. Ms. Bennett demands this of all children who want ice cream. I personally know many children who have willingly made this trade."

A beep went off and an orange light above the baggage carousel began blinking. The first pieces of luggage appeared and began their slow, circular journey.

"There's no way anyone can fall for such crap," Victor said.

"I'm less sure," said Vanessa. "People like mobs and conformity."

"They made up what the little girl was saying," Oliver said. "That's so obviously propaganda, Mom."

"See?" Victor said to his wife. "The teenager gets it. Anyway, I'm glad we're far away from the insanity of the election. There's one of our bags." He leaped forward to grab it.

"Didn't you and Dad once have to deal with the guy who's running against Bennett?" Oliver asked Vanessa. "Senator Dick Head?"

"Oliver!" Vanessa chastised him. "His name is Richard Redd and he's a United States senator."

Victor returned with a piece of luggage. "Why are you talking about Senator Dick Head?" he asked.

"You see?" Oliver said to his mother. Vanessa gave Victor a stern look.

"What?" said Victor.

Vanessa said to Oliver: "A few years back, your dad and I worked together to stop a terror plot in Georgia. The mastermind behind that operation was a West African named Omar al-Suqqit, and he was funded by a Middle Eastern prince. That same prince was a generous donor to Senator Dick Redd, who is now the Republican nominee for president. In an effort to keep the money flowing into his campaign coffers, he went out of his way to block our investigation."

"And that's why you call him Senator Dick Head," said Oliver.

"Can we please not discuss the election?" Victor said, dragging the last pieces of luggage toward Vanessa and Oliver. "That nonsense is far away." He looked at Vanessa. "You don't have to deal with it anymore."

Vanessa hoped he was right. Senator Redd had again crossed her path recently in Washington. She had been working in the FBI's counterintelligence division and had been assigned to a small, discreet task force, nicknamed "The Eagles." The group had been handed the unenviable task of investigating malign Russian actors, who, the Eagles believed, were trying to influence the upcoming presidential election, and, worse, whether they were helping the campaign of Senator Richard Redd.

She had spent her summer, before packing up the apartment and boarding the plane to Rome, surveilling Diana Abrams. The sophisticated and petite Diana Abrams was actually Diana Abramovich, a Russian intelligence officer living deep undercover in Washington. Diana worked as a real estate agent, but, like other Russian illegals, her sole objective was to collect intelligence for and work to advance the agenda of Mother Russia.

One day, Vanessa had tailed her to a quaint neighborhood near Glover Park, in Washington's northwest district. There, she had observed Diana walk up the front stoop of a light blue, brick home and ring the bell. A few seconds later, a thin, brown-haired woman answered the door. Vanessa had nearly choked when she saw her. She was Ashley-Anne Wynscott. The woman had done some past work for Russian oligarch Nikolai Surikov, but she was currently campaign manager for presidential candidate Senator Richard Redd. Vanessa recalled holding her breath as she had watched Redd's campaign manager welcome Diana Abrams, née Abramovich, into her home.

Exactly what had transpired inside might never be discovered. Vanessa did know, however, that the house had sold a week later for $3 million, about three times the average home price in the area. Maybe Diana Abrams was an outstanding realtor. On the other hand, the buyer was Dimitri Rostov, the head of New Russia News for North America.

Victor spoke to Vanessa again. "It's not your problem anymore. We're in Italy!" He spread his arms wide, gesturing all around him. "*Andiamo!*"

They grabbed their bags and walked outside, where they spotted a man in a black suit holding a sign that said, "CARO." They piled in the car and the embassy driver shot down the autostrada then turned off into the southern part of the city. They passed the Circus Maximus, where chariot races were once held, drove around the Colosseum, and entered the heart of the city's historic center. Victor and his family took in the sites with wonder and excitement. The car passed through leafy Villa Borghese, one of the city's main parks, then deposited the Caros in front of a ritzy yellow building in the upscale Parioli neighborhood.

They entered the apartment that would be their home for the next two years. Like most traditional Roman apartments, it was made up of an immensely wide hallway, with rooms running off the sides. Oliver ran down the corridor. "I could skateboard in here." He turned to his parents. "Or we could bowl."

None of their belongings had arrived yet, so the place was temporarily furnished with the cheapest, most basic furniture the embassy housing office could find. Sparing every expense, the office employees had brought in the bare minimum the family would need. The small square dining table was accompanied by exactly three chairs. The living room was sparse with only two faux leather seats.

"Oliver's young," Victor said to Vanessa. "You and I get to sit. He can stand."

They peeked in the kitchen. All the temporary plates and kitchenware sat wrapped in paper inside a flimsy box that had been unceremoniously dropped in the middle of the kitchen. A knife was sticking out through the cardboard.

Victor, Vanessa, and Oliver didn't care. They ran through the apartment calling to each other to check out this or that space and assigning rooms. "This one's mine!" Oliver said from the biggest bedroom at the end of the hallway.

They had the weekend to enjoy before they had to report to their respective offices, and they spent those days traversing the city streets. Victor's enthusiasm was palpable and contagious.

"Everyone loves to do operations in Rome," he said to Vanessa, pointing out locations for brief encounters or dead drops as they turned down tiny alleys and discovered hidden courtyards. "Do you know why everyone loves running operations in Rome?"

"It's centrally located and easily accessible?" Vanessa shouted over the sound of the taxis and buses rushing by.

"It's total chaos!" Victor responded. He jumped out of the way to avoid colliding with a passing motorcycle. "Think of all the opportunity there is in chaos."

They entered an ice cream shop as a blue car passed by, going the wrong way down the street.

"Do we get to keep our kidneys at this ice cream place?" Oliver asked.

"Stop," pleaded Victor, determined not to let anything kill his Roman buzz. "We are far from all that election crap now. Let's enjoy."

The blue car passed by again, going the right direction but in reverse.

They walked into Piazza della Rotunda, where the Pantheon's granite columns and concrete dome loomed over the throngs of tourists, whose babble of different languages filled up the square. Gaggles of pigeons gathered near the fountain then shot into the air as a toddler bowled into them laughing. Several men circulated through the crowd selling selfie-sticks. Seagulls cackled overhead.

The three Caros sat on the steps of the fountain eating their ice cream. Victor leaned in toward Vanessa. "We can use the chaos of the city as cover for our clandestine operations. Look at that guy," he said, pointing to a Russian-looking man in an Adidas track suit with a young woman on his arm. "Is he on holiday, or is he checking in on his money laundering business? And that guy." He indicated a Korean-looking man with a briefcase. "Is he taking an ice cream break, or is he a North Korean diplomat on his way to meet a contact from the Italian mafia in hopes of selling him weapons in exchange for cold, hard currency?" He looked at Vanessa with a grin. "In the chaos, anything is possible." He gestured to the crowd around them. "These people have no idea what clandestine operations are going on right under their noses." Church bells across the city began to chime the hour.

Victor kissed Vanessa and hugged Oliver as the cacophony of the streets enveloped them. Thoughts of kidneys and politics, of Washington, DC, and Director, receded into the distance. In many ways, he was home. He was embarking on his ultimate tour with the intelligence agency of the country he had chosen, posted to the country of his birth. He could see the next two years stretching out in front of him. Strolls through Villa Borghese, aperitifs in Campo dei Fiori, and carefree sailing on the Mediterranean, not to mention the fertile hunting ground Rome was for spies. He felt his adrenaline rise. The next two years would be the best of his career, serving the mission while enjoying the wonders of the Eternal City and gliding to the retirement finish line. Nothing, he felt in that moment, could burst his bubble.

***

Three months later

"President Dick Head," Vanessa whispered as she slid into bed next to her half-slumbering husband.

Victor opened one eye. "You're not serious."

"President Dick Head," she said again. "Go back to sleep. It's five a.m. We'll discuss it later."

Victor rolled onto his back, both eyes now wide open. "Fuck." It was the only word that would come out of his mouth, repeatedly, for the next several hours. He got out of bed and pulled on a sweatshirt, before shuffling down the long hallway to the kitchen to put the coffee on. "Fuck!" he shouted. While he knew he needed to set aside his personal distaste for Richard Redd, he knew from experience the man was unethical and willing to sell his grandmother if it benefited him. What would this mean for the country, to have a man ready to change public service into personal greed? "Fuck?" he asked aloud, wondering if all the ridiculous rumors about Willa Bennett had actually affected the outcome of the vote. "Fuck," he sighed with resignation, realizing it was nearly time to head into his office, where Director would surely be in a tizzy, handing down taskings related to what had just come to pass.

Vanessa walked into the living room, wrapped in a fleece robe to protect her against the cold emanating from the old, decorated tiles of their Roman apartment. Victor was sitting on their couch, now in a dress shirt, boxer shorts, and Top Siders without socks. His hair was a mess and his eyes looked drawn behind his reading glasses, a recent acquisition after he realized his arm was no longer long enough to hold reading material at the necessary distance. He placed his coffee cup on the table and looked at her. "Fuck."

"You should consider putting on pants before you go to the office," Vanessa said, sitting down across from him.

"I'm preparing for my retirement."

"How bad do you think this Dick Head thing is going to be?"

"Fuck," he said again, despondent. "It's possible he won legitimately, right?"

"Possible," Vanessa said. "Russia interfered. We know that. We know they hacked emails from the Bennett campaign. But we don't know what effect it had. We also don't know if Redd's campaign worked with Russia or knew what Russia was doing." She again saw Ashley-Anne Wynscott welcoming Diana Abramovich into her home. "Although I have an opinion."

"You know who is going to be in charge of tracking down intelligence on what exactly Russia got up to?"

"The CYA, where you work."

"Who will be in charge of tracking down intelligence on what exactly Dick Head's campaign did or did not do as Russia got up to what it got up to?"

"The FBI, where I work."

Victor stared out the window. Things had been going smoothly. He and Vanessa had settled into their respective offices. Oliver had easily transitioned to his new school. The waiter at the best pasta restaurant around the corner had learned their names and regular orders.

A tram bell rang in the distance. Victor continued looking out the window. "What do you do when the president is a counterintelligence threat?"

He turned to look at her for a brief moment then dropped his head, as a grim reality set in. The world, and Victor's world in particular, had just gotten a lot more complicated. No matter how much he loved Italy, or how much pasta he ate or wine he drank, the next two years were going to be an enormous challenge. A man Victor already knew from experience had no scruples and who was prepared to put his own quest for power above the national security of the United States, was about to become the American president. He had likely vaulted himself into the Oval Office with foreign help, which meant he owed someone powerful something in return. Yet Victor and his CYA colleagues, not to mention his wife and her FBI colleagues, would have to track down intelligence on that same foreign influence in order to uphold their oath to the Constitution. But anything they did, any asset they recruited, any intelligence they collected, could be known by the man who was about to become the commander in chief, the very man who, it seemed, had benefited from this foreign influence. All his hopes for Rome were dashed.

This tour was going to be trouble.

CHAPTER TWO

Victor and Vanessa headed out for the short walk to the embassy. Normally, they loved their commute, a twenty-minute walk through Villa Borghese, a public garden filled with towering umbrella pine trees and rows of Roman statues, many of them with nothing but a strategically-placed fig leaf to hide their nakedness. But today, they walked quickly without taking in any of the beauty. The surprise win of Senator Richard Redd had left them stunned, and they were sure Russia had had a hand in the victory. It was a sad tale, Victor thought, as he and Vanessa walked along a crunchy dirt path. Instead of democracy taming a corrupt Russia, the corruption had infused the democracy, and President Vlastov seemed intent on spreading that corruption westward.

"Do you think it would have made a difference if the president had revealed publicly that Russia was behind a lot of the fuckery we saw, like the hacking of Bennett's emails?" Victor asked. He looked at Vanessa, "Or the tremendous home sale for Ashley-Anne Wynnscott?"

"He was in a tight spot. He endorsed Bennett. Revealing publicly that the government was aware of Russian attempts to help

Redd beat her might have destroyed any faith in the democratic process the Russians did not manage to destroy with their influence campaign," Vanessa responded.

"But now we're in an even tighter spot as a nation."

The two flashed their badges at the Italian security guards at the front gate of the embassy and entered the compound at the main entrance of the chancery. Palazzo Margherita was a grand, pink edifice overlooking Rome's swank Via Veneto. The palace had been home to the widowed mother of King Victor Emmanuel III before Benito Mussolini requisitioned it.

Victor and Vanessa climbed the wide, majestic staircase of the palazzo, light shining in through oversized windows and reflecting off the golden ceiling, the thick marble handrail cold to the touch. At the top of the first flight, they arrived at Vanessa's office. "*Forza*," she said, using a common Italian word of encouragement.

"Fuck," Victor replied, before continuing on to his office. He walked through an enormous hallway, its high, wood-carved ceiling decorated with scenes of pink cherubs. He stopped at a large panel on the wall that was covered in golden fabric. He swung it open to reveal a fascist motto Mussolini had carved into the marble. It was one of several panels along the corridor, designed by a curator who understood the need to preserve, but not promote, the history. Like the fig leaves on the statues in the park, it was something pretty to cover up the dirty parts everyone knew existed but was too polite to discuss.

"Blood moves the wheels of history, and the dirt of our native land will soak it up for glory," Victor read. He closed the panel on the fascist screed.

He moved on, finally reaching an isolated, closed door. He punched in his cipher code and entered Rome Station. He walked down a wide corridor, past two shredders and a framed photograph of Rome under a rare snowfall. He felt a jolt of adrenaline as he turned left into the bullpen he shared with a handful of other officers, the people he'd be teaming up with over the next months to shake down the Russian threat and protect America. Hell, to protect democracy. To protect Western civilization! An energy stirred within him at the thought that they truly were, in that moment, the pointy tip of the spear, the nation's first line of defense against a formidable and determined adversary.

He stepped into the bullpen. Everyone was tapping away on their keyboards, reading through morning cable traffic, and scrolling through their emails. It looked like any other day. Were people avoiding discussing the election? Did no one grasp the intelligence attack Russia had just pulled off against the United States? He looked around the bullpen. This was the CYA, right?

"Victor, I'm so glad you're here. Drop everything. I need your focus. Now. This instant." Mary Driscoll was the deputy chief of station, a bland, petite woman with a penchant for unflattering pantsuits in various shades of beige. He perked up, relieved that a top manager was about to burst the bubble of serenity that seemed to encircle the bullpen when Victor felt sure everyone needed to be acting, brainstorming, *doing something* in that instant. Here was the deputy chief of station to hand down some marching orders about how they planned to confront the Russian menace. Mary locked eyes with Victor. "I haven't received your performance review. Without it, we can't forward anything to the promotion committee. If you don't aim for promotion this time around, you are drastically narrowing your career choices moving forward."

Victor glanced around the bullpen. "Russia attacked the United States. How many of you right now are working on your performance evaluations?" No one turned away from their computer monitors, but they all raised a hand. Victor turned back to Mary, who had satisfied look on her face.

"Today, Victor."

Victor had never cared about promotion before, which was why he had become CYA's longest-serving GS-13 officer. He now had managers who were many years younger than him and with much less experience. He knew this was an awkward dynamic. New managers tried to assert their power over him from the start, but most learned quickly that he was an asset, not a threat, and his experience and knowledge, if channeled well, were valuable for the office they worked in and for the agency as a whole. If the manager channeled Victor's energy badly, however, that meant trouble all around. Victor also knew he was retiring in less than two years, so promotion meant even less this year than it had over the previous twenty.

He looked at everyone tapping away on their keyboards, probably inflating their achievements in order to stand out to the promotion panel, writing how they had thwarted terrorist attacks at the last minute or singlehandedly prevented a genocide, while receiving an exceptional performance award for showing up on time five days in a row.

Yet, all the while, Russian President Darko Vlastov and his proxies had been nudging here, provoking there, helping anger percolate just under the surface of the American electorate. That anger, combined with a cascade of disinformation messaging—including, it seemed likely, accusations that Willa Bennett had been stealing children's kidneys to make ice cream—had polluted the public square, making reasoned discussions impossible. All of which had helped Richard Redd win his upcoming elevation to the Oval Office. Everyone in the bullpen should have been developing ways to figure out what Vlastov wanted in return for his help.

He looked at his colleagues typing away. Mary Driscoll looked at him expectantly then made a gesture as if inviting him to sit down at his own desk. As she exited the bullpen, he shook his head as he realized that stopping the promotion cycle would be even harder than stopping Russian disinformation.

"Pssst."

Victor turned around. Patrick Newell, a counterterrorism analyst, was leaning in toward him with a conspiratorial look on his face. He and Victor had become friends over the past few months. They had recently discovered a corner bar with outside seating that offered excellent happy hour specials on Fridays. The owner was constantly high, allowing Victor to talk down the price of each bottle of wine. Patrick tried to get Victor's attention in the most inconspicuous way possible. Victor leaned toward him.

Patrick glanced around the bullpen. When he seemed convinced everyone else was too busy typing, he said, "What the fuck happened? Did Russia elect Redd?"

Victor shrugged. "Russia did something, but I'm not sure they elected the guy."

"You don't think he's controlled by Darko Vlastov?"

"That seems a little too clear cut. At the very least, Russia tried to help him get elected. Redd may feel he owes Vlastov now. Or Vlastov may feel Redd owes him something."

Matt Patteson, another case officer, got up from his desk and walked toward them on his way to exit the bullpen. Victor and Patrick both sat upright. Patrick said loudly: "Wow, so that AS Roma team. Wow. Quite something. Right?" Matt left the bullpen and Patrick leaned in again toward Victor, then said quietly, "I don't know anything about soccer. But it feels kind of weird to openly doubt the legitimacy of the incoming president when I'm sitting in an American embassy." He glanced around again. "Do you think Redd knew he was getting a boost from abroad?"

"He's taken foreign money for campaigns before," Victor said. "He learned a long time ago, like everyone else in Washington, to run donations through limited liability corporations and funnel the money into SuperPACS. He was taking money from a Crown Prince in the Middle East back when I was chasing terrorists around West Africa. He had his own dark money organization called Dick's Socially Active Citizens PAC."

"Dick's SACPAC?"

"He pushed to keep buying oil from the Crown Prince's fiefdom. The Crown Prince used that money to help spread a perverted version of Islam, which created terrorists but bought the Crown Prince some harmony at home with his hardcore religious faction. Those terrorists then attacked us, so he had to appease some of our politicians by contributing generously to their political campaigns. If Redd had anything to gain by cutting a deal with Vlastov, he'd do it."

Patrick said, "He had the presidency of the United States to gain."

***

Victor was back in the bullpen later that week. He kneeled down and glanced under his office chair. He saw three separate levers, but no clear indication of what any one of them was for. He sat down again and fumbled for one of the levers. He jiggled it and felt a sharp pain in his lower back. He pumped another one and almost fell over backward as the back of the chair reclined too far. He moved the third lever and the arm rests dropped from under his elbows. He pushed and pulled some more, each time contorting his body to fit the chair's new shape. With another yank, the back sprang up, making a *whack* sound. He rolled forward and placed his elbows on the desk. The chair was protruding into his lower back and the back of the chair pitched him so far forward he had to dig his feet into the floor to stop from sliding out of the seat.

Victor rolled his shoulders and stretched his neck. He reached for the levers under his chair. He tugged at one and dropped several inches while pitching back.

"You're lucky they let you have an ergonomic one." Victor turned to look at Patrick. The counterterrorism analyst spun away from a link chart on one of his two monitors. "Support switched your chair out this morning for this fancy one," Patrick said, pointing to Victor's chair.

"I haven't had the best of luck with chairs," Victor said. "I like the one I had."

"It didn't roll."

"Where am I going to roll? I've got a two-foot radius in each direction before I hit someone. What did they do with it?" Patrick shrugged. Victor glanced at his link chart, mapping out a terrorist cell in Syria. "How's the Total War on Terror going?"

"I think we've got the TWOT almost wrapped up. A few more link charts and we will have definitively not crushed them, but at least categorized them. Anyway, who cares about terrorists now? It's all about Russians."

"For twenty years we've been building capacity to fight terrorists. You couldn't get a promotion without going to the war zones. Now we're surprised to find out Russia's intelligence services weren't just kicking back in Sochi schadenfreuding over our quagmire in Rubblestan. They actually stayed busy." He glanced at the clock on the wall. Chief of Station Wilcox had called an all-hands meeting for 9:00 am. "I hope we're finally going to do something about it."

They walked down the hall, joining the other Rome Station officers piling into the front office. COS Wilcox had a solid, square body, sported a bushy beard, and tended to wear no-iron khakis with quick-dry, button-down shirts. Today, he sported running sandals with toe socks. He had made a name for himself fighting the war on terror over multiple tours in Rubblestan—hunting terrorists and directing drones to send them explosive gifts once he found them—and had thus far shaken off neither war zone fashion trends nor war zone operational habits, despite now living in Italy.

"Ladies and gentlemen of the Directorate of Operations, a wounded nation turns its lonely eyes to you, our frontline intelligence officers, the pointy tip of the spear in our country's first line of defense."

Victor saw Patrick scratching marks on his notepad, as if keeping count. Victor nudged him and gave him a questioning look. Patrick wrote at the top of his notepad, "Number of platitudes." Victor gave him a thumbs up.

"Over the last several days since the presidential election, the United States intelligence community has worked tirelessly to assess the degree of foreign influence in said election." Wilcox cracked the knuckles on one of his hands. "In short, the United States intelligence community has assessed with high confidence that Russia interfered in our presidential election and that Russian President Darko Vlastov personally ordered the operation." He paced back and forth as he spoke, like a general before his soldiers. "To be clear, Willa Bennett did not, in fact, kill children in order to harvest their kidneys to make ice cream. She did not kill children at all. That was a conspiracy story started by Russians sitting in an office building in Saint Petersburg. The one in Russia, not Florida. The White House has placed a high priority on collecting on the Russian target. We need to know why they did this, how they did this, and if they plan to continue doing this. As such, I am calling on you to rise to the occasion and face this challenge, a challenge we thought we would not have to face again after whooping ass in the Cold War. We won that war, and since that glorious victory, the world has hungered for freedom. We have quenched that thirst." Victor and Patrick looked at each other, confused by the mixed metaphor. Wilcox continued, "Democracy is like peanut butter. It's American, and the entire world loves it. Like smooth peanut butter, we have been spreading democracy around the globe. We spread it in Rubblestan. We spread it in Iraq. Like the United States Postal Service, we have delivered democracy through rain, sleet, snow, and Hellfire missiles." He paused, looked down at the floor, and took a deep breath before looking back up at his troops. "Now it looks like maybe we didn't win the peace. It looks like Russia wants to bring back the Cold War. My response?" He looked out at his intelligence army, as if preparing to send them to war. "Bring it. Bring on Cold War two point oh! We beat the Russkies then, we will be beat them again now. I can hear you all asking, 'Cliff, how are we going to do that?'"

Everyone looked around trying to figure out who Cliff was, then seemed to understand all at once that was Wilcox's first name.

Wilcox continued, "All of you can contribute to this mission. No matter your creed or color, your country needs you." Victor could hear Patrick marking up his notebook. "We need intelligence now. We need sources now. What is Russia planning? What is President Vlastov planning? We'll have to be creative." He paused a moment, reminiscing. "When I was in Rubblestan, we had to be creative. Hell, I once recruited a goat herder to provide intelligence on the comings and goings of a suspected terrorist in a mountainside village in Rubblestan." He looked at the faces around the room. "I need each of you to go find a goat herder."

Victor looked at Patrick and mouthed the word, "What?"

Wilcox then made a fist, which he hit into his open palm to help emphasize his next words. "It will not be easy. It will require sacrifice. But you represent the greatest intelligence service in the history of our country or any other in the history of mankind or any other species."

"Chief, what if this is nothing? Redd was elected legitimately," said one officer from the back of the room.

"That may be true, but Russia still carried out operations, and the current president wants to know what else they have planned. Also, remember, recruiting a Russian really impresses the promotion panel. Now I want each of you to get out there and recruit yourself a Russian intelligence officer!"

A number of Victor's colleagues punched the air and yelled, "Fuck, yeah!" as they filed out to return to their desks to develop plans for this new mission. Victor stayed seated a moment. The chair he was in was better than the one he was heading back to. There were a number of holes in Wilcox's plan, first and foremost being that recruiting a Russian intelligence officer was really hard. And it did not happen overnight.

Victor had been developing ideas to approach potential targets since his arrival three months earlier, in anticipation of the exact scenario he and his CYA colleagues now found themselves in. Victor had pored over Rome Station's book of suspected Russian intelligence officers, studying the faces and backgrounds of every-one posted to the Russian embassy or any of its cultural institutes around town. He knew who liked to play violin, who had an advanced degree in molecular chemistry, and who had tried the paleo diet once but decided it wasn't for him. He knew everything about them, but was never convinced he'd be able to turn one of them. Victor had even dragged Vanessa out to the seaside town of Ostia, where a purported journalist working for New Russia News lived, trying to ascertain her movements and manufacture an introduction. He was never able to connect with her. He kept getting stuck.

Victor went back to the bullpen. "Do you like Russian cinema, Victor?" Patrick was scrolling through an email and didn't bother to turn around as he asked the question. "Or maybe you prefer a Russian cooking class? There's a vodka tasting Thursday. You should definitely do that one."

Victor sat in his chair. The seat sank slowly toward the floor, even though he wasn't touching any of the levers. "What are you talking about?" The seat was so low Victor's knees bent in toward his chest.

"The targeters made a list of events around town where you guys might be able to bump into Russians. DJ Faber-Jay will be spinning music in Testaccio Saturday at a Young Diplomats event."

"We're going to look like idiots if we all run out at once and start bumping Russians. We'll be the laughing stock of the Rezidentura," Victor said, referring to Russia's intelligence station. "This used to be a gentlemen's game. There has to be a better way for us to go about this."

"You could just hop down to your local bazaar and pick up a Russian recruit. That's how COS Wilcox seems to think it works."

"If you guys could find me a goat herder in town, that would be great."

"How about an energy conference?" Patrick asked. "The Italian energy company GasItalia is hosting a conference next week on the RosAlleman project."

"That's perfect," Victor said.

"What's the RosAlleman project?"

"It's the pipeline they're building between Russia and Germany. It's turning into a massive headache for the European Union. But I also think it's part of why President Vlastov is carrying out all this fuckery with the United States, and why I think he's planning to carry out similar fuckery here in Europe."

Patrick looked confused. Victor pulled up a map of Europe on his monitor and said, "Look. At the moment, Russia runs gas to Ukraine." Victor pointed to the country on Russia's southwest border. "It used to be the jewel in the Russian Empire's crown. Ukraine then sells the gas to Germany, up here. Two years ago,

Vlastov started feeling like maybe Ukraine liked Europe more than it liked him. So, he did what any jealous friend would do."

"He invaded the country."

"Right. But the United States and Europe didn't really appreciate Vlastov grabbing land by force. It broke a few international laws and brought back some unpleasant memories about another dictator in Europe and appeasement and a world war."

"So, the US and Europe sanctioned Russia."

"That's part of why Vlastov is so pissed off."

"Why does Germany want a pipeline with Russia, if Europe has taken a stance against Russia?"

"Vlastov has a nasty habit of using gas as leverage over states it wants to keep under its control. If a country doesn't do what Vlastov wants, he shuts off the gas supply." Victor turned to look at Patrick. "If Ukraine insists on building ties with Europe, rather than with Russia, Vlastov might turn off the gas to Ukraine."

"Leaving them no gas to sell to Germany, meaning Germans would have a very cold winter."

"Ukrainians, too. But Germany just cares about cold Germans. Hence, a direct pipeline between Russia and Germany."

"But then Vlastov could just turn off the supply to Germany," Patrick said, perplexed.

"The German government thinks Vlastov would pull that shit with a former Soviet state, but would never try it with a European power like Germany. Plenty of others in Europe disagree. They also feel like they owe some protection to the cold Ukrainians. The whole thing is testing the bonds of the European Union, which Vlastov loves. The more division, the better." Victor looked back at Patrick's monitor. "There will be good targets at that energy conference."

Victor marked the details of the conference down on a piece of paper. He squeezed out of his chair, contorting his body and pushing against the arm rests and the desk to pry himself loose. He walked out of the station to Vanessa's office. He found her at her desk, sitting on a large, inflated, blue exercise ball. He could see one of her colleagues at another desk sitting on a ball, as well. He stood for a moment, looking at the scene of her perched atop it.

"How did the FBI get such big balls?"

"We have a good support officer," Vanessa replied.

"I want a giant ball."

"Ask your support officer if he'll give you blue balls. Maybe phrase it differently. What's up?"

"We're going to an energy conference Thursday."

"I was just saying to myself I don't go to enough energy conferences."

"There will be lots of targets. I need your help spotting and bumping people."

"Let me guess. You want to bump a Russian? Russians are all the rage now."

"That's the problem," Victor said. "Everyone wants a Russian. I've got a different idea."

CHAPTER THREE

Ruslan Bebchuk shivered as the motorboat ferried him through the freezing arctic waters of the White Sea. The Solovetsky Islands faded in the distance behind him as the boat captain gently maneuvered to attach the dinghy to the side of a large research vessel. Bebchuk clambered on board, a cold breeze blowing through his brown hair, causing him to raise his buff shoulders up toward his ears, as if closing in on himself for warmth. He briefly acknowledged the film crew he had put together, then crossed to the starboard side of the vessel. He peeked over the side into the depths of water.

There, President Darko Vlastov was floating in the calm sea, outfitted in a handcrafted white scuba suit designed to make him look like a beluga whale. On his head was an underwater speaker that released whale sounds derived from Vlastov's own voice. Dozens of beluga whales swarmed around him, caressing him. One whale nudged Vlastov's chin, looking like he was giving the president a kiss. The film crew was capturing it all.

"We've gotten excellent footage," the director said to Bebchuk. "Maybe even better than the footage we got of him taming the polar bear that was threatening the Siberian village."

"Keep up the good work," Bebchuk said, pleased. He looked back as the sixty-five-year-old president who had ruled Russia for nearly two decades dove deep under the water, surrounded by the playful pod.

Bebchuk had known Vlastov his entire adult life. They had gone through the KGB's training academy together, later running clandestine operations to distribute large busts of Lenin to remote groups around the world in support of the Soviet cause. After the USSR ceased to exist and Vlastov was appointed to lead the new Russia's intelligence agency, he had chosen Bebchuk as his right-hand man, a role he maintained when Vlastov became president. Currently, Bebchuk was in charge of all state-run media, with a special eye on the newly-created New Russia News, or NRN, where he played an important role helping to cultivate the president's image and securing the loyalty of his subjects. Among his most recent projects was a ten-part documentary called *Our Great President*, which featured Vlastov demonstrating his virility by doing such things as swimming with endangered whales.

"Ruslan, my friend! It is good of you to come join me. The water is perfect!" President Vlastov stepped out of the water as a member of the crew wrapped an oversized towel around him. He was in a good mood.

"It is my pleasure, Mr. President," Bebchuk said, as if he had had a choice in the matter.

"Come with me," Vlastov said, leading Bebchuk past the film crew and inside. Bebchuk was relieved to be where it was warmer. Vlastov removed his equipment, stripping down to a tight swimsuit bottom, then opened a door, motioning for Bebchuk to follow him.

Bebchuk nearly choked on the dry heat of the sauna, as Vlastov settled onto a wooden bench. "This feels so good after a swim in the arctic waters," Vlastov said.

Bebchuk nodded in agreement, as he took off his jacket and fleece, leaving him in jeans and a T-shirt.

"Do you remember those early days of the new Russia, Ruslan? What a shift in history that time was. So many of our allies—former Soviet states and Eastern bloc countries, *our* allies, countries under *our* influence—began to feel the evil lure of the West."

"I remember it well, sir, and not fondly." Bebchuk grabbed a towel that was stacked nearby and wiped his brow. "The West claimed they had won the Cold War, and the North Atlantic Treaty Organization, under the guise of democracy, promised those countries prosperity, stability, and security."

"NATO promised to protect them from *us*. From their own brethren. One by one, our historical friends fell for the ruse." Vlastov sneered at the memory. First to go had been East Germany, which automatically became part of NATO with the reunification with West Germany. Soon after came the Czech Republic, Hungary, Poland, and then—more painful, as they had once been part of the USSR, under direct Russian control—came the Baltic states of Latvia, Lithuania, and Estonia. Vlastov was president by that time, making the betrayal even more acute. "So many self-righteous countries maneuvering to be part of the West's military and morality club, preaching equality, free elections, and fair competition, taunting us from right across Russia's border."

Vlastov scooped water out of a large wooden bucket and poured it over the sauna's hot rocks. They sizzled and steamed. Bebchuk pulled off his shirt. "Ruslan, when I was running for president, an American journalist asked me—I remember her words exactly—'In the years since Russia lost the Cold War, the transition to capitalism has been rocky. As president, how would you clamp down on the corruption that has plagued your country? And how do you plan to rebuild relations with the United States, which is now the sole superpower?'"

"I recall, sir. She demonstrated the hypocrisy of western capitalism and the arrogance of its practitioners." Bebchuk wiped his chest with his shirt.

"Do you remember how I responded? I said, 'What about corruption in America? Look at your military-industrial complex, which your President Eisenhower warned about. Your Pentagon insists we are still a threat. There is no more Soviet Union, but you keep building B-2 bombers and nuclear weapons. Programs you began in your fear of communism, they continue today, when there is no more communism in Russia. Why? I will tell you why. Your defense companies need to keep building weapons. Your senators and congressmen need them to keep building weapons, too. A lot of money and jobs are associated with these weapons. That is capitalism, no?'"

"I remember. You were furious. But you hid your anger well. Although I also recall we hit the judo mats after that and you beat the shit out of me." They both laughed.

"She painted such a humiliating portrait of Russia. She implied it was a lesser country, that it had lost its status, was no longer worthy of respect and admiration, and that the United States was the only influence that mattered anymore. I couldn't stand for that." He poured more water on the rocks. "Do you know what these experiences taught me, Ruslan? First, capitalism is inherently corrupt. Anybody can be bought. Second, the truth is relative. Objective truth serves no purpose. Third, the West wants to humiliate Russia. When I became president, this country was a sad, deflated version of the Russia I loved. It was a great nation whose global power was being overshadowed. I vowed to resuscitate Russia's glorious imperial past." He turned to look at Ruslan. "And I would use the West's greed to do so."

Bebchuk was sweating profusely. "I think it is fair to say you have succeeded. You've placed a malleable narcissist who pines for your approval in the Oval Office."

"I can't take sole credit," Vlastov said cheekily. "America was ripe to be toyed with. We just found the right fissures to stick a wedge in and crack the country open. Gun rights. Gay rights. Vegan rights." He wiped his shiny brow. "Nor do I relish working with Redd. He's a clown, but one who is easy to manipulate. An ego stroke here, a dick stroke there." He winked at Bebchuk. "He will be a good tool to knock the United States down a peg." He took a deep breath, sucking in the dry sauna air. "However, we cannot get ahead of ourselves, Ruslan. The election in the United States is a good step. We have more work to do. I plan to conquer *all* of the West. The United States, Europe, the Western sneerfest of liberal democracy and the hypocritical pursuit of happiness through racial harmony, equality among genders, and drug-free sports. I will tear it down, and the great Russian empire shall rise like a menacing grizzly protecting her cubs, the Russian people. Here is what I want you to do."

CHAPTER FOUR

Ness stood in the middle of Piazza di Pietra, looking frantically for the Chamber of Commerce, where she was supposed to meet Victor five minutes ago for the energy conference.

"Remember that piazza we went to once? It's right near there," Victor had told her that morning as the family prepared to head out to their respective destinations for the day.

"I'm going to need a little more information than that," she had said.

"The one with the columns."

"We're in Rome. That doesn't narrow it down."

"You know. Where we ate that one time."

"Which time?"

"Oliver, you remember. You really liked it." Victor said to his son, who was packing his backpack.

"The place with the gnocchi with the boar ragù, or the one with penne alla vodka?" Oliver asked.

"Gnocchi with boar ragù."

"There's a statue in the piazza," Oliver said.

"Yeah, that place." Victor turned to Vanessa. "You know that place."

Ness stared at her husband and son. "Oliver, how do you know what he's talking about?"

"I had the gnocchi. I never forget food. It was the place you had the strozzapreti with pesto and talked about it for the next hour and you didn't even want gelato because you kept talking about the strozzapreti."

"Oh! That place!" Ness exclaimed.

She stared up at Hadrian's Temple, which lined one side of the piazza. The nearly two-thousand-year-old structure maintained eleven of its original columns, soaring toward the sky and framing the entrance to the Chamber of Commerce. She walked into the grand space, which had been converted into a modern meeting hall but was marked on one side by an original temple wall. She found Victor sitting in the back row, where he could keep an eye on who was coming and going. She sat down next to him.

He leaned in to kiss her on the cheek and whispered, "Look."

She followed his eyes. To their right and four rows forward was a box of a man. His shoulders, his jaw line, everything was square. Ness recognized him as Kirill Ovetchkin, officially a political secretary at the Embassy of Russia but a suspected Russian intelligence officer. His picture was included in the book in Rome Station of known and suspected Russian intelligence officers based in Italy. Victor and Ness had studied the book for days before coming to the conference. Ness felt Victor's eyes move and she followed them. Several seats down and two rows in front of Kirill was Grigoriy Stepanov, a cultural attaché at the Russian embassy suspected of handling other tasks. Two seats down from Grigoriy was Matt

Patteson, a case officer from Victor's office. Across the aisle and a few seats in was Olivia Yeardley, also a case officer. Ness spotted three more case officers from Rome Station, making them six in total to fight over a handful of Russian targets. Victor and Vanessa scanned the rest of the attendees, wondering if there were more intelligence officers than actual audience members.

"Welcome to today's conference hosted by GasItalia," said the woman presiding over the event. "We are pleased to have this opportunity to discuss several energy-related topics as they affect both Italy and Europe, and to look at some of the politics, here at home and internationally, that might affect European energy policy going forward. Allow me to present our panel of speakers. To my right is Isabelle Tourneau, an expert in European politics from Sciences Po in Paris. To my left is Aldo Conti, head of the MussoRusso Cultural Association here in Rome."

Victor knew about the MussoRusso Cultural Association. Conti had launched the organization three years earlier to celebrate shared values between Italy and Russia, specifically sovereignty and tradition. Those two concepts had energized a number of activists in Italy, which had recently suffered from a weak economy and seen a large influx of immigrants, a combination that made many Italians susceptible to calls to return to an idealized past. The association's nod to Benito Mussolini, the fascist dictator who ran Italy for two decades, gave even the casual observer a pretty good idea about how the organization interpreted those values.

"Europe is at a turning point in deciding its energy security," said the panel moderator, who looked tiny next to the Roman columns rising behind her. "I'd like to pose the question simply, and allow each panel member to respond. What should Europe's energy policy be, and how can it develop energy independence? Signore Conti, from the MussoRusso Cultural Association, let us start with you."

Aldo Conti leaned in toward his microphone. A small, meek man in his fifties, he was dressed in a Herringbone suit.

"*Grazie*. It is a pleasure to be here. There can be no discussion of European energy independence without discussing the RosAlleman pipeline. It is surely the most reliable path to reach energy independence, as Germany will be well placed to manage the project in an efficient manner. The project, as well, provides an opportunity for Europe to improve relations with Russia, which I believe is an important step for the future of European sovereignty. The better we get along with our neighbor, the more sovereignty we achieve."

"How can you equate the pipeline with independence?" asked Isabelle Tourneau, the French academic. "The name of this project is not the European pipeline, or the German pipeline. It is the RosAlleman pipeline, for Russia and Germany. Russia will be in full control of how much gas arrives in Germany. This is the opposite of independence. This is subjugation and dependence. The Russian disinformation campaign that has accompanied Darko Vlastov's attempts to sell this RosAlleman project only makes clearer that Vlastov sees this as an opportunity that will be beneficial only to him, and detrimental to Europe. Additionally, we have lessons to learn from what we have just witnessed in America. It is Russian policy to manipulate elections of sovereign countries. By agreeing to move forward with this project, we are accepting Russia's actions and tacitly giving President Vlastov permission to continue with this behavior. Furthermore, the project cuts off funding for a switch to renewables, like solar power. Coincidentally, who does support this project? Luca Callieri."

Luca Callieri, Victor knew, was the charismatic head of the nationalist Italian political party Da Italia. He was a divisive figure but his party was gaining popularity as elections in Italy loomed. Callieri preached sovereignty above all, telling his adherents, "Italy for Italians!" He had spoken loudly and often in support of the RosAlleman pipeline, equating it with sovereignty, because it would be financed in large part by GasItalia.

Literally, Da Italia meant "from Italy," which played well with Callieri's "Italy for Italians" message. Until three years ago, though, he had not managed to spread the message much beyond a few conservative provinces in northern Italy. Then Callieri went to Moscow. By a flash of good luck, Callieri's party was suddenly flush with money, and Callieri was able to convert his regional party into a national one. Critics liked to say the "Da" in Da Italia actually stood for the Russian word for "yes," since Callieri's policies—particularly after he returned from Moscow with abundant sums of money—often aligned with the traditionalist and conservative agenda of President Vlastov and members of his party. The MussoRusso Cultural Association, whose creation coincided with Callieri's Moscow trip, supported the same agenda.

Tourneau and Conti debated back and forth, until finally the moderator opened up the discussion to questions from the audience. A young woman raised her hand. She stood up. She had long, red hair, which she wore over her shoulders so it swept across her large bosom. She wore a slim, white dress, hemmed well above her knees, with a giant red heart on it. She sported a pair of librarian glasses and held a leather portfolio with a notepad in her left arm.

"*Spasibo*," she said, taking the microphone from the moderator's helper who was circulating through the audience. "I appreciate all the viewpoints you have shared with us today," she said in heavily Russian-accented English.

"Who the hell is that?" Victor asked Ness.

"*What* the hell is that?" Ness said.

"First, I have a comment regarding Ms. Tourneau's discussion of solar power. Many people believe the Cold Sun theory makes any use of solar power impossible, so natural gas is our best option."

Victor and Vanessa looked at each other, confused.

Isabelle Tourneau said, "The Cold Sun theory is a conspiracy theory that is not based in science. The sun is hot and its energy can be captured by solar panels here on Earth."

"This has never been definitively proven," the redhead said, before quickly turning to Aldo Conti and speaking over Isabelle Tourneau's protestations. "Is it not true that the RosAlleman pipeline represents a huge sacrifice for President Vlastov and the Russian people, who have suffered greatly under illegal sanctions? Should Europe consider other sharing projects with Russia, including intelligence sharing and the lifting of sanctions because President Vlastov is being so generous?"

Conti nodded his head. "Absolutely, Italy and Europe should view this project as a starting point for a renaissance in European-Russian relations. Luca Callieri certainly views it that way. Lifting sanctions and working more closely on other security issues, including intelligence sharing, would be very welcome next steps."

At the end of the discussion, the group adjourned to the back of the grand room, where two waiters had opened a bar. Victor and Vanessa each took a glass of prosecco.

"What was that Cold Sun nonsense?" Ness asked, as the two of them moved behind the crowd for a better view.

"I have no idea," Victor said. "It sounds as ridiculous as the idea that Willa Bennett steals children's kidneys." He took a sip then looked alarmed. "Although that one actually caught on."

They observed the room. The redheaded Russian quickly went to work on the Italian government officials who had attended the conference. She snapped selfies with them, the men enjoying the touch of the young woman as she wrapped her arm through theirs and pulled each one close.

Olivia Yeardley, one of the case officers from Victor's office, was eyeing Kirill Ovetchkin. As she was weighing her approach, Matt Patteson, another case officer, walked up to Kirill and spilled his drink on him. Victor and Ness could see he had been trying to make it look like an accident, but he wasn't graceful enough to pull it off. Victor winced. Vanessa choked down a laugh. "It's promotion time," Victor said to Ness. "They're trying to outdo each other." Olivia swallowed her wine in anger and turned her attention to the other side of the room.

Victor and Vanessa followed her gaze. Olivia was now contemplating Grigoriy Stepanov, the other suspected Russian intelligence officer. He was up by the dais, where the speakers were gathering their belongings and chatting with members of the audience. Next to Aldo Conti, Victor noticed a man in his midforties, well dressed in a dark gray, traditional-cut suit. He was standing patiently at Aldo Conti's side, holding what appeared to be Aldo's briefcase and fedora. Grigoriy walked toward them and, while Aldo continued chatting with a member of the audience, Grigoriy approached the man and struck up a conversation with him. Slowly, almost imperceptibly, Grigoriy maneuvered the man away from the main group until the two of them were alone by the wall. The man listened intently to Grigoriy, and after a few minutes, the two exchanged business cards. Grigoriy returned toward the bar. The man returned to Aldo Conti's side and handed him his briefcase and hat. Olivia made her way toward Grigoriy. Victor handed Vanessa his drink and said, "I'll be back in a minute."

He crossed the room, pretending to look for the bathroom. He asked the man for directions. As he explained where they were located, Victor glimpsed his name tag. He thanked the man and headed off. He returned to Vanessa's side a few minutes later. Matt was still chatting up Kirill, and Olivia was now flirting with Grigoriy. His entire office was trying to recruit a Russian intelligence officer within the confines of a makeshift bar in a lobby.

Victor grabbed Vanessa's hand and led her out into the piazza.

"Leaving so soon?" she asked. "There's probably still a Russian or two in there that hasn't been spilled on or dry humped."

"I have a different idea," he said, smiling.

He didn't plan to recruit a Russian intelligence officer. Rather, he would recruit the guy the Russian intelligence officer intended to recruit. And he had seen from his name tag, his name was Massimiliano Brevi.

CHAPTER FIVE

Victor stood examining his chair. The back was hanging loosely off the frame. He pried it off, leaving only the chair's seat, and sat down on what was now basically a stool.

"I'm getting a blue ball, Patrick," he said.

"I'd love to help you, but that's not something we should do at work and is probably more appropriate for your wife."

"Not blue balls. A blue ball."

"You were able to conceive with only one?"

"To sit on. A blue exercise ball."

"Oh. That's both disappointing and exciting at once."

"I spoke to Ralph in support about it. You should get one. It's good for your back. Everyone in Vanessa's office has them."

"The FBI has blue balls?"

"How's the Total War on Terror? Have we won yet?"

"We're turning a corner," Patrick said. "Our soon-to-be president insists he will defeat the terrorists."

"Does he say how?"

"I'd say it's more of a stated objective, at this point, and less of an actual plan to achieve it. You know he doesn't love details. Analysts at Director are red-celling different approaches to briefing him, to see what might help him absorb the information best. This week, they introduced Dickie the Doll. It's a doll that looks like him, dressed in a suit and everything, and the analyst holds the doll and makes it walk across a very big, simple map. Each country is a bright color, but they only put the names of the countries they'll be discussing that day, and there's a big White House indicating Washington. The doll walks from the White House to whatever country they have to brief him on. Then, the analyst uses an Elmo-like voice." Patrick cleared his throat, then continued in a high-pitched voice: "Today, Dickie the Doll gets to travel to Russia, where evil Pickled Bear hackers are attacking America!"

"Please tell me you're joking."

"I'm joking. They would never brief him on Russia. The rest of it is true, though."

Victor perched on his stool and turned to his computer. He flipped a switch that changed his system from the classified one to the unclassified one, allowing him to access the internet. He googled Massimiliano Brevi. Having watched the interaction between him and Grigoriy Stepanov at yesterday's energy conference, Victor was pretty sure the suspected Russian spy was looking to ensnare Massimiliano. He wanted to know how and why.

He immediately found Massimiliano's Facebook page, LinkedIn account, and Twitter profile. He giggled to see that Massimiliano, among his friends, went by the name Max. His last name, Brevi, was Italian for "brief" or "short," which his first name, Massimiliano, most definitely was not. Max's Facebook page was crowded with photos of him involved in Russian cultural activities. He posed in Russia's Red Square, Saint Basil's Cathedral's colorful onion domes in the background. Another photo showed him at the entrance of an Orthodox church in Saint Petersburg. Last year, he had participated in a Russian folk dance festival. He posted several photos of himself dressed as a Cossack doing a squat dance. Victor's knees ached looking at it. In another picture, Max was standing in the falling snow, holding a bottle of vodka and wearing an ushanka fur hat that was slightly askew, while a cute, blond woman playfully kissed his cheek. He wore a giant grin.

According to his biography on the MussoRusso Cultural Association website, Max had studied international relations at Moscow State University briefly in the early 1990s, as the Soviet Union unwound and a new Russia emerged. He had made a handful of appearances on small news outlets, speaking about European energy policy and criticizing an overbearing European Union. At the cultural association, he had worked as an assistant to Aldo Conti, the director, for the last two years.

Victor wanted to know more about MussoRusso itself. The association's website featured photos of Conti with Luca Callieri, head of Da Italia. In one, the two of them posed merrily in front of the Kremlin, with Callieri wearing a T-shirt with the face of Russian President Darko Vlastov on it.

From what Victor could tell, Conti served as an informal advisor to Callieri. He did not officially work for Callieri's campaign; Da Italia nowhere listed him as a staff member. But Callieri appeared frequently at MussoRusso events, and clearly, Victor saw, their views aligned.

Victor discovered the association got some financial support from the Russian Cultural Center, officially an arm of Russia's foreign ministry. Unofficially, Victor knew, such cultural centers served as cover for Russia's intelligence services. He thought again about Grigoriy Stepanov.

MussoRusso also had a relationship with Konstantin Dudnik, an informal advisor to Vlastov who seemed to style himself after Rasputin, a mystic whisperer to Russia's last czar, Nicholas II. Victor clicked on a video of Dudnik addressing an audience at the MussoRusso Association. "It is only through our common roots, our common values, our shared traditions, that we find strength as a society," he said. He was tall and lanky with greasy gray hair and an unkempt long beard. "This is how we throw off the shackles of slavery and find true freedom. True sovereignty."

Dudnik also rejected science, calling it a false art. He had launched a program called Cold Sun, which promoted the idea that the sun was not hot and did not provide light to Earth. According to the main Cold Sun website: "Hot sun hoaxers want to curb your freedom by making you feel dependent on an external source for heat and light. They do this to maintain control over you. Sunlight is a man-made construction and those with power use it, providing it to you only when they wish. Some countries have become greedy and have sunlight all day long. Why is this fair?" Victor recalled the redheaded Russian woman at the energy conference who had floated the Cold Sun conspiracy.

He continued reading about Dudnik. He also ran a major charity, which donated millions to the Orthodox Church, and was a proponent of patriotic media. He believed those two components, the church and the media, were integral to rebuilding the empire on traditionalist values. He had shared that view with Vlastov, catalyzing the launch of New Russia News and similar outlets over the past handful of years.

Last year, New Russia News voted Dudnik the Second-Best Flatterer of President Vlastov for stating, "Darko Vlastov is vital to humanity. His graciousness and intelligence make him an indispensable force for the Russian people and the human race at large. If anyone stands against this angel, that person deserves to live out the remainder of their time in a padded cell, for clearly that person is not right in the head. Vlastov is also very handsome." Victor saw that NRN's winner of Best Flatterer had gone to Olga Pepuchik, a twenty-three-year-old negligee model who wrote a song about wanting to marry Vlastov. He clicked on the music video. Olga, in a white, see-through, baby doll negligee, was on her knees on a four-poster bed that was in a forest, its sheer silk curtains blowing in the wind. A bear paced through the snow in the background. "No more weakness. Other men are pathetic. I want strength and boldness. I want someone like Vlastov," she sang, as she simulated masturbating to Vlastov's photo under the watchful gaze of the bear.

"You know you're still at the office, Victor, on a government computer," Patrick said.

Victor was startled and paused the video. He looked at Patrick then back at his own monitor. "It's research."

Patrick looked disappointed. "I only ever get to watch terrorist training videos."

Victor switched to his classified computer system and started digging. Here, the story was different from Dudnik's public persona. Dudnik was known to have ties with the Russian mafia and to be laundering money through his charity and his Cold

Sun project. Running the money through shell companies in the Netherlands and Malta, Dudnik had cleaned an estimated half a billion dollars. He had a home in Monte Argentario, a seaside paradise in Tuscany, and another in Sardinia, and once tried to buy a private island in the Virgin Islands, but was outbid by Jeffrey Epstein.

Max seemed to exist in the background of all of this. His place of employment, the MussoRusso Cultural Association, looked to Victor like a cover for covert Russian influence—taking money from Dudnik and the Russian Cultural Center and promoting Vlastov's favorite talking points about tradition and sovereignty—but it had to run a few legitimate programs as cover, a sort of fig leaf. For now, at least, that was probably where Max fit in the Russian operation. Victor assessed Max loved Russia and its people, but not necessarily its government. Nor did he post anything or partake in activities that clearly placed him in the category of Da Italia supporter. He was conservative and traditional, but Victor was not convinced he was fully on board the Callieri-Vlastov train.

He was certainly deep inside the hornets' nest, though. He had access to and knowledge of many of the major players helping Vlastov carry out his destabilizing activities. He had also caught the attention of Grigoriy Stepanov, a suspected Russian intelligence officer. Victor began putting it all together in his head. It was a complicated web weaved by intelligence officers, politicians, journalists, mobsters, and oligarchs, all in the service of President Vlastov.

He leaned back to think, but forgot he had ripped off the back of his chair. He fell backward. Patrick glanced down at him on the floor. Victor cleared his throat and sat back on his perch. He looked at a picture of Max smiling in front of the Hermitage Museum in Saint Petersburg.

Given the company he kept, approaching Max was going to be risky. But, Victor felt sure, he was going to make a great target.

CHAPTER SIX

Valeriy Chekhov, the Russian propagandist who had won an Academy Award for the movie *Blackhouse*, and Ruslan Bebchuk, who ran New Russia News, sat at an isolated, brown table in a dreary cafeteria whose speckled linoleum floor was stained with coffee spills. Bebchuk grabbed the chilled bottle of vodka that stood between them and poured them each a healthy glass. He picked his up and said, "Here's to us." The two men smiled at each other. Bebchuk winked as they clinked their glasses. They each took a long sip.

"I didn't think we could outdo ourselves on *Blackhouse*," Chekhov said. "But now, President Richard Redd." He laughed and took another sip.

"I'd love for us to take all the credit, but a lot of people voted for him because they genuinely liked him," Bebchuk said.

"Many Americans came to genuinely like him because we helped convince them Willa Bennett was slicing out children's kidneys and smashing them into a delicious frozen treat."

"I still don't quite believe it myself."

"That she murdered children?"

"That Americans fell for it." Bebchuk leaned forward and placed his elbows on the table. A serious look crossed his face. "Now, we need to discuss our next steps."

Chekhov downed the last of his vodka and said, "Well then, let's head upstairs to the war room."

They exited the cafeteria and walked toward a small stairwell that smelled like fish. At the top of the stairs, they entered a large room with brown, industrial carpet and cheap brown wood-paneled walls. The expanse was filled with rows and rows of computer work spaces. A poster on the wall showed a picture of a cute troll doll with bright pink hair, standing under a rainbow. At the troll's feet was a graphic showing the United States and Europe smashed to pieces. The poster said, "Be the chaos you want to see in the world!"

"Welcome to the heart of Facts and Knowledge University," Chekhov said. "FaKU, a private company owned by Nikolai Surikov, quietly run by Russia's intelligence services, with a vision to pollute the information space to our advantage. Behold." He swept an arm out across the room. Dozens of people of all ages and sizes hovered over computers and pecked away. One middle-aged man was dressed in dark green camouflage and kept a long Nerf rifle slung across his back. A woman in tight distressed jeans and a midriff top was typing away with freshly manicured nails. Three young men sitting together in a row wore all black and had several tattoos and piercings between them. No one looked like they had seen much sun recently. "These are our keyboard warriors, battling the enemy for the heart and soul of the Motherland," Chekhov continued. He pointed to a pimply young man with enormous glasses and a faded, dark red polo shirt whose collar was fraying. "That guy convinced the world Willa Bennett's campaign was working with an Iranian monkey to lure children into her ice cream shops so she could slice out their kidneys and then used those proceeds to fund Iran's nuclear program." The young man sneezed and his glasses jumped down to the tip of his nose. He sniffled, wiped his nose with the back of his hand, and pushed his glasses up before hunching over his keyboard again.

Bebchuk chuckled. "That monkey was cute, wearing a little turban."

Chekhov pointed to the woman in the jeans. "She started the rumor that Bennett had gone sand-dune surfing with the head of a major terrorist group before beheading a child and sipping blood out of his skull."

Bebchuk nodded. "We got a lot of play out of that one, especially after Kip Lawson at Facts News ran with it."

"We're recruiting a number of new employees, given President Vlastov's desire to extend our capabilities," Chekhov said. "We'll need hundreds more warriors, with the packed electoral calendar. First up, Italy."

They walked along the cubicles, looking over shoulders to see the work of the meme warriors. An older woman with graying curls and swollen ankles was putting the final touches on a meme she had designed. It was a cartoon of a grimacing Uncle Sam, looming tall, hurling the stars of the European Union flag at a tiny, frightened, cute, sad bear.

"Looks great, Alina," Chekhov said. He turned to Bebchuk and said in a low voice, "She does amazing work. Last week, she made a video of an enormous bald eagle crapping on the Colosseum, the Eiffel Tower, Buckingham Palace, the Brandenburg Gate, just shitting all over Europe, and each dropping splattered out and created little letters that spelled freedom."

"Genius," Bebchuk said. "Any tension we can create between the United States and Europe or between European countries is great."

"An angry populace is a pliant populace," Chekhov said with a grin. "Keep everyone so angry that no one can compromise."

The three young men dressed in black rolled their chairs into a triangular formation and started gently slapping their thighs with their palms.

"Oh! You're in luck!" Chekhov pulled Bebchuk back to observe the group. "They are preparing for battle."

The three men slowly increased the speed and intensity of their beating, building up to a fervent slap fest. Then one placed his right hand over his heart. He was now beating one hand on his heart, the other on his thigh. The other two followed suit. They hit harder, louder, faster, their eyes bulging with anticipation. Sweat trickled down the forehead of one of them.

"They are going to launch a meme," Chekhov whispered.

Bebchuk watched them, entranced.

The three became frenzied, beating their hearts and thighs, breathing deep, eyes wide. Then all three, at the same time, made double fists and yelled—unintelligible, guttural shrieks—pumping their fists in the air. Bebchuk thought they looked like men about to run into a firefight. Their arms raised like marauding warriors on a rampage, and still yelling, they each used their feet to roll their chairs back to their computers.

"Are we ready, comrades?" one barked, as he placed his finger on a computer mouse.

"Loaded and ready, sir!"

"On my count," said the third.

Bebchuk and Chekhov tensed. They held their breath, as if standing on a cliff edge, waiting for massive destruction to be unleashed on the enemy.

"Three, two, one!"

Click.

The guy with his finger on the mouse released the meme. The group turned to each other and high-fived, as their weapon hurled through the internet toward its intended targets.

Both Bebchuk and Chekhov audibly exhaled.

"You can read about battle," Bebchuk said, "but you can't capture the intensity. I feel like I need a cigarette." He took a few deep breaths, imaging the wounded enemy on the other side. "President Vlastov will be pleased. Now, for the next stage . . ."

"Do you want to coordinate talking points?" Chekhov asked.

"You seem to have a good handle on the general direction President Vlastov would like to go. I believe I sent you the list of our preferred candidates in Europe."

Chekhov nodded.

"And anything you can push about the RosAlleman pipeline."

"Yes, of course. It's already proving a very divisive issue. Just last week, Alina created a meme showing the chancellor of Germany hugging a bear that was eating the chancellor's pet, which was named 'Values.'"

"Excellent. We'll pick up on your material and feed it through our media network to bring it center stage."

"And we'll pick up on your reporting and make sure it trends."

"Of course, other parts of the intelligence services will be hacking into the accounts of several European politicians. You'll pick up on those stories, too."

"That goes without saying. The same accounts that spread the Willa Bennett emails will handle all that."

"On our side, we'll also be recruiting a number of human sources to help push the same narratives on New Russia News and elsewhere. It really helps drive the message home for Europeans and Americans when it comes from one of their own. I am also on my way to see Surikov, to set up a few other machinations." Bebchuk was pleased. He could see the tentacles of the operation spreading. All of them—Russian intelligence, Russian official media, Russian oligarchs—were working together to achieve President Vlastov's objectives. He clapped Chekhov on the back. "We exceeded expectations in the United States. Let's see if we can do it again in Europe."

CHAPTER SEVEN

Ruslan Bebchuk looked down at the glimmering blue of the Mediterranean Sea, as the private Gulfstream touched down at the Aeroport du Golfe du Saint-Tropez in the South of France. Nikolai Surikov, the head of Russia's prized RosGaz energy company, had sent the jet to Moscow when he learned that Bebchuk, President Darko Vlastov's emissary, hoped to meet with him. After the jet taxied to a stop next to an exclusive, private terminal, Bebchuk transferred to a helicopter that would bring him to his final destination.

Bebchuk did not anticipate a tense discussion with Surikov. Like most of his wealthy counterparts, the oligarch understood his role in the delicate ecosystem in which he existed as one of the wealthiest men on the planet. He knew that he might be called on at any time to serve Mother Russia, to act as an extension of the normal levers of state power. This was the implicit trade-off he made in order to be able to continue plundering the state-owned RosGaz.

The helicopter lifted off, blowing the tall umbrella pines sideways. Bebchuk surveyed the palatial homes along the coast and the mega yachts dotting the sea below. Russia may be a great place for someone like Surikov to make money, Bebchuk remarked, but when it came to investing and spending money, he and his contemporaries were stolid supporters of the West. How could they trust any Russian institution to keep their money safe? After all, look at everything they had managed to steal.

The helicopter slowed to a hover over a yacht. It was massive. Bebchuk counted four deck levels. A crew of young men was tucking two jet skis into a compartment on the side of one of the lower decks. What looked like a sophisticated radar system rotated on top of the yacht, and Bebchuk noted several men dressed all in black looking outward from various lookouts. He assumed they were Surikov's security team. The helicopter lowered to the helipad on the yacht's top deck, its trajectory perfectly aligned to avoid any contact between its circling blades and the boat's radar equipment. A young woman holding a clipboard stood on the side of the helipad, oblivious to the wind swirling around her. She stepped forward to greet Bebchuk as he descended from the helicopter.

"Welcome aboard Mine's Bigger, Mr. Bebchuk." She wore a smart red skirt and a crisp, white polo shirt—collar up—with "Mine's Bigger" embroidered in red capital letters over the breast. Despite the wind from the helicopter, her hair was immaculate. "Mr. Surikov is pleased to host you. Would you like to hydrate after your long trip?" She held out a bottle of ice cold, thrice-purified mineral water from a glacier stream in Iceland. "We just had it flown in today."

Bebchuk took the bottle and nodded a thank you as the helicopter blades slowed to a stop.

"You have some time before Mr. Surikov can see you. I will show you to your cabin." She led him toward a spiral staircase with a gold handrail and they went down to the main deck. "Mine's Bigger is the world's largest privately-owned superyacht," the woman said, as she ushered Bebchuk toward a large sliding door.

Bebchuk already knew this factoid. Surikov had made no secret of his dream to hold the title of owner of the world's largest yacht. He thought he had fulfilled that dream five years ago when he built a 538-foot motor yacht that he named Belonging, to signify his rightful place among an exclusive subset of the world's richest people. Belonging featured a wood-carved mermaid at the bow in the likeness of Surikov's mistress. The three-level ship could entertain eighteen guests with a crew of forty-seven. But within two months of christening her—a celebrity-filled event that featured a private concert by the hot Russian DJ Faber-Jay—a Silicon Valley tech mogul unveiled his mega yacht, Unicorn, which was three feet longer than Belonging. Surikov was livid and immediately commissioned a new yacht. Mine's Bigger, at 590-feet, made the other yachts look like dinghies, and Surikov felt confident the added length would limpen the competition for several years.

The glass door slid open and they walked into an air-conditioned living room with two half-circle, white leather couches. A bowl of fresh fruit was perfectly centered on a low table between them. A photograph of Surikov shaking hands with President Vlastov hung on the wall. Next to it was a photo of Surikov stroking a rare albino giraffe. In the distance was a large, wrought iron gate with gold letters weaved into it spelling "Zoorikov." At the end of a long corridor, the young woman clicked open the door to Bebchuk's cabin. He glanced in and saw a king-size bed, atop which were several towels rolled and folded to look like swans.

"Mr. Surikov has asked we do everything to make you comfortable, Mr. Bebchuk. Shall I make an appointment for you at the spa? It features a steam room infused with incense derived from lapislyptus, a rare orchid found on a single mountain peak in Nepal that blooms only two days a year. Its powers include increased stamina and libido. Perhaps a visit before tonight's social activities in the disco?"

"I'm fine, thank you."

"Very good. I'll leave you to freshen up. I shall return in one hour to escort you to your meeting with Mr. Surikov."

Bebchuk took a long shower then lay down briefly on the 1000-count, Turkish cotton sheets, while wrapped in a soft bathrobe with the Mine's Bigger logo across the left breast. He got dressed just before the young woman rapped on his door.

"Mr. Surikov is waiting for you in the Ice Palace."

He followed her down another corridor to an elevator, which took them below deck. When the doors opened, Bebchuk could hear the din of air conditioners. The young woman removed a white, puffy parka from a coat hanger on a hook. The jacket was emblazoned with the same Mine's Bigger logo. "I suggest you wear this," she said, helping him pull it on before motioning to a sliding glass door that looked like it was made from glistening ice.

Bebchuk entered the Ice Palace, a full-size ice rink nestled in the lower levels of the yacht. Surikov was on the ice, wearing red ski pants with Mine's Bigger spelled out in small white capital letters all over them. He was practicing sweeping the ice. Without looking up, he said, "Come throw a stone."

Bebchuk stepped onto the ice, his arms out for balance, and gingerly stepped toward the granite stone used for ice curling. "You see the target?" Surikov said. Bebchuk looked down the ice at the red and blue circle. "Now slide the stone."

Bebchuk grabbed the cold handle and shoved the curling stone down the ice. The force made him slip. Surikov took no notice of Bebchuk's face-plant and began sweeping the ice vigorously. "Hurry!" he yelled, still sweeping in deep concentration, trying to lead the stone to its target. The stone veered off to the left, slowed, and came to standstill about thirty feet away from the target. "I'm improving," Surikov said, pleased.

Bebchuk, on his feet now, looked at the stone, then at the target, still a long way off. "Very close, sir."

"I find sweeping ice soothing," Surikov said. He was fit for middle age, although his hair was beginning to thin. "Do you know the Vancouver Turtles? I own them. All my compatriots are outbidding each other on football teams in Europe. Not me." He took a deep breath of cold air. "I love the sound of the stone gliding across the ice." He stepped off the rink and hung his broom on the wall. "President Vlastov must be pleased with the results in the United States." He began taking his gloves off.

"Indeed, he thanks you for your generous support of Facts and Knowledge University," Bebchuk said, rubbing his hands together to keep them warm. "FaKU was instrumental in spreading much of the disinformation that angered and confused the American electorate—and the media—creating the right environment for a Redd victory." Although it remained unsaid, they both knew, as well, that putting a privately-owned façade on FaKU had kept the Kremlin at arm's length from the operation, providing at least a fig leaf of plausible deniability for Vlastov.

"Do those Americans really believe Willa Bennett makes ice cream from the kidneys of children? I'll never understand cult psychology," Surikov said.

"Leave the psychology to our security services. They've had generations of practice."

"If you're here, Vlastov must have another project in mind. Why don't we discuss it as we warm up?" Surikov disappeared behind a door.

Before Bebchuk could respond, Surikov's assistant appeared again. "Mr. Surikov requests you join him for a jacuzzi," she said, sliding the winter parka off Bebchuk's shoulders and placing it on a hook. "This way." She escorted him up a different elevator and to a private changing room. She indicated a pair of swim trunks, the Mine's Bigger logo tastefully printed across the front. "Mr. Surikov requests you keep the swimsuit as a gift when your voyage with us has concluded. I will allow you your privacy. When you are ready, you may exit through that door." She indicated a door on the other side of the changing room, then left him alone. He changed out of his clothes and exited through the back door. He found himself on the main deck. A large hot tub was there, on the back of the yacht, providing a glorious view upon the sea.

Surikov was already enjoying the heat and bubbles. "Grab some maqui berries before you come in," he said jovially, pointing to a bowl of the small, dark fruit. "They're a natural superfood, particularly this kind. They only grow in one valley in Chilean Patagonia. I just had them flown in today."

Bebchuk helped himself to a handful. They were deliciously sweet. He took a few more then slipped into the hot tub.

"Now, what can I do to serve Mother Russia?" Surikov asked.

"As you noted, President Vlastov considers the election of Richard Redd a great success. He has a larger objective, however, and hopes RosGaz might be willing to offer some support."

Surikov leaned his head back on a cushion, relaxed but listening intently, as Bebchuk outlined what Vlastov had in mind. When he was done, Surikov lifted his head and smiled at Bebchuk.

"Mr. Bebchuk, nothing gives me more pleasure than to serve my country." He popped a maqui into his mouth. "It is also an honor to serve our esteemed President Vlastov. Of course, I also have private business interests that must be protected. Wholly unrelated to matters of state. Sometimes they require, shall we say, unconventional methods to ensure their success." He ate another berry. "I trust the president understands this."

Bebchuk gave a small nod. He understood perfectly. Vlastov needed oligarchs like Surikov to maintain his power. But the oligarchs also needed Vlastov, in order to maintain their wealth. "President Vlastov understands how difficult and cutthroat your line of business can be, and I can assure you, he wishes you nothing but success in your private endeavors. Although, it is always kind to remember those who helped you get to the top, particularly those who are humble servants of the state, such as President Vlastov."

Bebchuk doubted Surikov needed reminding that a certain amount of business profits needed to go to Vlastov. Officially, Vlastov earned little money. The man had never married or had children, because Mother Russia was his bride and the Russian people were his children. Whether he was communing with a wild bear or building a shelter for children by hand using trees he had planted himself (all of which was conveniently caught on camera for future episodes of *Our Great President*), he lived to serve the Russian people, not to enrich himself.

Privately, however, Vlastov had become one of the richest men in the world. He allowed the oligarchs to loot state coffers, and they, in return, handed over 50 percent to the man who allowed them to do the looting in the first place. They also agreed to do what was needed to keep him in charge, so that he would continue allowing them to loot the country.

"I have deep appreciation for the support President Vlastov provides," Surikov said. He motioned to his assistant, who scrambled to grab his robe and hold it open for him.

Surikov stepped out of the hot tub and turned to Bebchuk. "Please, enjoy the amenities of Mine's Bigger." A young blond woman in a gold-colored tankini appeared from a lower deck and slipped into the whirlpool next to Bebchuk. Surikov indicated the woman and said, "Nastya will see to all your needs. I'll see you after dinner."

That evening, Bebchuk and his new escort joined the rest of Surikov's guests in the disco. Nastya, now in a short-dress version of her gold tankini, ran her hand along Bebchuk's chin then stepped out on the dance floor. It was built on a gyroscope to maintain an even keel even if the boat was moving. Bebchuk watched Nastya in her high golden heels, swaying to the electronic music of DJ Faber-Jay that piped in through the speakers. Groups of Surikov's guests—some friends, some business partners, some hired for the night—gathered on low sofas scattered about the disco, silver bowls of caviar and bottles of vodka set on small tables around the room. Surikov sat in a back corner, nuzzling a woman.

Bebchuk sat on one of the stools at the bar and ordered a glass of Dom Perignon champagne. He ran a hand over the seat of the stool next to him.

"They are covered in beluga whale foreskin," the bartender said, indicating the stool where Bebchuk's hand was. He gave Bebchuk his drink. "One of the softest materials on Earth."

The wooden dance floor retracted, revealing a glass floor. Nastya squealed with delight, as barracuda and medusas swam through the yacht's blue underwater lights. She and several other young women, hired, Bebchuk presumed, to keep the guests entertained, gyrated together to the electronic beat. Their hips swayed sensually. Their heads fell back, and their backs arched, as they lost themselves in the thumping music. An octopus swam into sight, gliding just under Nastya's high heels.

Suddenly, the octopus released a cloud of black ink. The water turned turbulent, white bubbles rising and spreading under the glass floor. As the bubbles cleared, Bebchuk saw in the water a man in a suit, his hands and feet bound with heavy chains. He stared up at Nastya and the other women, grinding away to DJ Faber-Jay on the other side of the glass, oblivious to his torment. Bebchuk made eye contact with the terrified man. A final bubble escaped his mouth before his eyes—and the rest of him—went dead.

Bebchuk turned to look at Surikov, still in his corner, a glass of vodka in hand. Bebchuk understood the message. Surikov would continue to help Vlastov, as long as Vlastov left Surikov free to handle his business as he saw fit, even if that meant using unconventional methods to achieve his goals. Bebchuk had no problem with this. Neither would Vlastov, he knew. Such unconventional methods might come in handy one day to carry out unconventional statecraft, as well. Bebchuk raised his glass toward Surikov. The oligarch lifted his with a small nod of acknowledgment. Together, though separated across the room, they drank, implicitly sealing their deal.

CHAPTER EIGHT

"I need you to make sure I don't get kidnapped," Victor said. He and Ness were walking through Villa Borghese on their way to the embassy.

"That sounds like fun and nothing I should worry about."

"I'm meeting that Max guy we saw at the energy conference. He hangs with an interesting crowd, some with ties to not the nicest people."

"What kind of not nice people are we talking about?" she asked.

"Russian mafia."

"They're very nice! Good dressers, too. Mostly athleisure-wear. Why am I providing security and not someone from your office?"

Victor looked straight ahead and kept walking.

Ness stopped. "Does your office know you're meeting with him?"

"Of course, my office knows I want to meet with him."

"That's not what I asked. What are you up to?"

Victor recalled for her the conversation he had had with COS Wilcox the previous afternoon. After determining Max had good and relevant access, Victor had developed a plan to approach him, and he had met with Wilcox to pitch the idea.

They had walked across the street to a local cafe. Victor ordered an espresso, then Wilcox ordered a Frappuccino. The barista looked at him, confused. "FRA-PO-CHEE-NO!" Wilcox enunciated loudly. Wilcox turned to Victor and said with a wink, "I got top scores on my language test." The barista looked like she wanted to cry. "Now, Victor, what's your big plan?"

Victor gave Wilcox a rundown of Max's background then said, "I'd like to approach him as an Italian academic, a researcher interested in learning more about the conservative movement in Italy."

"You can't pass as Italian!" Wilcox said dismissively. Victor was, in fact, Italian. And his maternal language was Italian. Even after working for the US government for two decades, he still had an accent when he spoke English. Some people at the embassy thought he was a member of the local staff. Wilcox continued, "I heard you talking with our Italian colleagues and I couldn't understand a word you said."

"Chief, maybe that has more to do with *your* language skills?"

"Why do you want this Max guy anyway? I told you we need Russian recruits." The barista set down a cappuccino in front of Wilcox. He looked at it as if she had put a plate of dog poop on the bar. "Ee-chay?" he asked, annoyed. She looked very confused. He pointed to the coffee and said again, louder, "EE-CHAY." He looked at Victor. "What do I have to do to get ice here?"

Victor held down a scream. He turned to the barista and asked for some ice. *"Ghiaccio, per favore."*

"What kind of shithead wants ice for his cappuccino?" she asked him in Italian. Victor apologized profusely as she left to get the ice, still cursing loudly.

"We're going after HVTs here, Victor," Wilcox continued, meaning High Value Targets, a term used in the war zones to refer to high-level terrorists. "I need you to identify an HVT, hone in with superior force, and recruit the motherfucker. You tell them you love America and you know they love America. Everyone loves America! They're just waiting to be asked. And paid. We're ready to pay a lot."

"I understand throwing cash and the Star-Spangled Banner at people in the war zones often works, but I feel like this might require a little more nuance."

The barista returned and threw a bowl of ice down on the bar.

"You want nuance?" Wilcox said, as he dumped the ice in the coffee. The barista glared, horrified. Victor gave her an apologetic smile. "I've got the world's biggest military ready to drop a Hellfire missile on your nuance. As soon as those Russians hear you're offering them an out from their shitty Russian lives, they'll take it."

Victor was less sure a one-way ticket to Des Moines to live in the suburbs and work as a dental receptionist was as alluring as Wilcox painted defection to be.

"Look, I got people in Washington breathing down my neck to get Russians. When they needed me to find terrorists, I found them terrorists. I won't let them down this time either."

Now, as they strolled through the park, Victor turned to Ness, "Unless I'm planning to drone a Russian in the middle of Rome, I'm not sure Wilcox is going to be the best leader for this operation. But if I get the operation going and can prove to him this guy can provide the intel we're looking for, then Wilcox will have to accept it. So, again, will you please make sure I don't get kidnapped?"

"I'm honored you trust me enough to ask me," she said.

"You're my wife."

"Exactly."

"I've already scoped out the meeting place. Here's what we're going to do."

CHAPTER NINE

Ness sat at an outdoor table in Piazza Barberini and ordered a bottle of water and a small sandwich. The Bernini Bristol Hotel was wrapped in lights for the holidays, looking like a giant present tied with a sparkling bow. Scores of tourists gathered around Bernini's Triton Fountain in the middle of the square, water pouring down the ripped torso of the merman perched upon two shells balancing on the heads of fish. Ness maneuvered to see around the crowd. As the city's church bells began to ring in unison, marking 1:00 pm, she saw Victor arrive on the other side of the piazza and stand in front of the cinema.

She had heard stories of him meeting assets in abandoned parking lots in West Africa, surrounded by nomads and camels. He looked decidedly less out-of-place here. He blended in with the other Italians out on the street for a smoke, belying the fact that he was at enormous risk. He was waiting to meet Massimiliano Brevi, who worked for an association that had ties to the frontrunner candidate to be the next prime minister of Italy, as well as ties to the Russian government and the Russian mafia, in order to try to recruit him to provide intelligence on all of those same people. Would Max come? If he did, what precautions would *he* take? Would Max show up with an entourage of bullies? Would a strongman pull Victor into a car waiting at the curb, whisking him away to be asked questions in between beatings? Vanessa was running through every possible scenario, gripping the bottle of water, shifting to see through the crowd, and watching her husband like a hawk.

The church bells went silent. A tourist bus pulled into the piazza, directly in front of where Victor was standing. Ness could no longer see him. She threw money on the table and walked quickly to the north side of the piazza to try to see around the bus. Another group of tourists blocked her before she could get a view behind the bus. Then it drove away. She stared in horror at the empty spot in front of the cinema. She looked left. She looked right. Nothing.

Victor was gone.

***

Ness spent the afternoon on tenterhooks. She sat on her exercise ball and tried to read cable traffic, switched to a normal chair and scrolled through some news pages on the internet, checked her phone, called Victor's office, called his cell phone, bounced the exercise ball, then sat on it again. She repeated the routine for three hours before giving up and going home.

Oliver was at his desk. His Italian language textbook was open in front of him but he was on his phone speaking a language Ness thought she recognized but that, as far as she knew, her son did not know.

"*Suka blyad*," he said. "Wait, say it again." He paused. "*Suka blyad*, like that?" He turned to Ness. "Oh, hey, Mom."

"Come out when you're off the phone," she said.

He gave her thumbs up, as he said again into his phone, "*Suka blyad*. How's my accent? *Suka blyad*."

Ness walked down the long hallway of their apartment to the living room, where she sat on the couch and rubbed her temples. She could still hear Oliver in his room. Did he know he was cussing in Russian?

He joined her a few minutes later and sank into a chair. He was in the middle of a growth spurt, so his body was out of proportion. His feet were too big for him and flopped as he walked. "His shoes are bigger than a Manhattan apartment," she had recently said to Victor.

"Can Nat come over this weekend?" he asked.

"Sure. Who's Nat?"

"She's a friend from school."

"Is Nat short for Natalya? Is that who you were talking to?"

"How'd you figure that out?"

"You know what I do for a living, right?"

"You and Dad ruin everything."

"That's our job."

"She was teaching me Russian."

"I heard. Do you know what *suka blyad* means?"

"I have no idea but I think it's bad and it's really fun to say."

"It means fuck bitch."

"Awesome. *Suka blyad*." He repeated the phrase.

"Your mother is sitting right here. Maybe tone down the cussing."

"It's in another language, one that none of us speaks for real, so it doesn't count."

"That's an obscure rule, but I'll allow it. So, Nat's a Russian friend from school? What do her parents do?"

"Mom, I know you and Dad freak out about this stuff, but kids don't ask each other what their parents do."

"Did you tell her what we do? You know the cover story for Dad, right?"

Ness and Victor had only recently told Oliver about Victor's job. They had held off, knowing that anyone who finds out thinks it's very exciting to be in on the secret, at first. Only later, as they realize they now have to lie, too, do they understand what a burden it is. For years, Oliver had asked questions. Where was Dad? What was he doing there? Why couldn't he discuss the attacks on the homeland without crying, like a normal dad? Like his friends' dads? Each new trip to an obscure location to carry out a clandestine operation got harder to hide from their son. They also got tired of hiding it.

So, shortly before they left Washington for Rome, the three of them had gone out to Oliver's favorite restaurant. There, in a secluded corner booth, over cheeseburgers, Victor revealed to his son what he actually did for a living. Vanessa had never seen Oliver look at his father the way he did in that moment. With those three little letters, CYA, Victor had gone from nerdy dad in reading glasses to coolest dad ever. They had spent the rest of the dinner sharing exploits and telling Oliver how he, too, had been involved in operations. He just didn't know it.

"I took you in your stroller to fill a dead drop," Victor told him.

"We once used you to get unregistered mobile phones," Ness said. "We claimed our passports and phones had been stolen, and we really needed new phones to keep in touch because I was scared.

This was in a country where you couldn't buy burner phones, you had to register with identity documents. You started to cry, so the guy selling the phones felt bad for us and felt pressured to move fast. It worked. You were great!"

They had also highlighted for him the need to keep this reality a secret. It was a terrible responsibility for a teenager, but both Victor and Vanessa knew Oliver could handle it, and all three felt better knowing they were in it together.

Oliver's reverence for Victor's clandestine life had not lasted long. By the time dinner was over and they had walked home while wrestling each other, the son once again saw Victor for who he really was: his dad. It was glorious.

"Mom, I just told you. Kids don't ask each other what their parents do. I know Dad's cover story, but none of my friends care. We don't talk about you."

"Not even a little?" Ness asked. "You don't tell your friends how cool your mom is?"

"Oh my god," Oliver said. "Maybe I don't want Nat to come over."

"Have Nat come over. We'd love to meet her!" Ness meant this. She really did. But she also knew it meant both she and Victor would have to write cables back to Washington. Officially, they were not allowed to fraternize with anyone who was Russian. And here they were discussing having a Russian visit their house. Ness knew it was innocuous. Were Russian spies going to use their daughter to befriend a boy in order to target his parents? Not likely. But a bored desk jockey in Washington might have an overactive imagination and try to put an end to the relationship.

Oliver headed back to his room, repeating his new Russian phrase. Ness was glad the kid was so carefree. She, on the other hand, still felt a weight on her chest. She looked at her watch. It was past 6:00 pm, and she still had no word from Victor. She berated herself for not moving fast enough when the tourist bus arrived, for not maneuvering through the crowd in the piazza more efficiently in order to keep eyes on him. She had failed him. And now what? Was he in a dank basement being threatened and beaten by Russian mobsters? Or on a plane, being taken to Russia to undergo interrogation? She looked at her watch again and wanted to scream. Where was he?

CHAPTER TEN

Victor caught a glance of Vanessa across the piazza as he stood under the cinema marquee. He heard the church bells chime 1:00 pm, then saw Massimiliano Brevi come around the corner. He wore his hair long but pushed back with a small amount of hair product. He wore round spectacles and a tweed jacket with an olive-green scarf tossed casually around his neck. Victor was checking out everyone else around them, watching the lunchtime crowd pass by and noting the tourists that got off a large bus that had pulled up in front of him. Max approached Victor with a gentle smile and shook his hand.

"It is a pleasure to meet you, Mr. Caro. Come, I know a great restaurant up the street," Max said, motioning Victor to a road off the piazza. Victor followed him and they made small talk, but Victor remained alert to anyone who might be following them. They entered a crowded restaurant, filled with Romans enjoying a midweek lunch. They managed to grab a table, and Victor began to relax a little bit. Max had shown up alone. They were meeting in a public place, surrounded by people who would all be witnesses if someone tried to kidnap him now. The scenario didn't seem likely.

"Tell me, how did an American embassy official come to speak Italian so well?" Max asked, as the waiter poured them each some sparkling water.

COS Wilcox had been so adamant that Victor not present himself as an Italian national that he had prepared a cable for Director's lawyers that, if Wilcox decided to send it, would be sure to unleash a bureaucratic torrent on Victor. He had had nightmares of being put to the test to see whether he was Italian enough to pass as Italian, as judged by a lawyer from Virginia. He had had visions of being forced to take a language exam speaking only with his hands and being asked if he still lived with his mother. Instead, he had decided to give a little to make the operation more palatable going forward. As such, he had decided to tell Max he was an American embassy official, but one who was considering taking a sabbatical from service to pursue a PhD in Italian politics. It wasn't a great cover, but it would be easier for Wilcox and Director to swallow. Once he decided to tell Wilcox he had gone ahead and met with Max against the chief's order, that is.

"My mother was Italian," Victor said to Max. "It's my first language."

"So, as an Italian, then, you can understand: Italy for Italians."

"On the contrary," Victor replied. "I was born and raised in Italy but now work for the US government. It is that embrace of diversity that makes us so strong."

"Not everyone in the United States is embracing such differences these days," Max said, in a clear reference to President-elect Redd.

"But I'm here to ask about Italian politics," Victor said. "Luca Callieri is the strongest nationalist candidate we've seen in years. What triggered the movement?"

Max launched into a tirade about the European Union. "The technocrats in Brussels are on a permanent vacation funded by us," he complained, referring to the EU commission in Brussels, which handed down EU policy to its member states. "Showering themselves with tax-free salaries at our expense to eat fries with mayonnaise on the terraces outside their subsidized condos on the Grande Place, while telling the French all cheese is the same and the Italians that pasta is like any noodle you find in a British pub, slathered with brown sauce. We are forgetting our identity. Italians are Italian. The French are French."

"Yet Callieri turned to Russia for funding for his Italian nationalist party."

"Russia understands the need to embrace our differences in Europe, which makes them a better partner for Italy than the European Union," Max said, taking a sip of the Primitivo wine they had ordered. "Like us, Russia has a strong culture, a long history of which to be very proud. They do not apologize for it. Nor do they force it upon others."

"The people of Crimea might disagree," Victor pointed out, reminding Max that Russia had, in fact, quite recently forced itself on a sovereign nation.

"There are Russians in Crimea," Max responded. "They voted to be part of Russia."

"In a fixed referendum, surrounded by Russian military. It wasn't exactly a fair vote."

"I will concede to you this point," Max said. "But you must concede to me this: Russia's history with Ukraine and Crimea is not the same as Russia's history with Italy."

Victor raised his glass. Max did the same.

"*Cin cin*," Max said, toasting Victor. He took a long sip then placed his glass on the table. He fiddled with a breadstick, as he continued, "This is why the MussoRusso Cultural Association has been keen to work with Luca Callieri. Da Italia puts Italy first, not Brussels, not Europe, but Italy. He is not looking to standardize the size of bananas throughout Europe, setting up a commission to study precisely how long, how curved, and how yellow a European banana must be. Italy for Italians. It's very simple."

"How does your association with Russia help Italy for Italians?" Victor asked.

"We share our traditions and heritage with them. They share theirs with us. We share, together, an appreciation for family, for religion, for tradition. I will give you an example. Grigoriy, who is a Russian diplomat and works at the Russian Cultural Center, has asked me to help him develop a cultural exchange between young Da Italia supporters and Russia, so they can visit Moscow, see Orthodox churches, and learn some of our shared traditional history."

Victor perked up when he heard the name Grigoriy. Max must have been referring to Grigoriy Stepanov, the Russian intelligence officer—under diplomatic cover at the Russian Cultural Center— whom Victor had seen approach Max at the energy conference. "Is the Russian Cultural Center a large donor to MussoRusso?"

"We get donations from a number of international groups with whom we share similar values, similar ideas to promote," Max said. "Including, yes, the Russian Cultural Center."

It was as near a confirmation that Victor could get that Max was a target of the Russians. Moreover, Victor assessed, they were using shared ideology as their hook to reel him in. They were also using a tried-and-true lure: money. As Max went on explaining the many synergies between Italian and Russian culture, Victor's mind raced over the opportunities the recruitment of Max would bring. Max could provide information on how Russian intelligence officers were running their operations in Europe and what their objectives were. What were the Russians' plans and intentions in the European political sphere, and how were they going about achieving those objectives? Given the recent events in the United States—the fact that Russia had just interfered in those elections—Russian modus operandi in Europe was a high priority. And Victor believed he had found the right target.

Max and Victor stayed at the table eating and talking until it was nearly dark outside.

"I'm afraid I will have to end our lunch here," Max said, looking at his watch. "Although I have greatly enjoyed sparring with you for the last four hours. We will do this again, no?"

Victor was pleased. Max was suggesting a second meeting. Things were going well. They said their goodbyes and Victor meandered slowly back home through Villa Borghese as the sun set. The cool air and long walk helped him digest all the food he had eaten with Max. He felt satiated and relaxed, but also excited at the progress he had made. He opened the door to the apartment. Ness jumped off the couch, ran over to him, and threw her arms around him. He gave her a quick hug back.

"Four hours at the table!" he said. "It was delicious. We have to go to back to that place. I'll show you. They had wild boar with a chocolate sauce. Why are you rolling your eyes at me?"

"I spent the afternoon worrying about you, while you had a four-hour lunch? A bus blocked the view, then you were gone. I was having visions of you in a Russian basement surrounded by men in track suits and caps. I tried your phone."

"I had it turned off. Interesting guy. Excellent food. Hey, Oliver. What's up?"

"Not much. Nat's coming over this weekend." Oliver was passing by on his way from the kitchen to his room. "*Suka blyad,*" he repeated quietly, still trying to master the accent on the new phrase he had learned.

"Is he cussing in Russian?" he asked Ness. "Who's Nat?"

"I'll explain later. Get me a glass of wine. I'm glad you weren't kidnapped."

CHAPTER ELEVEN

Victor took the long way through Villa Borghese on his way to work the next morning. He walked by Piazza di Siena, where carabinieri law enforcement officers were training on horseback, surrounded by stone pine and cedar trees that shot up toward the sky. He thought about his lunch with Max the previous day and how he was going to write it up to present it to his management.

Victor had rather enjoyed sparring with Max. He was bright, curious, and open to new ideas, all of which Victor assessed as assets in his pursuit to recruit him. Now he had to sell it to his management. Normally, he would also have to sell it to Director, but given the sensitivity of the subject—a potential asset to provide intelligence on how Russia was funding and supporting political parties outside of Russia—and the current political situation in Washington—namely, an incoming president who was under investigation for possibly winning his position because of that same Russian help—Victor knew he'd have to be very careful about how he presented Max to the CYA bureaucracy. The Agency was very good at compartmentalizing information and keeping secrets among small groups of those with a need to know. But in this case, a number of people who could claim a need to know, including any incoming Director and the soon-to-be-president himself, possibly had a reason not to want *anyone* to know the intelligence Max could provide. What Max knew was a threat to any politician who had benefited from Russia's largesse. How would Redd and his aides react to a case officer working to prove Russia had placed them in power? What would stop them from shutting down the operation now that Redd was poised to hold the most powerful office in the world? How far down the chain would he be willing to crush individual civil servants who might uncover information that painted him in a bad light? Victor needed to tread carefully.

He arrived at the embassy and went up to his office, focused on how he was going to maneuver through this difficulty and protect his source, possibly from his own president. It was not a position he ever imagined he would be in. He walked into the bullpen. Ralph Fleiss, the support officer, was waiting for him.

"Good morning, Victor!" He was very perky for such an early hour. He was dressed in wrinkled chinos and a light blue, button down shirt that was not buttoned correctly. Each button was one hole off. The pocket had a large ink stain. "We need to discuss handling your ball."

Patrick, staring at his computer screen, giggled. "Handle your ball," he said, under his breath.

Victor glanced at him, annoyed and amused at the same time.

"Your ball is not a toy," Ralph continued. "It is an ergonomic piece of functionality meant to enhance and encourage spinal health and well being."

"Right, it's good for my back. That's why I want it."

"If misused or if your ball is handled improperly, the consequences can be devastating. Because this will be a government-issued ergonomic office enhancement, you are required, according to Regulation FURN-12874, to successfully complete an online safety course outlining proper use of this equipment."

"I have to pass a test to sit on a ball?"

Ralph took a tape measure out of his pocket and wrapped it around Victor's head. "Upon successful completion of the course, I will issue you protective head gear, in the event you should fall off your ball."

Patrick stifled another laugh.

"We take workplace safety very seriously," Ralph said, marking down Victor's head size on a notepad. "I've already sent you the link for the course. It will automatically notify me once you complete it. Good luck!"

Ralph walked into the hallway, and Victor noticed Mary Driscoll, the DCOS, standing by his desk. She had blended in so well with the beige wall behind her that Victor had not seen her before.

"I'm still waiting on your papers for the promotion panel, Victor. I'm starting to think you don't take your job very seriously."

"On the contrary, Mary. I take my job very seriously. It's my career I don't care about."

"You haven't been promoted in fourteen years. That should bother you."

"Should it?"

"I'd like to see you exceed your potential."

"That's not possible."

"If our officers aren't committed to their careers, it becomes difficult for management to represent you and the station as a whole in a positive light to Director."

"The more of your officers who get promoted, the better you look, thus increasing your chances of making it into the senior service."

"That may be true, but it's a very cynical approach, Victor. I care about your career. More than you do, apparently."

"My career is over. I'm retiring after this tour."

"Everyone says they will retire at fifty and no one does. I want you to keep all your options open."

"While keeping you in the running yourself. Don't worry, Mary. I'll fill out my promotion papers. Should I do that before or after I write up my meeting with a potential recruit on Russian influence tactics?"

"I can't believe you have to ask."

"Neither can I."

She looked at him, waiting. When he didn't say anything, she said, "The promotion papers are due next week."

She disappeared into the hall, blending in with the linoleum floor.

Victor sat on his broken chair and opened his email. He saw the link for the security course for the exercise ball. Patrick rolled up to his desk on his chair.

"Don't start anything yet," he said.

"How come your chair rolls so smoothly?"

"They like analysts better. Check this out." He clicked on the CYA's internal home page. Victor's eyes widened when he saw it.

"I knew you'd love it," Patrick said. "The annual gingerbread house competition has gone global! It's not just for officers at Director anymore."

The CYA annual gingerbread house competition had long been a thorn in Victor's side. The time and effort Director's minions in Washington gave to the competition had once delayed Victor's efforts to exfiltrate a source in West Africa.

"I think we're too late to turn in our own, and anyway, who the fuck wants to do that?" Patrick said. "But we can vote!"

He began clicking through the entries. An entry from a base in Yemen showed an airplane made of wafer cookies covered in icing, with Oreos for engines. Little gingerbread men were standing outside the plane. A windowless gingerbread van idled on the side.

"Is that a gingerbread rendition flight?" Victor asked. "The gummy drop airstrip is jolly."

"Look at this one." Patrick pointed to a simple, unadorned gingerbread house. Its windows were covered in black licorice, as though the curtains were drawn, and the door was simple and clean with small chocolate chip doorknob. "How boring."

"How unassuming," Victor corrected him. "It's a safe house."

Patrick clicked through to the next one. "Wow."

This entry featured a large tank made of graham crackers with a cigarette cookie as the barrel of the gun. An enormous American flag, made out of red, white, and blue tart candies, was mounted on top of the tank. The gingerbread artist had even given the flag a waving effect, as if it were blowing in the wind. Behind the tank were beige and gray mountains crafted from colored dough. Surrounding the tank, gray rock-like candies made piles of rubble. Small gummy bears gathered on the side, bearing gifts for whoever was arriving by tank. Some of the gummy bears were draped in blue taffy.

"Please tell me those aren't supposed to be niqabs on those gummy bears," Victor said, referring to the traditional female covering ubiquitous in Rubblestan.

"Those are totally supposed to be niqabs on those gummy bears," Patrick said.

Hovering above the tank scene, held in place by some kind of hook contraption, was a drone created out of marshmallows. In the corner of the scene on the ground was a small house with a single gingerbread man inside, appearing to hold a control stick while watching a tiny monitor made out of chewing gum.

"Is he piloting the drone?" Victor asked.

He and Patrick leaned in for a closer look. Patrick's mouth dropped open. He pointed to the name of the entrant: Cliff Wilcox.

Victor rubbed his temples.

"They're showing some of these on the public website, trying to make the agency seem more human," Patrick said.

"I'm sure our adversaries will be happy to see how much time we spend not going after them. I came in here to write about a potential asset who can provide intel on Russian influence operations that threaten our national security, and instead I just spent the better part of my morning being berated by one manager for not trying to get promoted while the COS apparently has time to craft a complex war scene out of cookies."

"Don't forget your ball."

"And I have to do a safety course to learn how to sit on a ball."

"You're a scrooge. I mean, you're 100 percent correct, but you're also a major downer. I'm going back to my desk. With my chair that rolls. I have a war on terror to win. Right after I vote for my favorite gingerbread house."

CHAPTER TWELVE

N ess spotted Francesco Restani sitting at a table on the side of a piazza at the restaurant Da Luigi in Rome's historic center. He was dressed in a slim-cut suit, the pants barely at his ankles, chic bright green sneakers on his feet. Heat lamps were keeping the terrace warm against the January chill. She crossed over to him and he stood to greet her, motioning to the chair across from him. "I took the liberty of ordering a few small starters for us. I hope that is OK," he said.

She looked at the table and saw tomatoes drizzled with olive oil and a giant lump of fresh burrata cheese. "That is more than OK," she responded, her mouth watering.

Francesco worked for Italy's Information and Internal Security Agency, AISI, and was Ness's counterpart in the Italian government.

"I read your government's declassified assessment about the Kremlin's actions regarding your elections," Francesco said. "One week until inauguration, and everyone is discussing whether your future president is an agent of the Kremlin."

"I'm afraid it's a strange position for President-elect Redd," Vanessa said, wiping a stray piece of burrata off her chin. "And for us. We have very good evidence Russian intelligence approached his campaign. We are not sure yet how the campaign responded, although publicly they insist to know nothing about it. They claim they never spoke to a Russian, which we actually know is not true."

"Perhaps Redd fears appearing illegitimate."

"That may be part of it. I helped investigate some Russian illegals, and we saw strange things. I'm not sure how clear a picture we will ever get. As you know, any influence operation like this would have plausible deniability."

"Ah yes, the ever-present fig leaf." Francesco pointed to the statue in the middle of the piazza. It was a naked man with a strategically placed fig leaf. There was no question what was underneath it.

"Even if we actually saw a Redd campaign aide in the same room talking with a Russian intelligence officer, unless we had audio or an eyewitness to the conversation, we would never be 100 percent sure what was said." She thought of Ashley-Anne Wynnscott opening the door to let Diana Abramovich into her home.

"We have similar—how can I say this?—dynamics here in Italy," Francesco said. "Are you aware of the Russian Cultural Center?"

"Near Largo di Torre Argentina, where Cassius and Brutus assassinated Julius Caesar."

"You know your Roman history."

"I know the history of dictators and traitors."

Francesco gave her a sympathetic look. "We believe the center is doing more than celebrating Russian culture."

"Isn't that cliché?" Ness asked. "The Russian Cultural Center as a front for Russian intelligence?"

"Clichés exist for a reason." He took a sip of red wine, as the waiter placed a dish of rigatoni amatriciana in front of Ness and a plate of spaghetti with clams in front of Francesco. "The director's daughter is a dual-citizen. She is quite something. Hard to miss. She ran for local office recently, although she did not perform very well."

"The daughter of the director of the Russian Cultural Center, which you believe is a cover for Russian intelligence, ran for political office in Italy?"

"This is Italy, Vanessa. We've also had a porn star and Mussolini's granddaughter in parliament. The Russian Cultural Center has worked closely with the MussoRusso Cultural Association," Francesco said. A small bit of clam sauce flicked onto his tie. "*Cazzo*," he swore.

"I've heard of the MussoRusso Association," Ness said, recalling the energy conference she had attended with Victor and half the spies in the city.

"Then you know the head of this association is an occasional advisor to Luca Callieri, head of Da Italia, who is hoping to be our next prime minister after our elections this autumn."

Vanessa connected the dots in her head. Russian intelligence services, using the Russian Cultural Center in Rome as cover, were supporting the MussoRusso Cultural Association, which was promoting Luca Callieri in his campaign to be Italy's next prime minister. Now it was her turn to give Francesco a sympathetic look.

He continued, "Given the assessment that President Vlastov helped to elect Redd in the United States, I can imagine it is awkward for someone in your position, because, you see, we have very similar questions about one of our main candidates, as well.

We hope we do not find ourselves in the same awkward position as the United States."

The waiter returned with a small spray can and brush. Without a word, Francesco held out the tip of his tie, where the clam sauce had stained it. The waiter sprayed it and brushed it, and the stain was gone. "*Grazie*," Francesco said.

Given his official position, he could not state clearly what he was trying to say, but Ness understood. Employees of the interior ministry, which oversaw Italy's security and intelligence services, hoped not to find themselves like Vanessa and Victor and their colleagues: having to investigate if their own leaders were being influenced by the Kremlin. It was, she had to agree, awkward.

He continued, "I did want to share more with you about the daughter of the director of the Russian Cultural Center. Her name is Svetlana Zharkova." He handed Vanessa a photograph of a young woman with long red hair. It was the same woman she and Victor had seen at the energy conference asking manipulative questions to Aldo Conti from MussoRusso and sidling up to the Italian officials who were in attendance.

"Her name is Svetlana?"

"As I said, clichés exist for a reason. She has become rather popular among conservative politicians here in Italy." He then handed Vanessa a piece of paper with a photocopy of both Svetlana's Italian and Russian passports, as well as a flight itinerary. "She's just bought a ticket to Washington, DC. I thought you and your colleagues would like to know."

CHAPTER THIRTEEN

Svetlana Zharkova stared at herself in the mirror. Her long, green-sequined dress accented all the right places, and she was having a good hair day. Her red locks spilled over her shoulders with just the right amount of curl. Tonight would be her first big event in Washington, DC. She took a deep breath. She was ready.

The chief justice of the United States had sworn in Richard Redd as president a few hours earlier. "This is such a huge crowd," Redd had said during his inaugural speech. She knew that was untrue. In fact, it had had the lowest attendance of any presidential inauguration on record, including that of President Kermit Lillipew III, whose inauguration was held in the middle of a rampantly contagious plague, but she understood the large crowd lie was now fact, and she was prepared to repeat it as such to everyone.

She had only recently begun circulating among the American conservative social crowd, but already she sensed most political players in Washington agreed Redd was not fit to be president. They found him brash, unethical, and not classy. The recent US intelligence community assessment that had been declassified and released publicly added to their trepidation. The intelligence community had assessed Redd had been elected with the help of President Darko Vlastov of Russia. The Washington Establishment, as she had learned this group of people was called, was befuddled about how to respond to his surprise win. She laughed at their attempts to remain above the fray, not to dirty themselves. She understood human nature and knew it was only a matter of time. Those same players very much enjoyed proximity to power, and no one was more powerful than the person who occupied the Oval Office. As one pundit who had spoken badly about Redd during the campaign said earlier as Redd—wearing a warm ushanka hat to protect him against the January cold—walked down Constitution Avenue from the Capitol to the White House: "I think Washington is ready to welcome him, and Congress is eager to help implement his agenda. If he succeeds, we all succeed."

The city was alight with several inaugural balls that night, but the most exclusive was at the Kosmopolitan Hotel in downtown Washington, and Svetlana had secured herself a ticket. She was staying at the hotel and checked herself one last time in the mirror, then took the hotel elevator down to the lobby.

The recently renovated hotel was owned by Ken Grandy, a real estate magnate and bundler for the Republicans, meaning he raised money—a lot of it—for the party. Svetlana entered the ballroom. Grandy's staff had gone with a Russian theme for the evening. Chilled vodka ran through an ice sculpture of a bear standing on its hind legs. The table centerpieces featured miniature towers with bright-colored onion domes. A hostess handed her a goody bag and welcomed her to the party. Svetlana peeked inside. Among the goodies were cookies in the shape of matryoshka dolls—each cookie smaller than the next—and a gift certificate to the Kosmopolitan's spa, called SpaSibo.

She grabbed a Moscow Mule from the bar and nibbled on a mini blini covered with caviar. She circled the room and took note of the attendees, trying to figure out who was who. She watched the journalists gathered at the door and gauged who was important by their movements. Whenever a VIP arrived, a shoving match would erupt as they tried to maneuver for better access. She listened as one TV reporter grabbed Senator Kyle Lewis, who was head of the Foreign Relations Committee now that Redd had moved to the White House, and interviewed him about the day's events.

"Senator Lewis, you ran against President Redd in the Republican primary. At that time, Redd accused you of murdering a puppy. He also called your wife ugly and implied you were the reason she got cancer and died. Yet, here you are at his inaugural ball."

"It's time to let bygones be bygones and focus on the future," Senator Lewis told the journalist.

"Do you find it odd that the ball has a Russian theme, given the accusations against the president?"

"I find it very festive," Lewis responded, before walking away.

The reporter turned to her camera. "There you have it. It's Washington on the Moskva and everyone seems ready to celebrate together and close the wounds of a hard-fought campaign."

Svetlana continued rubbing elbows with Washington's movers and shakers, but kept an eye on the door. When a loud commotion broke out, she knew the guest of honor had arrived. President Redd swaggered in with a young woman on his arm. He still wore the ushanka hat he had sported earlier. He stopped to pose for the cameras, making sure his date, with her short silver dress and her long pouty face, was in the photos with him. "This is Yulia. Make sure you get her in your shots too. Isn't she beautiful?"

"Mr. President!" one reporter shouted. "Given the accusations about you, that you accepted help from Russian President Vlastov to get elected, don't you think a Russian-themed inaugural ball is a little over the top?"

Redd replied, "I don't know what you're talking about."

"Thank you, Mr. President," the reporter said. "Have a great evening, and good luck!"

Svetlana went back to moving through the crowd, taking names and determining the pecking order by who sat where and who had access, for how long, to whom. She laughed again at human nature. All these people talked about being ethical, but in the end, the smell of power turned them into easily manipulated animals.

CHAPTER FOURTEEN

Grigoriy Stepanov sat in the Number One cafe on the outskirts of Rome's Trastevere district. He was tired. He had spent the night before with Olivia Yeardley, a suspected CYA officer at the US Embassy, drinking in Campo dei Fiori. Grigoriy suspected she was trying to recruit him, and he knew he was trying to recruit her. He had fantasized it would make for an intriguing and sexy dynamic. He had imagined the two of them rolling in the sheets at the chic Hassler Hotel before she handed him classified documents with details of all of America's assets in Russia. "Grigoriy," she would whisper into his waxed chest as he poured them more vodka, "take me here, then take me back to Moscow with you." In reality, she talked a lot about yoga and only drank filtered almond water. She had brought her own bottle to the bar in Campo dei Fiori, much to the waiter's consternation.

So, he really needed to move things along with Massimiliano Brevi. He sat at a table in a back corner and watched the traffic outside. A tram went by, then he spotted Max crossing the street to the cafe. The two sat, each with a cappuccino, although Grigoriy had added a little Sambuca to his, to ease his headache from the night before.

"Max, I have great news! The Russian Cultural Center would like to invite you to an upcoming conference on nationalist movements, in Moscow."

"I would love that, Grigoriy, but I'm afraid the MussoRusso Association doesn't have the budget to send me to Moscow."

"Perhaps I wasn't clear," Grigoriy said. "We would like to sponsor you to go. We will cover your airfare, hotel, and food expenses. It's really quite an opportunity. We only sponsor a few individuals each year. The conference is organized by Konstantin Dudnik. He is very particular about who we invite. He'll also be speaking."

"Konstantin Dudnik will be at the conference? Can I meet him?" Max was elated at the thought he might be able to meet the long-bearded mystic behind President Vlastov.

Grigoriy had no idea if he'd be able to arrange a meeting between Max and Dudnik. Dudnik had a reputation as a savant, but he was also a crotchety man with little patience. But Grigoriy needed Max to feel special. He needed Max to be pliant. Things were going badly with Olivia. Grigoriy's boss had been hounded by Moscow. He, in turn, put pressure on Grigoriy. Grigoriy pictured himself spending the rest of his career at a desk in Siberia, trying to type wearing mittens. He needed a recruit. "I am sure we can arrange that, my friend! He would love to meet someone with your love of traditional values and appreciation for Russian culture."

Max felt very special.

They discussed the details of the trip. Then, Grigoriy leaned back in his chair and looked at Max. He held up his hands, making a square frame with his thumbs and index fingers, and looked at

Max as though sizing him up with a camera. "You're a good-looking man, Max. Have you ever done television?"

Max was flattered. "I've done a few small interviews. I mostly leave that to my boss. He is a good spokesman for MussoRusso."

"I've got some friends over at New Russia News who are looking for people who can speak eloquently about how the European Union is destroying European countries. Italy for Italians, isn't that what you always say? Why not go on NRN and say it for everyone to hear? I've seen your boss, Aldo Conti, right? He is fine, but you are young and dynamic. Besides, he may be a figurehead for the MussoRusso Association, but aren't you the one who keeps it going every day? He's out meeting with politicians, but you're the one who really knows the people." Grigoriy waited as Max mulled this over. He again saw the image of himself in Siberia, his tea turned into a popsicle, his lunch consisting daily of frozen potatoes. He silently urged Max to agree with his proposal.

Max stirred his cappuccino then took a sip, as he contemplated. He had been feeling a little overshadowed by Conti. Maybe this was a good opportunity to step out into his own spotlight? He put his coffee cup down. "I'd like that, Grigoriy. I'll do it."

Grigoriy shoved the image of him in a freezing office in Siberia to the back of his mind. He exhaled. His boss would be pleased. Moscow would be pleased. He had clinched a new asset.

CHAPTER FIFTEEN

Victor and Max sat in a fish restaurant that was a shack on the beach in Ostia, outside Rome. Victor had not yet managed to move his meetings with Max into a private location. The shack was public but isolated, limiting the chances they would be spotted together by anyone who cared. Victor had taken the additional precaution of driving along back roads, avoiding tolls and their accompanying cameras, to arrive at the spot.

"We need to move past this idea that Russia is our enemy," Max said, as he dug into a plate of spaghetti with frutti di mare. "This is where I think Callieri is very strong. He recognizes that the Cold War is over. These systems we put in place to counter the Soviet Union, they are anachronistic now. We do not need a European Union. We do not need NATO. There is no threat anymore, so let us each be a sovereign state. I'll be speaking about this next week on New Russia News."

"Have you done interviews with NRN before?" Victor asked.

"This is new. Grigoriy, who works at the Russian Cultural Center, has asked me to speak about how Callieri hopes to restore a true sense of Italian nationality here."

"Why does the Russian Cultural Center care about restoring a sense of Italian nationality?"

"They fund a number of our programs. The concepts of true sovereignty and cultural tradition are shared by both Italy and Russia. They are also hosting me in Moscow in a few weeks. I will be attending a conference organized by Konstantin Dudnik on autonomy, how we can promote our autonomy over institutions like the European Union."

"What are your thoughts on Dudnik?" Victor asked. "You can't possibly buy into the idea that the sun is cold?"

"Of course not. Only a very small minority of people believe in this, but the mainstream media latch onto it and hype it up, as if it is a major movement."

Victor assessed that Grigoriy Stepanov was manipulating Max into delivering the Kremlin's exact anti-European Union talking points. Such a pro-Russia agenda would come off softer when delivered by an enthusiastic believer who didn't realize he was being manipulated. He also wondered if the Russian would try to set Max up in a compromising position while he was in Moscow.

"You'll have a great time, I'm sure. Moscow is a fantastic city," Victor said. "But avoid plugging your phone into any USB ports, and check for cameras in your hotel room."

"You Americans are always so paranoid when it comes to the Russians."

"That doesn't mean we're wrong." Victor popped some fried calamari in his mouth. "How does appearing on a Russian news channel help Italian sovereignty? Look at the United States, where Russia just interfered in the elections. Does that help American sovereignty? Isn't that actually an attack on American sovereignty? You don't fear the same behavior here in Italy?"

"Again, you read too much of this mainstream media, my friend. What you say is more of this Russophobia. Russia didn't do this to the United States. Redd is very popular, but the elitist newspapers, who are used to everyone following their opinion, steal the narrative and try to blame someone else for the loss of their preferred candidate. No outlet will tell you Redd is, in fact, very popular."

"Have you heard of Facts News?" Victor asked. "It's one of the biggest news outlets in the United States, and they can't stop singing Redd's praises. Anyway, none of that excuses Russia's actions."

"What about the EU?" Max asked. "We've been told for sixty years we must relinquish our sovereignty for the greater good of Europe, as if we are all the same. You will never convince me that spaetzle is pasta. Enough!"

"You can't compare EU influence on Italy, which is done through a transparent process in which Italy's representatives play an active role, with Russian covert influence on a sovereign nation's elections. Now you want to trust them with this RosAlleman pipeline. Callieri should be careful, and keep his eyes open. That's all I'm saying. Vlastov does not have Italy's best interests at heart. Vlastov has Russia's best interests at heart. In fact, really he has his own best interests at heart."

"I like to debate with you, Victor. You make me think." He dug the brains out of a langostino and slurped them up, as the small waves of the Mediterranean washed in and out on the beach.

Victor knew this was a delicate moment. He had walked Max to a line where he had started to question the premise of his own argument. It was best to let him digest the conversation and process his doubts, rather than risk him becoming indignant. Victor allowed the silence to sit between them, giving Max the choice of continuing or changing the conversation.

"Enough of these politics," Max said. "Much of the time, I would prefer to escape all those discussions." He pointed out toward the water. "Most days, I'd be happy to sit by the sea in Ventotene, eating a delicious, ripe plum."

"You know the Pontine Islands well?" Ventotene was part of a small archipelago off the coast of Italy, between Rome and Naples.

"I spent many summers there growing up. Have you been?"

"I haven't," Victor said. "I've been wanting to sail out there."

"Ah, a sailor. Odysseus sailed the islands. Ponza, the largest of the archipelago, is where he was lured in by the goddess Circe."

"I thought it was mostly penal colonies."

Max chuckled. "It is true, it has this history too. Many Roman emperors banished their enemies, some of them their own relatives, to the island of Santo Stefano. Benito Mussolini, too, sent criminals there. But the sea is beautiful and there is always a nice breeze. It is a lovely spot to be in jail!" He smiled as he reminisced. "One restaurant in Ventotene, near the old port—the old port was a Roman port, by the way, two thousand years old and it is still in good condition—this restaurant is run by a man named Benito. He is ancient! Almost as old as the port itself. I don't know how he stays upright. It is the best fish in Italy. You have to go. Bring your wife. She can dance with Benito at the island's discoteca when we all finish eating."

"It sounds like paradise."

"It is my paradise. One day, when I no longer have to worry about work and politics, Ventotene is where I will go."

Victor allowed Max to fall into his reverie, and they ended the evening there.

CHAPTER SIXTEEN

Svetlana Zharkova rearranged her boobs in her bra, pushing them up and out. Her nipples projected through her T-shirt, which sported a graphic of a Kalashnikov rifle across her now heaving chest. She hiked up her red pleather miniskirt, giving onlookers a scintillating peek at her semiconcealed thigh holster for her pistol. She teetered on stiletto heels toward the entrance of the grand ballroom of the Kosmopolitan Hotel. She had easily infiltrated the conservative social scene and today's event was the biggest and most important one on the conservative social circuit since the inauguration. She was about to attend the National Jesus Brunch. Here, well-connected and powerful elites—both politicians and private sector power brokers—would gather to pray to Jesus while eating delicious pancakes. It was an opportunity to influence and be influenced, as many attendees were richer than the Vermont maple syrup that flowed freely. In fact, this was the first time the maple syrup was from Vermont; previously, it had come from Maine, but the Vermont Maple Syrup Association had successfully lobbied the organizers to make the switch after providing a sizable financial donation.

Standing in the lobby of the Kosmopolitan Hotel in her Kalashnikov shirt, Svetlana put on a last hit of red lipstick before entering the National Jesus Brunch. Hundreds of people were milling around, politicians, social media influencers, billionaire CEOs, and Christian leaders. She saw an influential married businessman who had recently been outed for sending dick pics to his mistress, bowing his head with a priest who had done more paperwork than most to move underlings from diocese to diocese after too many altar boys had inexplicably quit the choir. Together, they prayed for the survival of the traditional family and the upholding of conservative values.

Svetlana popped a grape in her mouth and circled the crowd. She spotted Kip Lawson from Facts News, chatting with Florida Congressman Matt Donovan, who was head of the House Intelligence Committee. She sidled up to them and heard Donovan say, "So we send each newborn home with a gun. A blue one for boys, a little pink one for the girls. The nurses can tuck it in with the hospital goody bag, with a few diapers and swaddle blankets." He noticed Svetlana. "That's a great shirt," he said, staring at Svetlana's boobs. He and Kip Lawson maneuvered to make room for her in their circle.

"Thank you. I am very proud of Russia's contributions to gun development."

The men drank her in. "Russia has made some mighty fine contributions," the congressman said, giving her a wicked smile.

"I like how a Kalashnikov feels in my hands." She made a stroking gesture with her fingers, her bright red manicured nails fondling the air. Kip Lawson coughed a little. "You are both so famous. Can I take a picture with you?" She pulled out two chairs and motioned for them to sit, which they did. She sat on Kip's lap and crossed her legs across the congressman, the top of her thigh-high stockings peeking out from under her skirt. "Oh!" She looked at Kip as she leaned into his lap. "Is that a Kalashnikov in your pocket?" *Snap!* She took a photo of the three of them, lingered a moment, then stood up. "Maybe you will come to Moscow for one of our conferences on family values. In Russia, men are men. We women know how to take care of ourselves, but we like a strong man. Like our President Vlastov. You seem like strong men."

"I'd enjoy that opportunity," Donovan said.

"Or maybe a gun conference. I work with a big organization advocating for gun use in Russia. I will contact your office and we will arrange it." She started to walk away, then turned and gave them one last flirty smile.

"Please tell me she's over eighteen," the Florida congressman said.

"She just gave me a great idea for my show tonight," Kip said. He put on his television voice: "Progressives want a pussy in charge, but what we need is a real man."

Svetlana put a few cherries on a plate and weaved through the crowd. She saw Senator Kyle Lewis plopped in the middle of a group of admirers. He resembled a dollop of whipped cream, white and fluffy. With the exception of Lewis, the group had bowed their heads, listening intently as a priest in the group said a blessing. The senator noticed Svetlana sashaying toward him and said out loud, "Good lord!" The group looked up at him. The priest looked shocked. Senator Lewis tried to cover for his outburst. "Praise be to God, Father. Thank you for that wonderful prayer. Excuse me a moment." He strutted over to Svetlana. "Welcome to the National Jesus Brunch, young lady. I haven't seen you here before."

"This is my first time," Svetlana said, looking shy. "I am a Jesus Brunch virgin."

"I'm so glad I get to share this first time with you." He took a cherry from her plate and plucked it off its stem with his mouth. He grinned.

Svetlana took the stem and put it in her mouth. A moment later, she pulled it out. She had tied a knot in it with her tongue. He stared at it, his mouth agape. "Senator, I am loving Jesus Brunch. Perhaps I can convince President Vlastov to host a similar Jesus Brunch in Moscow. I could show you the ins and outs of Russia." She moved close to him as she said it, lightly brushing his groin with her hip. "You would come, no?"

Senator Lewis's body jerked. "I think I just did. I would love to visit Russia with you."

"President Vlastov would like you. He is strong leader. You are strong leader. You are in charge of Senate foreign relations. You must be so powerful, like President Vlastov."

"I admire him," Lewis said. "He is decisive, in control. A strong traditional leader. Hey, can we ride a bear?"

"Of course! All men in Russia ride bear. You, too, will ride bear. May I take a picture with you?" He moved closer to her. In her stiletto heels, she towered over him. "Shall I do the hard work? Or you prefer selfie?"

"Oh, I'm happy to let you take the lead," he said, as he hooked a stubby arm around her tiny waist and grinned like an impish leprechaun. *Snap!*

She looked at the picture on her phone and giggled. "You are so handsome!" She looked back at him. "Kyle, may I call you Kyle? Your committee will look at options for Crimea next week, right? Crimea is so privileged to have Russia helping it in its struggle for independence."

"I'm afraid I can't discuss committee business."

"I understand, Kyle." She dropped her chin and looked up at him. "It is my brother. He is Russian in Crimea. They treat him so badly because he is Russian. It makes me so sad." A tear formed at the corner of her eye.

Senator Lewis patted her waist. "It's going to be OK. Your brother is going to be OK."

"You are so kind. President Vlastov was right. He said you would be kind."

"President Vlastov knows me?"

"Of course, he knows you! You are famous American senator! Perhaps even next American president. You want to be president, no? One more picture, before you come to Moscow to ride bear with me." She held out her phone. *Snap!* She flashed a smile for the camera. Senator Lewis stared at her like an awestruck puppy.

CHAPTER SEVENTEEN

The plain but pretty woman in a pencil skirt and sensible heels crossed in front of a row of cubicles. She turned and smiled blankly at the camera. She held up a blue ball next to her face then said, "Today, I'm going to talk to you about how to use your ball safely and responsibly. Don't overinflate your ball. It could lead to pelvic injuries. Balls should be squishy for good overall health."

Victor's eyes glazed over as the video droned on. When it ended, he clicked it off and a quiz automatically appeared on the screen.

"What is the proper placement of your feet when using an exercise ball as an office chair?" the first question read. Answer A showed a graphic of a woman sitting on the ball with both feet on the ground in front of her. Answer B showed her balancing on the ball with her feet resting on her desk. Answer C showed her in a yoga headstand on top of the ball.

Victor was about to click on A when his instant message window popped up. It was Habibi, one of his oldest and dearest friends. The two had gone through training together back when they were young and their backs didn't hurt from sitting in an office chair all day. In fact, they almost never sat all day back then. They used to have to explain why they were in the office and not out in the streets meeting people. Nowadays, they had to explain why they *weren't* in the office.

Victor had seen Habibi shortly before moving to Rome last summer. They had reminisced about their exploits in Rubblestan, where one of Habibi's sources had provided key intelligence on members of Core Central, the terrorist group that had dominated the time and energy of a generation of CYA officers after the big attacks on the homeland. As Victor had been preparing to head to Rome, Habibi was returning from a stint in Lebanon, where he had helped flesh out the details of several money laundering networks. He had become quite knowledgeable about the flow of Russian money, and now that he was back at Director, he had taken a position in Russia House. Victor clicked on his instant message screen.

> Habibi: How many days until retirement?
> Victor: Too many. You?
> Habibi: Thirty days less than you, but still too many. Rome good? Send me cannoli. I can't eat anymore hot dogs out of vending machines.
> Victor: You've actually tried those?
> Habibi: I'm not proud of my actions.
> Victor: How are things at Director?
> Habibi: Things are great. No complaints.

Habibi stopped typing and Victor's green phone, the encrypted phone that allowed for classified conversations, rang. Victor picked it up.

"It's a total shitshow here, Victor." It was Habibi. He didn't want to write down what he was really thinking and leave a record that higher ups at Director—and beyond—could read. "Redd is naming Charlie Plotzki as the new Director."

"Redd's chief of staff from the Senate Foreign Relations Committee? What does he know about intelligence? Come to think of it, does he know anything?"

"He knows the sun is cold. He latched on to that conspiracy theory during the campaign. He also did a lot of kidney ice cream demagoguery."

"A guy who spreads conspiracy theories is going to run an agency that gathers facts to use as empirical evidence in order to reach logical conclusions?"

"You make it sound like it's a bad thing. I'm excited to get tasked to steal sunlight from Norway this summer. Maybe I'll score a free trip to the fjords. Do you want to know what Director Plotzki's first order of business is going to be?"

"I'm not sure I do," Victor said.

"He's arranging to meet with the analysts who wrote the assessment that Russia interfered in the election and that Vlastov himself ordered it. They're all lawyering up. Doesn't help when Redd tweets about a deep state cabal out to get him and then includes a hashtag CYA. Just be aware. Everyone is paranoid."

"We're spies. That's our job."

"Plotzki is bringing his own staff. He calls them commissars."

"No." Victor could not believe the new Director of CYA, appointed by a president whose ties to Russia were under scrutiny, would call his staff after Soviet officials who were responsible for political education.

"Do you think I could make this shit up? Retirement may be too many days away, but let's get there safely. If you've got anything sensitive, let's discuss it on the green line first, before you put anything in writing."

"Well, now that you mention it."

"This means you're about to make my life difficult." Habibi said. "Thank god. It's about time we get a little action around here."

"Habibi, you work in Russia House, right after the Russians interfered in our election and the president quite possibly helped them. The incoming Director is looking for anyone digging up the truth about it all, and you have too little action in your life?"

"Victor, I sit in traffic for three hours, then read cables for twelve hours, then sit in traffic for another three hours, then eat a vegan burrito from Whole Foods by myself, before going to sleep and doing it all again. Remember when we drove through rubble-strewn villages and had to dodge donkeys? Now I'm lucky if I get above fifteen miles per hour on the highway. So, whatever your operation is, it is a welcome challenge."

Victor explained how he was developing Max to provide intelligence on Russian influence operations in Europe. "The new administration is not going to love that," Habibi said. Victor could hear Habibi typing on the other end of the phone. "Normally, I'd have a desk officer set this up, but I think it's best if I handle it myself." Victor heard more typing, and Habibi didn't say anything for a minute. "Alright, I've set up a special compartment for Max, who we're encrypting QDCHESHIRE. All information and communications related to QDCHESHIRE will go into the compartment. I've limited the number of people, both at Rome Station and at

Director, who can access it. He might not be a popular asset with a lot of people around here."

"Thanks for setting it up. Try to get up and walk a little bit today, before you have to go sit in traffic again."

"I might never leave the office for the next four years. If no one comes or goes, Plotzki and his commissars might think it's just a janitor's closet behind the door. I have no desire for them to discover the existence of Russia House."

They hung up and Victor rubbed his temples. What did this mean for his development of Max as a source? He was currently being groomed as an asset by a Russian intelligence officer, and Victor planned to flip him in order to learn the modus operandi of Russia's intelligence services, who were assessed to have helped Redd become president. Now, Redd's people would be in charge of CYA and could have access to information about any operation or asset, including QDCHESHIRE. Victor also wanted intelligence on the MussoRusso Cultural Association and its director, Aldo Conti, and by extension Italy's possible next prime minister, Luca Callieri, and their relationship with Russian players connected to Vlastov. However, what he had learned so far about what was taking place in Italy looked remarkably similar to what had happened in the United States. If Plotzki, the new Director, and his commissars were looking for anyone who was digging into intelligence that might embarrass Redd—or worse, implicate him—how could Victor keep Max safe? He needed Max as a source to help protect US national security, yet the US national security apparatus was now headed by people who would see Max as a threat. Victor rubbed his temples harder as he contemplated the paradox. His head started to spin as he calculated the risks.

"Stop," he said out loud. He looked at his computer monitor and the safety question about how to sit properly on a ball. He clicked A and completed the quiz as fast as he could to get it out of the way. He had more important things to think about, and he needed to focus.

CHAPTER EIGHTEEN

Valeriy Chekhov and Ruslan Bebchuk sat once again with a bottle of vodka between them, discussing strategy. They were at the lone table in the opulent grand ballroom of the Russian Bear Hotel, adorned in red velvet with gold decorations on the walls and ceiling. Colored marble ionic columns, topped with golden, classical urns, lined the entire back wall, and red-and-gold silk damask hung from the ceiling, creating upside-down onion domes. The ballroom had sweeping views over the Moskva River and was the site, in 1967, of the mysterious death of the mistress of then-premier Leonid Brezhnev. Dressed in a fur stole and a diamond necklace, she had slumped over after sipping turnip soup, setting off a whirl of gossip and a complex game of machinations among a small group of particular women who hoped to be the leader's next mistress (while escaping her dramatic demise). The hotel was owned by Nikolai Surikov, who had poured millions into renovating it into a splendid, majestic, sparkling oeuvre in downtown Moscow.

"We are seeing good traction with the Russophobia talking points in the United States," Bebchuk said, fingering his glass of vodka. "Check out this new segment from New Russia News America." He pressed play on his phone and a video popped up.

"This is Igor Popov," the reporter said in English, "reporting for New Russia News from Newton, Massachusetts, in America, where Russophobia is reaching calamitous heights. NRN has learned that this primary school has banned beets from the children's meals, after parents expressed fear about exposing their children to this delicious root vegetable that is a base for many traditional Russian dishes." The screen showed the inside of the school cafeteria, young children pushing their trays along the queue, as Igor Popov continued his report. "As America reels from the election of President Richard Redd, whose unexpected victory last November has left many elitist Americans in a rage, the beautiful red beet is nowhere to be seen, banned out of ignorance and fear." The camera panned down to several trays full of food. "Look at these meals. Not a single beet in sight, indoctrinating children from a young age with a hatred of all things Russian." The camera cut to Popov, interviewing a child. "Do you like beets?" The child made a disgusted face and said, "Yuck!" Popov looked directly at the camera. "School authorities insist the lack of beets is not related to Russophobia, and that, in fact, beets will be served with a salad later this week. NRN has seen no indication that will occur, and such lip service seems to be too little, too late to curb the maniacal hatred of all things Russian by American isolationists too insecure to experience and embrace this wonderful culture. Back to you in the studio."

Chekhov refilled Bebchuk's glass. "It's a good segment, Ruslan."

"Kip Lawson at Facts News picked it up for his show last night, right after his segment on sex-crazed pandas turning people gay.

He's so eager to get Redd to watch his show, we don't even have to send him the talking points. He seems to just know which direction to run with our segments. Watch."

Bebchuk pulled up another video. Kip Lawson sat at his desk. A graphic to the side of him displayed the show's motto in bright red and blue letters, "Truth, the Right Way." Kip wore a blue blazer and a tie with a shield pattern, with the number 1620 on each shield.

"Is that a family coat of arms on his tie?" Chekhov asked.

"He had it designed last year."

"The tie?"

"The family coat of arms. He wants people to believe his family went to America on the Mayflower. In reality, his family arrived by steerage much later. His mother got rich selling frozen fish in the 1980s."

Bebchuk clicked play.

"Have we lost our minds, America?" Kip said indignantly. A still photo captured from Igor Popov's report was on a screen next to him. "Did I fall asleep and wake up in a Soviet gulag? Where food choice does not exist? Where the state tells you what you can and cannot eat? Who are school administrators to deny our children beets out of ignorance and xenophobia? This is Russophobia run amok. They're just beets, folks. They're not an invading Russian army. Yet, this school banned them? What have we come to? We see Russia everywhere, and it is literally killing us."

Bebchuk smiled at Chekhov. "That one got the attention of Redd." He held up a tweet from President Redd. "Children in Massachusetts are DENIED vegetables because the Liberals fear RUSSIA RUSSIA RUSSIA! Sad!"

Chekhov chuckled. "Do we even need FaKU? I don't know how my trolls can top this."

"It's almost too easy, isn't it?" Bebchuk agreed. "But hell, let's keep having fun. Nobody is doing anything to stop us, and Vlastov loves it. Look, I took the beet story further." He pulled up another video, this one featuring Lance Whitaker, the extremist vegan actor who had played Lawrence Blackhouse. "Igor and Kip help get the right wing angry. This one is to send the lefties into a fit." Bebchuk clicked play.

Lance Whitaker, dressed in distressed jeans and a black T-shirt, sat on a stool in front of a gray backdrop. He looked into the camera earnestly. "Establishment politicians and school administrators across the country hate President Redd so much they are ready to starve their own children of the nourishment of good vegan foods like beets. The elitists are so stuck trying to save the status quo, in which they thrive at the expense of everyone else, that they will do anything to try to take down this president, just because he wants to make changes, changes they fear will strip them of the power they have wielded for generations. This Russophobia, using beets, is an ugly extension of that, and one that only harms our kids and prevents them from having a healthy and balanced diet. This story disgusts me."

Chekhov and Bebchuk clinked their glasses and drank. Bebchuk leaned back in his chair and stared out at the river for a moment, pensive. "Valeriy, my friend, do you think it works? All this shit we throw out there." He gestured with his arms. "Does it work? Are we changing behavior? Changing how people think? I wonder sometimes if we are running on a treadmill. We are huffing and puffing as if accomplishing something big. But when we look up, will we see that we have gone nowhere?"

Chekhov smiled. "Ruslan, you worry too much. More to the point, you think too much. And many other people do not!" He shot back the rest of the vodka in his glass before pouring more for himself and Bebchuk. "Now I will share with you." He picked up his phone to show Bebchuk. "We've launched a new hashtag," Chekhov said. "We started with this tweet from @knejks9817263." He showed Bebchuk a picture of the account's profile page, which showed a beautiful, young blond, wearing an American flag bathing suit and playfully sticking her tongue out at the camera. "The account is actually run by Boris, a fifty-six-year-old former plumber who now works at FaKU. Nice guy. Smells like herring. He used this account and tweeted this." He showed Bebchuk a screenshot of the tweet.

"Left-wing fascists call Redd misogynist. No one loves women more than Redd! Here's a picture to show my support as a Real American Woman who loves my President! Retweet with your own pic if you're a Real American Woman who loves Redd!" Attached to the tweet was a picture of an enormous set of boobs nearly bursting through a low-cut, wet, white T-shirt with the phrase "RAW for REDD!" written in red letters across it. The tweet ended with a series of hashtags: #RealAmericanWomenForRedd #ShowYourTitsForRedd.

Bebchuk looked up at Chekhov. "I imagine with tits like that, it was easy to get it to trend."

"With tits like that, we immediately caught the attention of Redd." Chekhov swiped the screen to another screenshot of a tweet.

Redd had retweeted @knejks9817263 and her tits, adding the comment, "TRUE! No one loves women more than me!"

Chekhov started swiping through tweets. "It blew up. It's trending across America now. Thousands of women are tweeting pictures of their tits to show they don't believe Redd is a misogynist. Some are real. Some are fake."

"The tits or the twitter accounts?"

"Both." Chekhov put his phone down and reached for the vodka. "FaKU has been pivoting some of the same accounts to use in Europe." He grabbed his phone again and pulled up the profile for @SallySoftLove2867001, whose bio read, "Christian dog lover, veterans, 2nd Amendment 4 Life!" Her profile picture showed a bikini-clad woman lying on a pristine beach next to clear turquoise water. She had tweeted in English, "Callieri is love Italia! No be sheep for union of the Euros! Yes Italia!"

"Her profile doesn't look like she's from Italy. Also, shouldn't she tweet in Italian?" Bebchuk asked.

Valeriy sighed. "We've been working out the kinks in the system. Sometimes the younger ones are going so fast they forget to change the profile and their Google translate languages. But we don't really see a change in response. Especially with the bikini pictures. People just retweet without thinking, as long as the message fits their preconceived stance on an issue, and as long as the girl is hot."

"We're lining up a number of pro-Callieri messaging campaigns for Italy, as well," Bebchuk said. "We've got a new young man from one of our cultural associations who will be doing a number of hits on NRN. Massimiliano Brevi is his name."

Chekhov was jotting down notes. "Mas-si-mi-li-a-no," he sounded out, struggling, taking several seconds to write out the name.

"He goes by Max."

Chekhov looked up at Bebchuk, annoyed, then back at his notes. He drew a long line through the name Massimiliano, then said, "Max," as he wrote the three letters. "We'll be sure to amplify those," he said. "Any particular themes?"

"The usual. Italians against Callieri are guilty of Russophobia. He'll give a strong anti-EU message, I understand. He's a well-spoken chap. He comes across as very amiable and normal, which is quite a change from the usual guests we have. I think he will boost the credibility of our talking points, and Callieri's talking points, as well. Brevi will also be attending a conference here at the Russian Bear Hotel next week. Your colleagues from the security services have arranged some further cultivation of several of the attendees. I believe the room cameras are already installed, and Vlastov has requested we spare no expense on companionship services."

Chekhov's phone pinged. He read a notification and laughed. He turned the screen toward Bebchuk. "A new trend in the United States. People are sticking pins through their eyelids to symbolize how blind they've been to the corruption of the political elite." The notification showed #FinallyISee and #FreedomGouge trending in the United States. "I should get back to FaKU, before Boris gets the Americans to inject themselves with bleach with a disinfect and cleanse challenge. It's getting a little dangerous." He gulped down the vodka remaining in his glass. "And you were worried we weren't affecting behavior." He put his hand on Bebchuk's shoulder. "Sometimes, my friend, all they need is a little social pressure. Conformity is a strong drug."

CHAPTER NINETEEN

Max stepped out of the taxi and gazed up at the magnificent Russian Bear Hotel. A sweeping portico protected its expansive curved driveway. Mustached men in sharp red uniforms and gold caps lined the entrance, waiting to help the exclusive clientele out of their luxury cars and through the sparkling glass doors. One of the men took Max's suitcase and ushered him inside. Max drew in a sharp breath as he entered the lobby. The giant domed ceiling was covered in glittering stained glass, ruby red, golden yellow, emerald green, and sapphire blue, laid out in a geometric pattern accented with flowers and vines. Arches of gold motif framed a series of semicircular windows that lined the upper reaches of the wraparound mezzanine level, where revelers could observe the vast marble floor below. Natural light poured in through the glass dome, reflecting the bright colors down on dozens of small round tables and glinting on the white leather chairs that seemed to scoop up their patrons as they sipped their cocktails and nibbled on deviled eggs, surrounded by enormous, elephant-eared plants.

Max was stunned and delighted. The hotel had been less grand when he last saw it during his university days. It had still been considered a top hotel in Moscow back then, but the standards were a bit different. He recalled one of his professors telling him about an American business delegation that had come to Moscow in 1989, that tender year when Russia was emerging out of its cocoon. The professor had been one of the hosts of the delegation, whose members stayed at the Russian Bear Hotel. At the time, the hotel was drab, with water-damaged walls and peeling paint on the industrial ceiling. The hotel had no computer system, and employees had written down each guest's information in pencil in a thick notebook before sending them off to their assigned rooms. Since the hotel was large but the check-in system was lacking, many guests had found their assigned rooms were still occupied or had not been serviced. One member of the delegation, Max's professor had recalled with a laugh, found a dead fish wrapped in newspaper in the clothes closet.

A kind woman in a red velvet hat tapped away on a state-of-the-art computer system and checked Max in to his room. She then directed him to a table in a corner to check in to the conference.

A very tall woman in a very short black dress smiled at him from behind the table. "Welcome to Self-Determination Elation," she said. "We are very happy you are here." She handed him his name tag on a Self-Determination Elation lanyard along with a schedule of events. "I am Adriana. If I can help you with anything, you will let me know, yes?" Her long blond hair and blunt row of bangs framed her bright green eyes. "Anything. My colleagues and I are here to make sure you have a good time." She gestured out to the crowd, and Max noticed several young women in short black dresses flirting with men adorned with lanyards. He looked back at Adriana. "A very good time." She fluttered her long eyelashes.

Max nodded politely and made his way to the elevator. He glanced at the conference schedule. The following day's big event was titled, "The Demon of Democracy: How the liberal experiment enslaved us." The main speaker would be Konstantin Dudnik, Vlastov's spiritual advisor, who was also the organizer and host of this weekend's event. He would be introduced by Luca Callieri. Max had just enough time for a shower before the evening cocktail party—billed as "Autono-me, Autono-you! Come meet your counterparts fighting for autonomy across the world!"—officially began.

His room was tidy and clean. He searched for an outlet to charge his phone and computer. He spotted a USB plug next to the desk, where a copy of *Moscow* Magazine was prominently displayed. Its cover showed President Vlastov in a fine suit holding a puppy. "He'll melt your heart," read the caption, purposely making it vague if the magazine meant Vlastov or the puppy. Max was about to plug in his phone when he remembered Victor's warning that Russian security services use USB ports to compromise devices. He cursed. "Now he's got me being paranoid," he said. But still, he continued searching until he found a regular electrical outlet.

Max returned to the splendid lobby, clean shaven and wearing fresh clothes. Adriana was having a drink with a man with a lanyard. She listened attentively to the man and laughed on cue, her long, bare legs crossed in his direction. She wore stiletto platform shoes that were covered in metal spikes. Max was both frightened and aroused. He ordered a glass of champagne at the bar, then faced back toward the lobby to survey the scene. A rugged-looking man in a rumpled, olive-green linen shirt that was unbuttoned to his midriff saw Max sipping his drink against the wall and motioned for him to join his table, where two other men and one of the women in a short black dress were also seated. Max smiled and approached them.

"The night is too short to drink alone, my friend" the rugged man said. "Come join us. I will make the introductions. This football fan is Xavi," he said, pointing to a young man in the red-and-blue jersey of the FC Barcelona soccer team. "Xavi is fighting for the independence of Catalonia. This is Gustave." An older man with a weather-worn face and a beret nodded. The rugged-looking man continued, slurring a little. "Gustave is the head of the Occitan movement. This lovely creature," he motioned toward the young woman in the black dress, who was now canoodling him, "is Adriana." He nuzzled her neck before returning to the glass of pastis in his hand. "She doesn't give a shit about any of the struggles for autonomy."

Max was confused. "I thought she was Adriana?" he said, pointing at the woman who had checked him in to the conference.

"We're all Adriana," the woman said.

"They're *all* Adriana," the rugged-looking man laughed, giving Max a wink. "And I," he said, extending his hand, "am Battistu." He gave a little bow. "Crusader for the independence of Corsica. *Vergogna à tè chì vendi a tò la terra!*" He tossed back the rest of his pastis.

"I'm Max, from the MussoRusso Cultural Association in Italy."

"Italy? What is Italy?" said Gustave, adjusting his beret. "You took land from us and decided to call it part of Italy. What you call Piedmont, in the northwest of this, this, *entity*," he spit as he said the word, "is rightfully part of Occitania. For hundreds of years Occitania has laid claim to the entire arc of the northern Mediterranean, from your *Italy*," he said with disgust, "across France, and into Catalonia. The problem is the fascists in Paris who dare to tell us we are not free! Not to mention the fascists in Brussels, forcing upon us their fries with mayonnaise. What is this?"

"Catalonia is for Catalans," Xavi said. "I appreciate your Occitan movement, but Catalan speakers belong in a free and independent Catalonia. While I agree with you about the fascists in Brussels, the real problem is the fascists in Madrid."

"There are no fascists," said Max.

"Ha!" Battistu guffawed. "There are no fascists, says the man working at the association named for Mussolini." He leaned in toward Max. "No worries, mate. I love fascists!"

"The problem is much more nuanced than this," Max continued. "Brussels is, indeed, the problem. We don't need a European government telling sovereign nations what to do. Italy should be Italy, for Italians. And I agree, mayonnaise on fries is against the natural order of things."

"Brussels does have good waffles, though," Xavi said.

They all nodded in agreement.

"You don't want the European Union telling Italy how to be," Gustave said. "Yet you are fine with Italy telling Occitans how to be."

"Or for Spain to tell Catalans how to be," said Xavi.

"What do you think, Battistu?" Max asked.

Battistu laughed. "It's hard to form alliances when everyone's first priority is total independence." He grabbed Adriana's breast and let out a joyous "Woohoo!" He looked back at the others. "*Pffff,* the politics are too complicated. I don't give a fuck about any of it. I just like to blow shit up." He took a shot of vodka Adriana was holding out to him.

Max sat silently and let the others debate. As the evening wore on, he circulated among the crowd. He met a Texan looking to secede from the United States, a Californian who wanted part of the state to rejoin Mexico, and a different California secessionist with dreams of starting an independent vegan commune. He crossed over to another group, where he met the leader of a violent group from Lichtenstein who wanted to overthrow the monarchy, end the country's pledge of neutrality, and institute a standing army. "No one in Europe trusts us with weapons," he lamented to Max, as he tripped over his own foot and dropped his glass. Max went to the bar for another drink and met a man wearing a T-shirt with a flag that said "Fred Nation." "We all keep answering to higher governments," the man said to Max. "But to be truly free, shouldn't we each be able to assert our independence? Isn't that true freedom?" He took a sip of his drink. "I'm Fred, by the way."

Max looked across the sea of characters, each claiming some form of nationalism and sovereignty. All of them, Max was learning, were receiving the ideological support of Russian President Darko Vlastov.

After dinner, Max returned to his room alone, despite flirty protestations from one of the Adrianas. That night, he was restless. "Vlastov does not have Italy's best interests at heart," he recalled his friend Victor saying to him at dinner, shortly before he left for Moscow. Max had anticipated finding camaraderie among the many nationalist and independence movements who he knew would be attending Self-Determination Elation this weekend. Max believed in Italy for Italians. How could Gustave believe that an entire region of Italy should be incorporated into Occitania, a region that existed only in medieval texts? How could anyone view Occitania's claim to land across Italy, France, and Spain as legitimate? The notion was ridiculous, Max thought. Italy had been a sovereign nation since 1861. Claims to land from long before that were irrelevant. Italy was Italy, period.

Yet, he couldn't sleep.

He thought about history, about how one chooses when a story begins. If one looked back far enough, nothing belonged to anybody. It had all changed hands too many times. Vlastov, Max noted, was supporting all of it, every autonomous and nationalist movement across Europe and North America and probably elsewhere. He supported countries that wanted to get rid of the EU and be sovereign again, but also regions that wanted to get rid of national governments and be their own sovereign entity. "Vlastov does not have Italy's best interests at heart," he heard Victor in his head. He fell into a fitful sleep.

He awoke to a knock on the door. He glanced at the clock on his phone, 2:32 am. He went to the door but remained as hidden as he could as he opened it a crack, since he was wearing boxer shorts and a T-shirt. It was Adriana. He couldn't tell if it was one of the same Adrianas he had seen earlier in the evening or a different one. They all looked the same.

"*Zaichik*," she said, using a Russian term of endearment. She pouted a little. "You must be lonely. Why do you choose to go to sleep alone?"

Max moved behind the door even more; he could feel the start of an erection. "I appreciate your concern, Adriana. But I'm fine. I prefer to sleep alone tonight." He couldn't express, even to himself, why he was saying no, despite his clear temptation, which was now bulging inside his boxers.

"You don't like me?" She emphasized the word *like* by sticking out her breasts more when she said it. Her dress was very tight across the bodice.

"I like you very much," Max stuttered. "I would like to sleep, that's all."

"You are gay? I won't tell anyone, but perhaps it is best you prove you are not by having sex with me."

Max knew President Vlastov was very antigay; it was a big part of his conservative, traditionalist platform. Max, too, was conservative and traditional, and while he did not support Italy's attempts to legalize gay marriage, he was not so naïve as to think homosexuality was going to be prayed or brainwashed away. Adriana's statement put Max on edge, but still, he couldn't express why. Once again, he heard Victor. "Vlastov does not have Italy's best interests at heart." And what about Grigoriy Stepanov? Max wondered. Did he have Max's best interests at heart?

He closed the door on the pouty Adriana and returned to bed, alone.

The next day, he put on a fresh shirt and a new tie and headed out to the conference. He ran into Battistu in the elevator. He was wearing the same clothes as the evening before. Max spotted a pair of lacy women's underwear hanging out of his shirt pocket. He was singing a Corsican folk song. Max greeted him in Russian, "*Dobroye utro.*"

Battistu wiped his brow with the panties. "I'm sweating pastis, my friend! I love Moscow!" He put an arm around Max's shoulder as they exited the elevator. Max could smell the alcohol seeping out of Battistu's skin. Battistu spotted a short man with a briefcase in the lobby. "That's my guy, Max. I have to go. I'll see you later." He waved to the man with the briefcase. "Vlad! What do you have for me? AKs? Buks? Sniper rifles? Show me the whole lot! I love Moscow!"

Max went into the grand ballroom and looked for an empty seat near the front. The audience bubbled with excitement. Luca Callieri took the stage. He was tall, with flowing, brown hair that curled under at his shoulders. He had an easy manner about him as he introduced the organizer, host, and main speaker of the conference. "He has broadened our perspectives, reminding us to question so many narratives that the establishment feeds us and we, for years, have swallowed whole. Whether it is our absolute adherence to notions like 'the sun is hot' or 'women are as smart as men,' he reminds us to question what so many now accept uncritically. He has also reminded us of the true priorities for our communities, the values we should all embody to help usher in stronger societies. He has recognized and articulated the inherent weakness that diversity brings, and reminds us we are strongest when we work with those we most identify with. It is my pleasure to introduce Konstantin Dudnik."

The audience applauded as Dudnik walked on stage. He was thin and tall. He stroked his long, gray beard as he entered. He turned to the crowd, placed his hand on his heart, and nodded his humble acceptance of their fervor for him. He then crossed to where Callieri was standing with the microphone and embraced him, giving him three kisses on alternating cheeks. Callieri took a seat in the front row as Dudnik launched into his presentation.

"The world is changing too much, too fast, and we are told by the elite progressivists that we must accept this disruption or perish," he said. "What we need is not to look forward to a future we cannot yet understand, but rather to embrace our history and find stability in our traditions. Our bonds with those with whom we have common histories will allow us to weather the disruptions wrought by an unsure future, catalyzed by people who shun commonalities, shun tradition, and try to force us to accept that somehow, despite all our obvious differences, we are the same. It is only through self-determination, our tribal cohesion, working with those we recognize, whom we understand, who are like us, that we will prevail. This is how it has always been, and it has brought us great prosperity! The world is richer and healthier than at any time in history. If we lose our traditions and let crazy ideas ransack our minds, we will lose ourselves."

The audience erupted in cheers. Max clapped loudly, last night's restlessness dissipating with each smack of his hands. Italy for Italians, he thought. No more Brussels telling Italy how to be, what color its street signs should be, or how long to cook its pasta. Tradition! Keep Italy Italian!

The audience poured into the brilliant lobby, their chattering floating up and filling the glittering dome. A crowd gathered around Dudnik, everyone soaking in his aura and hoping for even a brief exchange of words with the sage. Max got a glass of tonic at the bar and mingled among the other attendees. When he saw the crowd around Dudnik dispersing, he approached. Dudnik was speaking to an attentive short man with a thick head of red hair and a red beard to match. Dudnik was stroking his own facial hair, as he expounded on traditionalism in Russia.

"This is why Chechnya is Russia," Dudnik said. "Crimea is Russia. Eastern Ukraine is Russia. Anywhere there are Russians, it is Russia. There is no question about this. Europe is a different beast. What is Europe, anyway? What makes someone European? No one is European. This is not tradition. Europe has long been fractured. Why do they try to force these differences into a single entity?"

Max leaned in. He liked what he was hearing.

"Russian blood is thick and pure. In Europe, everyone has mixed together over the years. I understand France wanting to limit who comes to France, who becomes French. But even that, who is to say who is French? Do the Occitans not have a claim to be independent? Does Catalonia not have a claim? This is for people in Europe to figure out. We Russians know who is Russian and where Russians are. We do not interfere in the internal business of other states."

Max pulled back. President Vlastov had spoken strongly in support of Italy's nationalist party, Da Italia, as well as other nationalist parties in Europe and the United States. Max had assumed Dudnik was on the same page. His restlessness returned.

He turned away from Dudnik and spotted Callieri, speaking with a group of Russians and a small man in a Herringbone suit and fedora, Aldo Conti. That was strange. Aldo had not told him he would be attending the conference. Max thought he was the only representative from the MussoRusso Cultural Association. They didn't have the money to send Max; he had been sponsored by the Russian Cultural Center. Did MussoRusso have a budget to send Aldo to Moscow? Why hadn't Aldo told him he'd be here? Max started toward them. Aldo and Luca Callieri were deep in conversation with two Russians. They didn't look open to receiving anyone into their group. But Max was too curious. He had to know what Aldo was doing here. He took one of the Adrianas by the elbow and led her behind a large, elephant-eared plant.

"Oh, *milyy*," she cooed. "Be gentle with me. You like to lose yourself in bushes? We could go upstairs?"

Max held her there but ignored her, as he tried to overhear the discussion.

"Our election is the best hope to change Europe," Callieri said. "Enough with the elites in Brussels meddling in our sovereign decisions. We want to work with other, like-minded political parties across Europe toward this goal. Russia will help make that happen. This is how we can decide our future, for Italians. There is an urgency, however, since our election in Italy is quickly approaching."

"*Dorogoy*," Adriana said. Max shushed her. She pouted.

One of the Russians spoke. "We will have GasItalia on one side and RosGaz on the other. The RosAlleman pipeline will be the conduit. We'll need at least two intermediary companies." He had a gravelly voice and scar across his right eye.

The second Russian, who was taller and had a small tattoo of a butterfly behind his ear, cut in. "One of those needs to be a major player, or we risk many antimoney laundering questions. We have several subsidiaries that can fill in for this."

"Stefano will handle it from our side," Aldo said.

Max wasn't sure why they were discussing the pipeline. Of course, it will be the conduit, the conduit for gas from Russia into Europe. So, what was this about? He looked at Adriana. She was checking her fingernails, bored.

"We'll discount it 40 percent, which will kickback approximately sixty million euros to Da Italia once it's all been cleaned," the first Russian said.

Max froze. He understood now, but he didn't want to believe it. These Russians were working out a deal with Callieri to siphon off financing from the RosAlleman pipeline and funnel it to Da Italia's coffers to help Callieri in the upcoming election. These two Russians were not doing this out of the goodness of their hearts, and there was no way they were helping the candidate of a major European political party without the knowledge of President Vlastov. What did they want in return? More to the point, what did Vlastov want in return?

"Vlastov does not have Italy's best interests at heart." He heard Victor again and again, ringing through his head, which was now pounding.

He glanced around the room. Dudnik was standing next to someone in a Braveheart T-shirt with a picture of Mel Gibson and the words "FREEDOM FOR SCOTLAND" in all caps. A woman waving a Flanders flag was saying to them: "Flemish independence is the natural next step for Belgium. Half the country doesn't understand our language." Max saw Dudnik was pushing solidarity among Russians, but encouraging every regional group in Europe to rise up and claim their independence. While this would weaken Europe, it would also weaken France, Spain, Italy, and others. It counteracted their push for a nationalist agenda in those countries, including Max's own. Now Vlastov was using a pipeline, which critics argued would make Europe more reliant on Russia, to feed Russian money to Callieri's political party, with Callieri making promises that he would move Italy to be closer to

Russia. The winner in every scenario was Russia, not Italy. Max was against Brussels and the European Union controlling Italy. But he wasn't looking to trade one dictator for another.

As the group disbanded, he stuffed a few rubles in Adriana's hand. She looked unimpressed and walked away. He rounded the plant and ran into Aldo.

"Hello, Max! Are you enjoying the conference?" Aldo said.

"You didn't tell me you were coming too. I thought I was the only one from MussoRusso."

"I'm not here in an official capacity. Luca asked me to join to provide advice on some business. Come, meet our future prime minister."

Aldo escorted Max to where Callieri was chatting with several conference attendees. Max saw the two Russians exiting the lobby.

"Luca, please meet my protégé, Massimiliano Brevi. A proud supporter of Da Italia."

Callieri shook Max's hand. "I'm happy to see you supporting the party here at the conference, Massimiliano. With enthusiastic supporters like you, our country has a bright future."

Aldo turned to Max. "How wonderful it will be to have Luca Callieri running Italy. Italy for Italians, once again!"

Max felt the restlessness creeping back. He wasn't so sure.

CHAPTER TWENTY

Victor walked down a small alley, his head down to avoid the ubiquitous security cameras. He ducked through a Roman archway and turned hard left down a dimly lit street. He weaved behind a row of orange trees, glancing behind him, and went into a hidden garden. There, he waited on a bench for two minutes, watching and listening. He exited the opposite side of the garden then circled back through a different ancient archway, which led to a small tunnel. He walked through it and came out on a small street in Rome's Monti district. He crossed the cobblestone street and slipped into La Carbonara, where he made his way to a quiet table in the back of the restaurant. He would have preferred a more discreet meeting location, but Max had returned from the Self-Determination Elation conference in Moscow in an agitated state and was anxious to meet. The small restaurant off the beaten path in the historic center would have to do. Victor could not take his eyes off the door. He hoped Max's trip to Moscow had been an eye-opening experience and that he could now help lead Max up to and over a blurry ethical line. Far-right nationalist parties across the world were gaining steam, it seemed with help from Russia, threatening to slide several countries closer to authoritarianism. Max would be able to shed light on how Russia was doing that. "The fate of the democratic liberal order rests on this recruitment," Ness had said to him that morning. "Don't fuck it up."

Max walked in, looking behind him as he did so, then glanced at the tables in the restaurant. He spotted Victor and crossed over to him quickly. He sat down, his eyes darting around. He was fidgety. Victor pushed his way into Max's line of vision, forcing him finally to make eye contact. At last, Max spoke. "Italy for Italians. That was Luca Callieri's promise." He shook his head. "Hypocrite. I love Russia, but not like this. You were right, Victor. Vlastov does not have Italy's best interest at heart. Worse, neither does Callieri."

"Why don't you tell me what happened at the conference."

Max was reticent. "I've never asked what exactly you do at the embassy." He took a sip of wine, as the waiter placed a plate of rigatoni carbonara in front of each of them. Max had enjoyed his conversations with Victor, whom he saw as a worldly, curious, intelligent man. But it had started to dawn on him during the conference that Victor had been warning him and offering him an alternative. "During my trip to Moscow, I began to wonder if perhaps your interest in MussoRusso is more than academic."

Victor nodded in understanding, but said nothing. The fig leaf remained, even if its hold was tenuous, barely disguising the truth of what Victor was and what he wanted Max to do. Sometimes, silence was best. It forced the asset to move forward on his own, so that dropping the fig leaf seemed like his own decision. Victor could tell, Max needed to confide in someone who could counter Vlastov's machinations in Italy.

"I suppose certain people at the US embassy would like to know about Russian efforts to influence our politics here in Italy," Max said. "But then maybe they, too, want a piece of Italy."

"We aren't interested in telling Italy what to do," Victor said. "That's the prerogative of Italians. Nor are we interested in telling you what to do. No one will tell you to appear on TV and what to say. But we are interested in how Russia is doing what it's doing." Victor watched Max continue eating. That was a good sign. He wasn't so agitated that he couldn't eat. Victor continued, "We are interested in what Grigoriy Stepanov tells you and asks you to do, and who he introduces you to."

Max wiped his mouth. "Grigoriy." He took a sip of wine. "He has been pushing me to do more editorials, more television interviews, to deliver his talking points. He has a list of people he wants me to contact."

"We are willing to pay for this information, but if you ever want to stop, you are free to. You might find that Grigoriy is harder to break up with." Victor paused a moment then said, "What happened in Moscow?"

Max saw the fig leaf slip away. He wanted to grasp it. He knew it was too late. And yet, as it floated away on the wind of the conversation, he succumbed to it. He felt himself embrace the raw nakedness of his situation.

He let it all out. He lamented Konstantin Dudnik pushing both sides of the autonomy issue in Europe, but not in Russia. "He caresses nationalist parties with one hand and feeds regional independentist groups with the other." He recounted the dozens of Adrianas milling about the hotel and how one had knocked on his door late at night.

"Maybe she was trying to put you in a no-win situation," Victor said. "If you didn't have sex with her, someone would start rumors that you were gay. Not ideal, given the traditionalists you hang around with. If you had had sex with her, well, then they'd have a video of you having sex with a prostitute. Maybe that's not a problem. Maybe it is. Maybe it becomes a problem later. But it's a convenient piece of kompromat to have tucked away. Did you bring any devices to Moscow?"

"I just said I didn't have sex with her."

"I meant computer devices. A laptop? A phone? Anything you plug in?"

"I saw the USB port and thought of you."

Victor smiled. He had made Max question so many of his assumptions. "You plugged it into an electrical outlet instead?"

Max nodded. "I still think you've seen too many spy movies. What are they going to do with a few pictures of pasta dishes or pictures of me with my friends?"

"Or your emails, or your bank information, or your call history, or your texts. They can use any of it out of context to make whatever narrative they want. They used an email about an ice cream recipe to convince people children were being trafficked through an ice cream shop."

Max was disconcerted, and he hadn't even gotten to the worst part of the trip. Finally, he recounted witnessing Luca Callieri accepting the bald money-for-influence scheme from two Russian mobsters working for Vlastov. "They weren't even discreet."

"They were on their own turf, but I agree, it would be nice if they made a little effort to hide their subversion." Victor thought about Svetlana Zharkova. He and Vanessa had been following her social media posts brazenly documenting her exploits with a who's who of conservative Washington and making no effort to conceal her efforts.

"What happens now?" Max asked.

"When do you see Grigoriy next?"

"This weekend. I'm sure he'll have a list of tasks for me."

"We'll meet the following week. But not here." He outlined his plan to meet in a more private setting.

That was it. Victor had recruited Max to provide intelligence on Russian operations in Europe. Once the deal was made, they changed the conversation, with Max regaling Victor with stories about his childhood in Ventotene. At the end of the evening, they walked out to the cobblestone street. A light rain was falling. They shook hands. Max had no trouble making eye contact now. They went their separate ways.

CHAPTER TWENTY-ONE

Ness and Francesco Restani sat on stools at a high table enjoying prosciutto with figs at Sogno Autarchico, a hole-in-the-wall nestled in between Castel Sant'Angelo and the Vatican. Francesco sported another dark, slim-cut suit that hit just above his ankles, this time contrasted with bright blue sneakers. His brown hair flopped over his left eye and he swept it out of the way every so often with his right hand.

"I brought visual aids," Ness said, pulling her hair back into a pony tail before reaching into her bag. She took out a folder and slid it across the table.

Francesco opened it and saw a photo of Svetlana Zharkova. She was in a pink ruffle miniskirt and purple sequined Uzi T-shirt and stilettos, showing a lot of leg and pointing a Glock at whatever schmuck was holding the camera. "Is this how you dress in America to go shooting?" he asked.

"It seems counterintuitive, but the stilettos help with the recoil."

"Who is this?" he asked, indicating the man standing next to Svetlana and holding an AR-15 pointing down, trigger finger extended but off the trigger. He wore more camouflage than a Walmart on Black Friday.

"Chad White, he's just been named an aide to CYA Director Charlie Plotzki. A commissar, as they say now." Francesco looked at her, incredulous. "There are plenty of other photos in there." He flipped through images of Svetlana with Kip Lawson of Facts News, Senator Kyle Lawson from the Senate Foreign Relations Committee, Congressman Matt Donovan from Florida who was head of the House Intelligence Committee, and even one with President Redd. Vanessa said, "She's sat on every conservative lap, at gun conferences, family values conferences, even the National Jesus Brunch." A group of priests passed their table and gave her a confused look.

"Are you supposed to be showing me these?" Francesco asked. A piece of fig dropped on the lapel of his jacket. "*Cazzo*." The waiter rushed out with a spray can and brush. Francesco held out his jacket. The waiter whisked away the stain.

"It's all on Instagram. There's nothing secret about any of it. Except . . ."

"Except she is establishing back-channel communications with some of these very powerful political operatives, hoping to influence them to influence American foreign policy." He took a sip of wine. "She did the same here. She floated around many conservative circles in Italy and got the attention of many politicians." He held up a photo of Svetlana in a black leather miniskirt, a red-lace bustier, red-leather stilettos, and orange-tinted eye protection glasses, shooting a Beretta. "She is hard not to notice."

"What did she do with them, once she got their attention?"

"A number of them attended various conferences in Moscow and Saint Petersburg. They returned to Italy more a Russophile than when they left. Did they fall in love with the culture, or were they compromised while there?" He shrugged. "Some, like Callieri, returned richer too. We are looking into it." He looked at Ness and leaned in toward her. "A very small group of us, that is. I am sure from your position, you can understand."

"Unfortunately, I can."

"It is awkward." Francesco stared off into the distance for a moment. "Your election may be over, and ours may be coming up, but I feel you and I are, perhaps, in similar situations."

Ness gave him a resigned smile. "It won't end after your election. It didn't end after ours. I appreciate the details about how Svetlana worked here. It is comforting, in a way, that the Russians are so lazy, they can't come up with new approaches."

"Why extend effort to develop new approaches when the old ways keep getting results? Our politicians, like yours, could end all of this foreign influence easily. They just don't want to. They are benefiting too much."

Ness looked down at the pile of photographs. There was Senator Kyle Lewis, the head of the Senate Foreign Relations Committee, looking like a beanbag chair for Svetlana, his squishy lap molding around her ample derriere. Francesco was right. Too many people were getting what they wanted from the current arrangement, be it power or money or both. "They really are ready to sell their souls for an immediate power grab," she said.

"They are ready to sell democracy's soul for power," he corrected her.

She shook her head. "I'm so goddamn tired." A priest sitting at the next table over looked at her. "Sorry," she said in Italian. He smiled gently and gave her a small blessing.

***

Vanessa exhaled and let the evening calm of Villa Borghese envelop her. She headed down a path under the umbrella firs. A man sat on a bench playing an accordion. The slow-building melody of "Bella Ciao," an anti-fascist Italian folk song, wafted through the air. She continued to the villa proper, now a museum called Galleria Borghese. It stood before her in all its grandeur. The renaissance building had been the country home of the wealthy Borghese family, which had produced politicians, princes, and popes. Cardinal Scipione Borghese had been a patron of the sculptor Gian Lorenzo Bernini, who was known for, among other masterpieces, a series of marble statues that captured a moment in time. They were now housed at the gallery.

The sun was setting. The garden's lamp posts flittered on. The accordion player was ratcheting up the speed and intensity of his rendition of "Bella Ciao." Vanessa circled around to the back of the gallery and walked into a small garden with geometric bushes surrounding a fountain. She went to the back door of the gallery, the pebbles of the garden crunching under her feet. The gallery's curators kept all the windows and doors covered and closed, with one exception. Vanessa approached the window. The sun was down now, and the inside gallery was lit up. There, in the middle of the room, was Bernini's Rape of Persephone, depicting the goddess's abduction to the Underworld. Though carved out of marble, Persephone's thigh spread under the heavy squeeze of her abductor, her foot twisted in fear and pain. A single moment in time.

Ness stared at it. She was here, now, in this moment, involved in an investigation against the president of the country she had sworn to protect. Her husband, too, was involved in an operation that would upset the White House and the new Director of CYA and his commissars if they were to find out about it. Unseen forces were sweeping them toward their own underworld. She took a deep breath before turning away. She walked home.

Outside her apartment, she dug into her purse to find her keys. She reached into the deep abyss of her bag and pushed aside crumpled receipts, lipstick tubes, and a closed extendable baton she kept in case she needed to whack someone. Just as her fingertips sensed the metal of a key, the front door of the apartment opened.

"Oh, hey, Mom."

Ness looked up at Oliver. Next to him was a teenage girl.

"This is Nat." The girl standing next to Oliver had shoulder-length blond hair with cute tendrils. She wore black sweatpants with a red stripe down the side and a T-shirt depicting Russian President Darko Vlastov riding a bear topless.

She smiled at Vanessa. "Hey, Oliver's mom." She turned to Oliver. "I'll see you at school tomorrow. Ciao!"

Ness went inside and dropped her bag. "Ask her where she got her shirt. I want one."

Oliver rolled his eyes. "Please don't embarrass me."

"I'm serious. I need that shirt. Next time she goes to Russia, tell me. I'll give her money to buy me one."

"Hey, Nat. Here's money from my FBI mom who hates Vlastov to buy her a shirt with him on it."

"I don't hate Vlastov. I just don't want him running the United States."

"She thinks he's awesome."

"Clearly, otherwise she wouldn't be wearing a T-shirt with him on it."

"You want to wear the same T-shirt."

"Yeah, but ironically."

"Would you wear a T-shirt of President Redd?" he asked. He followed her into the kitchen.

"Hell, no."

"So, I don't get it then."

"Redd is a moron. That's the difference."

"Well, a lot of women love him, and they're showing it."

"Oh, god. What did I miss?"

Oliver laughed. "This new trending hashtag is insane. That woman who lost the election?"

"Willa Bennett."

"Yeah, her. I guess she called President Redd an ass. So, now all these women are posting pictures of their asses in support of Redd. Hashtag ReddAss." He laughed, scrolling through his phone. "It's awesome."

"Show me." Vanessa leaned against the counter next to him. He started scrolling through hundreds of pictures of women's asses, some in Confederate flag bikinis, others in the Stars and Stripes. One showed a healthy—and flexible—young woman in high heels and a teeny red, white, and blue bikini bending over, her bottom toward the camera. She was looking over her left shoulder at the camera and holding a gun pointing at her crotch. Across her butt cheeks were scrolled the words, "Family Values."

"Why does this exist?" Vanessa asked.

"Don't look at me. I didn't create this world. You guys did. Look at this," he said, still scrolling through his phone. "@DreamUnicornScum732948365," he said, reading the bio of the flexible woman in the teeny bikini. "She believes the sun is cold, diseases do not exist in nature, and the hashtag Deep State uses bio weapons for population control. Oh, and she loves kittens. Look, here she is holding a kitten." He showed Ness a photo of the woman, naked, with an arm draped over her bosom and a kitten curled up in her crotch. "Hashtag pussy," he said. "Clever." Oliver kept scrolling through her timeline. "She apparently also speaks Russian."

Ness leaned over her son's shoulder. Several of @Dream UnicornScum732948365's posts were written in Cyrillic.

"Oh, and President Redd just retweeted her family values picture," Oliver said. "Why is the president of the United States following @DreamUnicornScum732948365?"

"What do you take from all this?" Ness asked him.

"The internet was supposed to be a democratizing tool but all the wrong people are messing it up for everyone."

She was impressed. "Where did you learn that?"

"I have dinner with you and Dad every night. You have no idea how much you guys drone on and on." He smiled at her. "I'm going back to my room. I have an idea for a TikTok video."

"TikTok is owned by the Chinese and they're stealing all your information so they can surveil you anywhere."

"You guys take the fun out of everything," he said as he walked away down the hall. "I'm also going to write my science paper about why the sun is cold, and I might post a picture of my butt for President Redd. Then I'm going to devise a plan to keep my kidneys safe from Willa Bennett." He disappeared into his room.

Ness took two wine glasses out of the cupboard. She filled them both and took one in her hand, leaving the other for whenever Victor came home. She moved into the living room and opened her laptop. She clicked on a video of Kip Lawson, his ever-present motto, "Truth, the Right Way," emblazoned next to him on the screen. The graphic on the bottom of the screen read, "The End of Civility?"

"Willa Bennett's comments, calling the president of the United States a three-letter word—I won't repeat that word, we are a family program—were demeaning, especially for a person who herself thought she had the gravitas to serve in the White House. It is only fitting that great patriots like DreamUnicornScum732948365 demonstrate their support for President Redd and the traditional values he stands for." He showed the photo of DreamUnicornScum732948365 bending over with a gun to her crotch, her Family Values tushy message emblazoned across the high-definition screen. "DreamUnicornScum732948365 is just like you and me. She believes in the traditional family and that family's right to protect itself. Just like President Redd does. So, go ahead, Willa Bennett. Call him names. Such debased behavior is fitting for an ex-candidate such as yourself. But President Redd and his supporters, like DreamUnicornScum732948365, will continue to stand up for our rights and our freedoms, in a civilized and dignified way."

Ness closed the laptop. She had a hard time wrapping her head around how diffuse the propaganda was. Oliver knew to be critical of what he was seeing, to an extent, but likely because his parents, as he had noted, droned on and on about the dangers of disinformation. Not everyone had intelligence officers for parents. How much were ordinary people influenced? Ness also struggled to find linear causation. Did Russian trolls start the ReddAss hashtag? Or did it start organically and they simply amplified it? Which came first? It was the chicken and egg question, but with dire consequences for democracy. Furthermore, as Oliver had asked, how did Redd see @DreamUnicornScum732948365's post? He didn't follow her. Who put it in front of him to retweet? And why? At what point did Kip Lawson and Facts News choose to cover it? Disinformation was coming from every direction, combined with actual anger on the ground in the United States, and seeded with both overt and covert attempts at manipulation of the president and his cohorts. It was a massive onslaught, and so few people understood it.

CHAPTER TWENTY-TWO

Grigoriy Stepanov blended in with the dozens of hams hanging from the ceiling of Pane Vino, a small trattoria hidden in a tiny piazza in Rome's center. A fountain featuring four tortoises burbled in the square, surrounded by couches and plush chairs so the locals could enjoy a comfortable break outside. Inside the trattoria, Grigoriy chose a table in the corner. He hit his head on a giant leg of prosciutto as he maneuvered into his seat. He rubbed his shoulder, which was sore from doing hot yoga. Although his relationship with suspected CYA officer Olivia Yeardley had never caught any real traction, she had gotten him hooked on centering himself through yoga. Practicing it calmed him, particularly when his boss got angry and Grigoriy once again feared being shipped east and the nightmare vision of him typing with mittens returned.

He saw Max walk in and waved, his thick arm smacking another ham nestled on the windowsill. He ran quickly again through his mental checklist of points to go over with his new asset. Max sat down across from him.

"How did you enjoy Moscow?" he asked enthusiastically.

"What is there not to love?" Max replied. "Such a dynamic city, and an enlightening conference."

"You know, Max, we don't sponsor many people to go to those conferences. You were very fortunate we deemed you worthy. I pushed for you. I want you to know that." He dipped a piece of bread in a small bowl of olive oil. "New Russia News would like to have you on next week, to talk about how the RosAlleman pipeline is going to be great for Italy."

"Certainly, GasItalia will make a fortune," Max said.

"Thanks to the generous terms agreed to by RosGaz."

"That goes without saying."

"But perhaps you should say it. The NRN audience will appreciate that."

Max nodded.

"I also was thinking it would be great exposure for you to write an editorial for one of the main newspapers in Italy. It would really increase your profile, don't you think? You deserve to have more people listen to you. What about a think piece on where you think the relationship between Italy and Russia should go? You could write about how Luca Callieri's desire to work with other strong sovereign and traditional nations like Russia, rather than bureaucrats in Brussels, is in Italy's interest. Or how all this openness to immigrants is tearing Italy apart, how Russia has become a superpower by focusing on Russians, and how Italy should do the same: focus on Italians."

"That's an interesting idea. I'll think about it."

"You should do more than think about it." Grigoriy stretched his sore arm, whacking another ham hanging on a hook behind him. "We were just reviewing the budget for the Russian Cultural

Center this morning. We're hoping to increase our donation to MussoRusso, which, of course, would help cover overtime payment for you, since you'll be writing these editorials and appearing on NRN. We understand your time is valuable."

"That's very generous. I'll get to work on all of that right away."

"Good man," Grigoriy said, his thoughts of Siberia melting away once again.

CHAPTER TWENTY-THREE

"Who's the potato in a suit?" Patrick asked, dropping his bag at his desk and leaning over the shoulders of Victor and Vanessa, who were watching a livestream press conference. "Not Redd, the other guy."

"That's Russian Foreign Minister Yuri Nebkov," Victor said.

"We think he played a big role in attempts to influence the Redd campaign," Vanessa said.

Nebkov and Redd were laughing and jovially patting each other on the back. Then Nebkov pointed to a reporter who wanted to ask a question. She asked it in Russian. Nebkov nodded and grinned and responded in Russian.

"What are they saying?" Patrick asked.

"We don't know," Victor said. "They only allowed in Russian press. No Americans."

Patrick squinted at the screen. "Isn't that the Oval Office?"

Victor and Vanessa nodded in unison.

Nebkov was still laughing then said, "I'll repeat that in English. We categorically deny any role in American elections. This idea that Russia somehow elected Redd, it is fantasy."

As he was talking, President Redd opened a drawer in the Resolute Desk and pulled out a doll. It was dressed in an ill-fitting black suit and had unruly, brownish hair.

"Oh, my god. I don't believe it!" Patrick leaned into the screen. "He's not really . . ."

Ness and Victor leaned in, as well. The three of them went silent.

"He's . . ." Patrick said.

"What is it?" asked Victor.

"Is that . . . ?" Ness's mouth dropped open.

Patrick stood up straight. "That is Dickie the Doll. The doll that gives President Redd his intelligence briefings."

Redd made Dickie the Doll walk through the air to Foreign Minister Nebkov. "*Privet!*" The doll said hello in Russian. The doll then stuck its head into Nebkov's ear, and Victor, Ness, and Patrick could see Redd whispering something to the Russian.

"Is he . . . ?" Victor started.

"Dickie the Doll is briefing the Russian foreign minister," Patrick said. "In the Oval Office."

The three of them were silent for a moment.

"You look pale, Victor," Ness said.

"Dickie the Doll is giving away secrets," he said.

"You know that doll can't talk, right?" Patrick said. Victor shot him a look.

Nebkov had a long, quiet conversation with Dickie the Doll, in front of the rolling cameras. He then turned to Redd and said, "President Redd, as a symbol of the close relationship we'd like to see between the United States and Russia, I would like to present to you Mischa the Matryoshka." An aide handed him a green, red, and gold matryoshka doll, which he held out as a gift to Redd. "Mischa is looking forward to joining Dickie on his adventures all over the world!"

Redd grabbed the matryoshka doll and held it up facing Dickie the Doll. He made voices, as the two dolls spoke to each other.

Victor had work to do, and the president of the United States was not making it easy. He waved Vanessa off as she headed back to her office. Patrick sat down at his desk and said, "Good luck with all that, Victor. I'll be over here working on terrorism. Much easier to tell the good guys from the bad guys."

Victor picked up his green line and called Habibi at Russia House.

"Did you watch that?" Victor asked.

"I'm still numb," Habibi said. "I keep slapping my face, thinking I'll wake up from a bad dream. But nope. This is all real."

"Do you know what Dickie the Doll said to Nebkov?"

"You know the doll can't talk, right?"

Victor didn't respond.

Habibi continued, "I'm guessing it wasn't a knock knock joke. Although with Redd . . ."

"How are things with the commissar?"

"The good news is, Ivan is an idiot," Habibi said. "I call him Ivan. That's not his name, but it sounds Soviet. He doesn't think it's funny, but what Soviet commissar named Ivan ever had a sense of humor? His name is actually Chad."

"Chad White?"

"He is White, yeah, but let's not be racist."

"I mean, his last name is White. Chad White is now your commissar?"

"Yeah, that's the guy."

"He's been meeting with Svetlana Zharkova," Victor said. The photograph of Chad White posing at the gun range with the redheaded Russian flashed in his head.

"Running Russian ops just keeps getting easier," Habibi said. "He mostly gives trouble to the analysts. Nobody upstairs, including Ivan or Plotzki, is happy when the analysts write that Russia is up to no good, because then someone has to go tell Redd and he flips out. The briefers get in a punching match over who will give the briefing. Ivan doesn't know anything about operations, though. When he comes to check on me, I type away like a good bureaucrat, and that seems to placate him. He thinks my job is to type. He's not wrong, but at least I've got a few people like you on the other side of my computer actually collecting intelligence against Russia. So, I can manage the commissar. Now, about COS Wilcox . . ."

Victor looked at the clock on the wall. "I'm ready if you're ready."

"Let me do the talking."

Victor hung up and went to Wilcox's office. "Chief, I believe your assistant told you we've got a scheduled call with Russia House."

Wilcox sat behind a heavy desk. In front of it was a small rug from Rubblestan decorated with tanks and rocket launchers. It was a standard kitsch item people who served in Rubblestan picked up as a souvenir. On a side table was a photograph of a smiling Ahmed al-Rubli, the head of a top terrorist group. The photo sat in a frame with crosshairs that marked the center of al-Rubli's forehead.

Wilcox, dressed in a camouflage quick-dry shirt, was pouring instant coffee grains into a mug of hot water. Victor winced. The world's best coffee was available right outside the embassy. Wilcox tasted the coffee, made a sound of disgust, then added two more scoops of coffee. He tried it again, satisfied.

"Have a seat." He saw Victor looking at a photograph of a Reaper drone on the wall behind Wilcox. He glanced at the picture then back at Victor. "I neutralized a terrorist with that drone. America can thank me for moving us closer to victory in the Total War on Terror."

"When was that, Chief?"

"Ten years ago. Then again three years ago. Then again last year."

"Nothing says victory like having to kill people year after year."

Wilcox's green line rang. He clicked it on speaker. Habibi introduced himself and explained that Victor's operation with Max was now a top priority for Russia House. In doing so, both Victor and Habibi hoped to avoid any anger from Wilcox, who had not wanted Victor to pursue Max in the first place. Habibi then described how the compartmentalization for QDCHESHIRE would limit knowledge of the existence of the operation. "The ultimate substance of what we collect will deal with Russia, but since the asset is Italian, we'll consider it first and foremost an Italian case," Habibi said. "We'll be limiting distribution, though, of both the intelligence reports and our operations cables. Especially the operations cables."

"You're going to have to explain this to me," Wilcox said, scratching the inside of his ear. He pulled out a piece of wax and rubbed it on his pants. "In my experience, more distribution is better. Sharing is caring, we say in the war zone. Why don't we share this with all of our European allies?"

"I understand the standard for sharing is different in war zones," Habibi said. However, with Russia we are dealing with a very different counterintelligence situation. The fewer people in the know, the better. This is rather standard procedure for operations involving a Russian target."

"You said it was an Italian target."

"Yes, but the intelligence collected is mostly about Russia, what Russia is doing in Italy and Europe and how Russia is prioritizing and running operations."

"I prefer clear lines," Wilcox said. He fiddled with an ivory-hilt dagger on his desk. "Like the border between Rubblestan and its neighbors, or between Iraq and Syria."

"That might be why we're still in those places," Habibi said. "The people on the ground don't view those borders quite as clearly as you do. In any case, QDCHESHIRE is an Italian reporting on Russia, so we need tight compartmentalization. We do need to share with Italy, though."

"You just said don't share!" Wilcox tried to drive the tip of the dagger into his desk, which was aluminum. The knife made a dull *ding* sound. Victor tried not to move.

"The Italians have an election coming up," Habibi said. "They might be targeting QDCHESHIRE too. Victor didn't pick the guy randomly. Chances are, the Italians are interested in someone like him, someone who can report on Russia's operations to influence the election and individual politicians, to help promote Russia's agenda. The Italians have the same concerns we have, so this is a compatible operation. We can't risk them targeting QDCHESHIRE and stumbling upon Victor running an undeclared operation in Italy. They'd be pissed. We tell AISI, but we make sure they compartmentalize too. The counterintelligence challenges are a little different than what you experienced in the war zones, sir," Habibi continued. "You're dealing with two sophisticated intelligence services. Both the Italians and the Russians have a lot of experience running complex operations. In addition, Victor will be operating on the Italians' turf. They run all the surveillance technology in the country. They can see all the CCTV footage, track any phone, track who rides what form of transportation from where to where. We cannot risk them discovering Max and Victor meeting. If we inform them now that this is going on, they can help ensure the safety of both Max and Victor. As for the Russians, if they find out Max is a double agent, they'll kill him, and possibly Victor, as well."

"I can call in a drone strike," Wilcox offered.

Habibi had no idea what Wilcox planned to blow up. "Why don't we hold that option in reserve, sir," Habibi said. "We also need to keep Max safe from any inside threats," he continued.

"Like a mole?" Wilcox asked.

"We've had our share of them in the past," Habibi said. "The more restricted information about him is, the less chance someone with access can misuse the information and, perhaps, share it with parties who, as I mentioned, would like to see Max dead."

Victor understood Habibi was sticking to a generic concept of a mole in his explanation to Wilcox. But he knew both he and Habibi kept picturing the image of Redd and Dickie the Doll laughing with Nebkov in the Oval Office and wondering if some case officer somewhere in the world would now have to extract a well-placed, sensitive source on a moment's notice because of the impromptu lovefest between them. He and Habibi were determined not to end up in a similar situation.

With the bureaucratic protections for QDCHESHIRE in place, Habibi hung up, leaving Victor to discuss the operational protections.

"I've scoped out a secure meeting location," Victor told Wilcox.

"You guys just lectured me about how dangerous this situation is. Why risk going out to meet him? Let's bring him in. Meet him here. Safest place in the country."

"Chief, this isn't Rubblestan. Italy is a safe country. If I take good counterintelligence precautions, I can handle him, no problem. He cannot come into the embassy. That would blow his cover. I'll run a two-day surveillance detection route on the way to the meeting. I've already briefed QDCHESHIRE about precautions he needs to take, as well."

"A two-day SDR? That's one way to get your sightseeing in, Victor."

"It's not a two-day vacation, sir. Have you ever run a multiday SDR?"

"Where was I going to go for two days in Rubblestan?"

"I can assure you this is the safest way to meet with QDCHESHIRE."

"Your colleagues are in here every day. You'll have to explain to them how two days away from the office is not a holiday. Do you need an armored car?"

"I'll drive my own car."

"Do you need a beacon? If you need to call in the Marines to get you?"

"Unless I choke on a piece of prosciutto, I think I'll be fine."

Wilcox stood up. "Go forth, Victor. Return to us safely." He saluted.

Victor stood up and gave an awkward bow with a half-salute and walked out of the office.

CHAPTER TWENTY-FOUR

Victor checked his rearview mirror. The silver Peugeot 307 was still there. The driver was a woman with a ponytail and a blue blouse. He memorized the license plate number and took a mental note of the small dent above the left headlight. If he were being followed, they could change drivers, or the same driver could change her hair and clothes, and the license plate could easily be switched out, in an effort to throw him off. The dent was harder to change. Unless the person switched cars, Victor would know the same person was following him.

The silver Peugeot was the only car he had noticed more than once since he had left Rome that morning. He pulled off the highway at the small town of Orvieto. The Peugeot drove on. He would continue his surveillance detection route on foot.

He parked his car and walked into the main piazza, where the fourteenth-century cathedral stood like a lace façade pointing to heaven. A cool fog enveloped the town, providing an ethereal aura to the medieval town. Victor passed a ceramics shop and turned down a small alley. Election day was several weeks away and political parties from across Italy had affixed their campaign messages on walls throughout the town. Victor spotted a poster for Da Italia, featuring a photograph of a large family standing in a field. Among them was an elderly man in a military uniform. "*L'Italia agli italiani!*" it read in screaming red letters. In slightly smaller type below, it said, "We honor our military." Something looked off. Victor recalled photos of his grandfather in his Italian military uniform. He scrutinized the Da Italia poster. The uniform was not the same. He looked more closely. Was that man wearing a Soviet uniform? He looked at the medals on the man's lapel. One had a large red star on it. Others had Cyrillic writing. That was definitely a Soviet uniform.

He walked on and entered an outdoor market filled with the smell of fresh basil and garlic. He glanced around before continuing on. He ducked into a small trattoria and ordered penne alla vodka. He watched the faces pass by the window as he ate.

After a delicious tiramisu, he walked back through the narrow streets, still taking notice of faces and cars, before once again getting in his vehicle and returning to the highway. He drove on to the town of Todi. There, with a view over rolling Umbrian hills, he had a pleasant stroll through its maze of medieval streets, before slipping into the fourteenth-century cathedral. He sat for several minutes, allowing the calm of the dimly lit space to embrace him. He was alone. After several minutes, he exited through a side door into an alley. With each turn on a road, with each stop—at the ice cream shop or the store selling truffles—he observed the faces around him.

He sat down at a cafe in the main piazza and ordered a glass of wine. Several of the locals had gathered as the evening set, discussing their views of the upcoming election, the different political parties, and the direction of the country.

"Giovanni, why did you take down the Da Italia poster I gave you?" an older man in a loose-fitting suit yelled from his table to the cafe owner inside. "You're probably going to vote for the Communists."

Giovanni stood in the doorway of his bar, drying a glass with a small towel. "The poster you gave me had a Soviet soldier on it, and you're worried about me voting for the Communists." He saw Victor watching the exchange and smiled. "Don't worry," Giovanni said to the older man. "You'll be forced to share your house with fifteen immigrants, but they won't make your goats gay."

"Communist." The old man stood up to leave, then turned back to Giovanni. "Don't be late for dinner. Your mother will kill you." Giovanni gave him a peck on the cheek. "Ciao, Papa. I'll see you in an hour." The old man put on a fedora and grabbed his cane before walking away. Giovanni looked at Victor, who laughed. Victor paid Giovanni, walked down the hill, and back up the other side to a restaurant with a view, where he ordered a divine osso buco.

Wilcox had been wrong that Victor was trying to make his SDR into a two-day vacation, but there was no reason he couldn't make the hard work more enjoyable. Any observer would think he was having fun, and he was. But he was paying more attention to every glance than anyone might notice. It was exhausting. Finally, he retired to a small hotel in Todi for the night.

He returned to the piazza the following morning. He ordered a pastry and coffee from Giovanni and grabbed a newspaper. He caught his breath when he saw the front-page headline, "President

Redd Compromises Israeli Intelligence Source." A large photograph showed Redd and Dickie the Doll whispering in the ear of Russian Foreign Minister Nebkov during the Oval Office press conference. He read, "Redd revealed specific intelligence about a terrorist plot. The intelligence had originated with an Israeli source, and the government of Israel had not given permission for the intelligence to be shared with any other government. Israeli government sources said the revelation could be traced to identify their clandestine source, whose life is now in danger. 'That the president of the United States did something like this is already bad,' one anonymous Israeli official said. 'That he used a doll to do it somehow makes it worse.' Asked about the incident, President Redd said, 'Dickie the Doll thinks we should be friends with Russia, which is why Dickie the Doll has invited Mischa the Matryoshka to all our intelligence briefings from now on!'"

Victor's head hurt. How would Max react to the news? Would it scare him off? Convince him the United States was no different than Russia? Would he even show up for their meeting?

He finished his breakfast and headed to his car, where he checked his list of license plates. He drove on, finally arriving in Spoleto nei Guai. The town was actually named just Spoleto, but it had acquired the nickname Spoleto nei Guai, literally meaning Spoleto in Trouble, after a series of earthquakes had damaged several of the town's main buildings. He parked his car, tucked his license plate list into a hidden compartment in his backpack, and locked up the vehicle. He began the walk up the hill to the town. He was exhausted, but it was worth it, worth taking the time and spending the energy to make sure no one—particularly no Russians, like Grigoriy Stepanov, Max's Russian intelligence handler—was following him. He arrived, at last, at the charming, but empty, Bellavista Hotel.

As its name would suggest, the hotel had a beautiful view over the city's Roman wall and onto rolling green hills accented with firs and cypress trees. It wasn't Tuscany, but it was as lovely and didn't suffer from tourist overcrowding like its more famous neighboring province did. The biggest patrons of the Renaissance were from Tuscany, but Umbria was just as worthy of eternal life in a painting.

Victor waited for Max in a room that had a small private garden with a table under a fig tree. He heard a knock and opened the door. He ushered QDCHESHIRE out to the terrace and poured him a glass of sparkling water.

Max threw a copy of the newspaper on the table. It landed face up, a large photo of Redd holding Dickie the Doll up to Foreign Minister Nebkov's ear prominently displayed. "President Redd likes to talk about sources, I see." Max held Victor's eyes for a moment before turning away, looking angry.

Victor was angry too. It was hard enough to recruit an asset, to convince someone to do something they knew they shouldn't be doing, something that could cost them their job, their livelihood, maybe their life. Max had agreed to provide information on Russia's actions and, in order to do so, to continue pretending he was working on behalf of Grigoriy Stepanov. If Stepanov, or any other Russian—or anyone friendly with Russia—were to find out Max was playing him, the consequences would be dire. President Redd's cavalier actions were making all of these dynamics more difficult to manage.

"Max, keeping you safe is my top priority," Victor said. "The minute I don't think I can keep you safe, or the minute you don't think I can keep you safe, this is over. That's why we've had our last supper in public and are now meeting here."

"I am afraid references to last suppers do not reassure me." He smiled, shaking his head. "It is one thing to keep me safe from Grigoriy, safe from the Russians who are here. What about the Americans? How many at the embassy know? Does the American president know about me? He can know about me, if he wants, no?" Max grabbed the newspaper and shook it in front of Victor. "The next time he wants to impress Nebkov, will it be my name he uses?" He threw the paper down again.

"You don't have to worry about President Redd. Or Dickie the fucking Doll," Victor said. He hoped he was telling Max the truth. "I know it doesn't always seem like it, but we do know how to keep secrets. I've made sure any information about you, and any information from you, is compartmentalized, available to only a handful of people, all of whom want to see you succeed."

"See me succeed." Max threw his arms up and shook his head. "I don't even know what this means anymore." He sat down. "Grigoriy has me writing two editorials for the Italian press, both about how the RosAlleman pipeline will be good business for Italy. For Italy? It is only for Callieri. And I must be on NRN tomorrow morning, discussing how the pipeline means energy independence for Europe. I don't know what I am doing anymore."

"Take a breath," Victor said. "Drink some water."

Max took several sips. Victor sat down across from him. Neither of them said anything. A cool breeze rustled the leaves on the fig tree. At last, Victor spoke. "Tell me about your meeting with Grigoriy."

Max recounted as many details about the meeting as he could. He told Victor where they met, how Grigoriy communicated with him, how Grigoriy had tacitly tied funding for the MussoRusso Cultural Association—and an increased salary for Max—to Max's performing the tasks assigned to him by Grigoriy. He told Victor the main points he was supposed to make during his NRN appearances and in his newspaper editorials.

Victor listened intently and took notes. Why was Grigoriy giving Max these tasks? The most logical reason was to make the message more palatable to the audience. It allowed Russia's agenda in Italy to be presented as though it was coming from an Italian. With Max as the messenger, the reader or TV audience would be more open to the policy ideas, not realizing the policies actually benefited Russia. As a respected academic, he also lent credibility to the agenda. Grigoriy was coopting Max into being part of Russia's messaging and influence campaign in Italy. Furthermore, it seemed like Grigoriy was priming Max, in case he moved into a more influential position, with the government, for example. If Callieri won, Max might become a government official, placing him in an extraordinary position to help influence Italy's policies in a way that ultimately served Russia.

When Max finished, he stood up and walked around the garden. "Is this information even helping you? Is doing this helping me?"

Victor reassured him, "These are minor tasks you need to keep doing for Grigoriy. In the long run, you are helping stop Russia from interfering in Italy, even if it doesn't feel like it in the short run." He looked Max in the eye. "You are doing a good thing. You are making Italy truly for Italians, and making sure Italy is not for sale to Vlastov."

CHAPTER TWENTY-FIVE

"I stand before you to make a great announcement," President Redd said, sitting at the Resolute Desk in the Oval Office. A framed photograph of himself hugging an American flag sat on the sideboard behind him.

"He's sitting down. How can he say he stands before us?" Vanessa asked Victor. They were watching a video of the president's speech, which he had given the previous evening in Washington.

Redd continued, "I am here to announce something no other president has ever announced before. This is the greatest announcement ever given from the White House. I, your favorite president, have defeated the terrorists! We have won the Total War on Terror! I grabbed that TWOT and I didn't let go until I was victorious!"

"We'll have to celebrate tonight," Ness said.

"It came together quickly at the end," Victor said. "I read a report yesterday about terrorists bombing a US convoy in Syria. It's amazing the difference a day makes. All our counterterrorism officers can go home now. Imagine all the free time they'll have. The gingerbread house competition is going to be lit this year."

Vanessa clicked through a number of social media sites. Redd's message was getting a boost across a number of platforms. Many voluptuous women in confederate bikinis and men who loved Jesus and guns were praising Redd's single-handed dismantling of a terrorist group that the US military had been unable to defeat in fifteen years and that, Victor and Vanessa both knew, was not defeated at all in real life. A number of terrorist groups were, in fact, alive and kicking and planning all kinds of new attacks. Redd would find a way to blame someone else if any of those attacks succeeded.

"Here's more good news," Vanessa groaned, summarizing a news article she was scrolling through. "A number of White House staffers didn't pass their background checks and investigators declined to give them clearances."

"That actually is good news," Victor said.

"Redd overruled them."

Victor ran his hand over his face, trying to stay calm. "Why didn't they pass their background checks?"

"We don't know. With this crew, I'd guess investigators had questions about their foreign financial ties." She glanced at her watch. "Time to head in to the office and share all our secrets with a White House staff that couldn't pass a background check and a president who, in the best-case scenario, won't condemn an enemy attack on the country and in the worst-case scenario is aiding and abetting it." She looked at Victor. He looked like he wanted to throw up. "It's going to be a great day!"

The two dressed and made their way to the embassy. At Vanessa's office door, Victor eyed her exercise ball.

"Your day will come, my love," Ness said. "You, too, shall have a giant blue ball." She kissed him on the cheek.

Victor continued to his office. He arrived in the bullpen and could not believe his eyes. There, tucked under his desk, inflated and blue and glorious, was his own exercise ball. He pushed his decrepit chair aside and rolled out the ball. He pushed on it. The pressure seemed good. Not good. Great. He bounced it. It made a satisfying and amusing *poing!* sound. Finally, he sat on it, bouncing a little on his butt. It was fun. He felt the pressure in his lower back melt away with the mere thought of not having to sit in his broken chair anymore. He rolled himself forward, placed his forearms on his desk, his fingers hovering above the keyboard. Then he spotted it. Sitting to the right of his keyboard was a neon blue helmet. He picked it up and chucked it onto his discarded chair.

He glanced around the bullpen. A few other officers were typing away. Patrick was not in yet, though. Victor had an idea. He logged into the unclassified computer, pulled up a number of sites, and clicked print. He ran over to the printer and grabbed the pile, looking around furtively. Patrick would be in any minute now. Victor scrounged through a desk drawer and found a roll of tape. He stuck the papers up around Patrick's desk and on his computer monitor, then rushed back to his new seat.

He was still giggling to himself when Ralph Fleiss, the support officer, walked in. He looked at Victor and exhaled. His shoulders drooped and his head dropped forward, as he shook it slowly back and forth.

"Victor, I'm disappointed," he said.

Victor was about to defend his handiwork on Patrick's desk, but Ralph had more to say.

"These balls can be extremely dangerous. You barely passed your online ball security course. Barely." He walked over to Victor's chair and picked up the neon blue helmet. He placed it on Victor's head and began adjusting it. "An officer in Malawi bounced himself off his ball and hit his head on the office's minifridge." He tightened the strap under Victor's chin. "Another one rolled off and banged his head on an open file drawer." He placed his hands on top of the helmet and shook it and Victor's head. "These regulations exist to protect you." He banged the top of the helmet. Victor winced. "There, that's better." He walked to the door of the bullpen and turned back. "Remember: Before you log in, protect your noggin." He tapped his index finger against his forehead then walked out.

Victor watched him go, perched on the ball, his neon blue helmet snug on his head. Patrick walked in.

"Cool helmet. Is Vanessa that worried about you banging your head against your desk?" He crossed over to his desk and laughed at the papers Victor had taped everywhere. They were headlines from various news outlets. "Terrorists Decimated!" he read out loud. "Redd Wins War on Terror!" He looked back at Victor. "This was a very funny idea to do to a counterterrorism analyst, but I'm guessing you didn't anticipate looking like such a doofus when it was time for the punchline."

"Ralph said I have to protect my noggin."

Patrick sat down and stretched over the back of his chair, his arms high overhead before he clasped his hands behind his head. "What the hell am I going to do all day now that we won the war on terror?"

"You could help me against the Russians," Victor said.

"That's a hoax. The president said so."

"You could start brushing up on your ventriloquism skills and land yourself a briefing job with Dickie the Doll."

"The briefers are trying to retire Dickie the Doll, ever since he became inseparable from Mischa the Matryoshka. But they can't get the guy to focus for more than a few seconds."

Victor pulled on this chin strap of his helmet. "What have they come up with?"

"You remember that Canadian weather girl who undressed as she gave the weather forecast?"

"How could I forget?"

"They're working on getting her top-secret clearances."

Victor started unbuckling his helmet. "It has to be awkward to read all these news articles questioning if Redd is a Russian agent and then go in and give him a classified briefing on Russia." He removed the helmet and ran his hands through his hair. "I guess in some ways it's a blessing he doesn't pay attention to the briefings."

"Until the Canadian weather girl gets her clearances."

"We can also take comfort in the fact that most of the White House staff has no business having access to classified information," Victor said. "I should just put a selfie of me and Max on MySpace. It would save us the time of having someone leak it."

"If you put it on MySpace it will remain classified. No one is going to see it. How old are you, Victor?"

"I had a flip phone until about six months ago when the Station made me get an intelligent phone."

"A smart phone."

"Whatever."

Mary Driscoll, the deputy chief of station walked in. If she hadn't been carrying a red notebook, Victor would not have seen her. Her beige suit matched her skin, her hair, and the cubicle fabric. Victor put his helmet back on.

"I've looked through what you've written for your performance evaluation, Victor." She tapped a government pen against the red notebook. "It's a good start. I particularly like this section." She read from her notebook, "Victor made enormous and relevant contributions in the decisive fight to end the Total War on Terror, or TWOT, when he volunteered to serve in an expeditionary capacity in West Africa, where he applied his native language skills to navigate the complex physical, cultural, and human terrain to harness a greater understanding of the multifaceted conflict and help lead it to a successful conclusion."

Patrick swallowed a laugh. Victor looked at him, smiled, and gave him a wink and a nod.

Mary looked up from her notebook at Victor. "I really like your use of the word expeditionary there. The panel will love that, and contributing in a hardship zone will certainly help your case. However, we're going to need to highlight your leadership skills a little more."

"I wrote in there that I trained a team of Nigeriens to get highly detailed intelligence about the plans and intentions of a West African terror franchise. That intel was briefed up to the White House, which loved it. So, I think I have the leadership part covered. Also, the president announced we won the war, so I get some of the credit, right?"

She smiled at him as if he were a child. "Victor, Director is very keen to highlight Leadership Where You Are." From the way she said it, Victor knew it was a new motto at Director. "You were part of a team with liaison in West Africa. We need examples of you showing your leadership here in Rome. You can't just coast through your tour."

Victor glanced at the clock on the wall. He had been hoping to write up his assessments and intelligence reports from his last meeting with QDCHESHIRE. He needed to think through the complications of keeping his source safe. Director had dispersed a commissar who was getting felt up at the gun range by a redheaded Russian known to be trying to influence conservative politicians in both Italy and the United States. The president of the United States was whispering intelligence secrets and giving away sources to the Russian foreign minister. Grigoriy was tasking Max and probably knew he would face a frozen future in Siberia if he messed up the operation, which Victor was actively trying to do. Any of them— Director, the commissar, the Russians—would want a piece of Max if they knew what information he was providing. Yet since he had arrived at the office an hour ago, he had been forced to wear a helmet and lectured on how his year spent away from his family while living twelve kilometers from a terrorist group that wanted to kill him wasn't a true show of leadership and wasn't worthy of promotion.

"You're right, Mary. I shouldn't think I can I just coast." He glanced at Patrick, who was biting his lower lip to stop himself from speaking.

"I've thought of a solution for you," Mary continued. "There is a big push at Director to be more transparent about mental health issues. You've spent a lot of time in some difficult places. Maybe you could put together a PowerPoint presentation outlining some coping mechanisms and advice for officers who might be going to those places for the first time."

"I'm not sure I'm qualified to act in a mental health capacity, Mary. I actively encourage yelling at idiots and drinking at the office on Fridays."

"I can't help you if you don't want to help yourself, Victor. I've made a suggestion. I think it's a good one. I can't force you to do anything, of course. But showing Leadership Where You Are is a top priority for the promotion panel."

"I'll take it under consideration, Mary. Thank you for your feedback."

Victor turned back to his keyboard, hoping to finally start working through the many challenges he had to keep Max safe. Mary left. Patrick let loose and laughed. "How did you finally manage to write your promotion essay?"

"Oliver and I fed certain words into an artificial intelligence site that writes essays and it spit our that paragraph. It makes no sense but has lots of buzz words."

"The promotion panel will love it," Patrick said. "Be sure to include some purple in your PowerPoint presentation."

"What?"

"I took an online course about creating effective PowerPoint presentations."

"There's a course about how to make PowerPoint presentations?"

"It's an online PowerPoint presentation that teaches you how to make an effective PowerPoint presentation. The fact that I remember you should include purple proves it was effective."

"Why purple?"

"It's soothing for the audience."

"According to whom?"

"Whoever made that online PowerPoint presentation about how to make an effective PowerPoint presentation."

"I'll get on it," Victor said. "Right after I figure out how to protect my asset from, well, from everyone."

"Priorities, Victor."

Victor pulled up the New Russia News website. The chyron on the livestream video read, "US Must Leave Middle East Now That Redd Claims Terror Victory."

"Of course, Russia deserves credit for our cooperation in defeating the terrorists," a Russian senator was saying. "But you won't hear any thank you from the West. They cannot show us any gratitude. Anyone who might thank us would be suspect. The liberal media would call them a Russian agent."

Victor was familiar enough with the war on terror to know that Russia had played a decidedly unhelpful role, in fact. But NRN was known for its revisionist perspective. He scrolled down and found a video of Lance Whitaker, the actor who had played Lawrence Blackhouse. He was speaking to Igor Popov, the NRN reporter whose work was often picked up by Facts News.

"It's not a question of supporting President Redd," Lance said to Igor. The graphic on the screen read, "Progressive Actor Denounces Russian Hoax." Lance continued, "I find him to be something of a buffoon, but I could not in good conscience vote for Willa Bennett, who had the support of the establishment political party and planned to continue policies that only further entrench the elites in our power structures. And now, this establishment cannot fathom that it lost and so is perpetrating a campaign of lies against President Redd."

"May I ask who you voted for?" Igor Popov said.

"I voted for the Green Party, the third party, to make a statement that I disagree with the entire political establishment. The Green Party is the only party pushing for progressive measures, trying to establish responsible vegan consumption, and supporting a regional California movement to allow our vegan communes to split off and function free from the tyranny of the overbearing, meat-loving state and federal governments."

"I can't believe how stupid everything is," Victor said to no one in particular. He recalled Max telling him about the many tiny groups, including a California vegan secessionist, who had been present at the autonomy conference he attended in Moscow.

Patrick turned his chair around to face Victor. "You go far enough right or far enough left and the two extremes actually meet."

"Why the long faces, guys?" Kelsea Greyco interrupted them. She was a young analyst with the National Security Agency. Like most NSA officers, she eschewed formal business attire. Jeans with a black T-shirt was her regular uniform. "Entertain me, I need a break. I've been stuck in a windowless room all morning. Nice blue ball, Victor. And the hat is fantastic. What's the gossip? Is that the guy who played Blackhouse?" she asked, looking at Victor's screen. She jumped up and sat on an empty desk. "Fuck that guy and his CCCP helpers. And his doppelganger actor. Vlastov has been manipulating us for years. Blackhouse was just part of it."

"No one would ever guess you've been sitting alone in a dark room with no one to talk to, Kelsea," Patrick said.

She gave him a sarcastic smile.

"If we don't do anything to stop it, they'll keep doing it," Victor said. "It doesn't help that the president of the United States has turned public service into a dirty concept. What the fuck am I supposed to tell my assets? 'Don't worry. We probably won't reveal your cooperation to the world, unless it's really helpful to the president politically.'"

"You may have to work on that messaging," Kelsea said.

"Maybe just hope our politics are too obscure for your assets to understand," Patrick said. "Try to convince them not to read American news. Or foreign news, because this president is so whacko everyone else covers it, too, just to feel a little superior, I think."

"I'm trying to protect a source from being discovered by the Russians and to protect him from our own leaders. And I am surrounded by chaos."

"Try to carve out a little time for the important things, Victor. You have that PowerPoint presentation to do, to be a leader where you are."

"You should use purple," Kelsea said. "I heard it's soothing and captures the audience."

CHAPTER TWENTY-SIX

Victor drove through the curvy roads of the Apennine Mountains, once again keeping a list of all the cars he saw along the way. There weren't many, as he stuck to back roads that wound torturously through the region of Basilicata, nestled in the instep of Italy's boot with coastlines on two different seas, the Gulf of Taranto to the south and the Tyrrhenian Sea to the west. He had spent the last two days making stops to visit sites, hike the mountains, and eat the famous local Lucanica sausage. There was no reason hard work couldn't also be fun. At last, he pulled in to a small hotel in the town of Maratea built into a cliff overlooking the Tyrrhenian Sea.

As planned, at exactly 1:00 pm, Max knocked on the door of Victor's room. Victor welcomed him out on the terrace, where the late summer sun sparkled on the sea as the cool air from the mountains swept down on them.

Max reached into a carrier bag strapped across his chest and pulled out two thick reports. He tossed them on the table. "I wrote these for Grigoriy."

Victor sifted through them and looked at their titles: "A Peace Plan for Ukraine: How Italy can lead the way to a solution" and "Energy Opportunities to Create Stronger Italy-Russia Ties."

"How much did Grigoriy write for you?" Victor asked.

"He suggested the themes. I pretended to be enthusiastic and support the ideas. I hammered out the main substance. It was rather clear what direction he wanted me to go. In some places, he dictated specific talking points. I am supposed to present these in a few weeks to a gathering of parliamentarians." He picked up one of the reports and flipped through it, then threw it back on the table. "Does this even work? Why does Grigoriy have me spending time writing obscure policy papers?"

"Let's say Callieri wins." Victor picked up the report outlining a peace plan for Ukraine. "He could propose this peace plan and say that Italy will recognize Russia's annexation of Crimea. Many parliamentarians, and many Italians, would be more ready to go along with it if the idea were already floating around in foreign policy circles. It makes it look like an Italian idea, when in fact, it is Vlastov's." He put the report back on the table. "Grigoriy might be hoping you'll be useful in other ways too. Especially if Callieri wins. You will play a role in shaping the actions of Italy's government. Which brings me to something I wanted to discuss with you." Victor pushed Max's reports aside and leaned forward. "I'd like to share our discussions with some Italian officials. I think this would be beneficial for both you and me."

Max exhaled and relaxed in his seat. "I am pleased to hear this. I have been feeling guilty, as though I am hiding secrets from Italy."

"I don't want you to feel that way," Victor said. "What you are doing is only going to help Italy, help your country maintain its sovereignty. By sharing your information with these officials, you can feel confident you are doing that. I told you from the start, I'm not here to make Italy do America's bidding. I just don't want Italy doing Russia's bidding."

Max patted the stack of papers on the table. "Like promoting a Russian peace plan that endorses the first annexation of land in Europe since World War Two?"

"For example." Victor smiled at him. "When is your next meeting with Grigoriy?"

"Next week."

"I'll meet with my Italian friend so we're all set up the next time you and I see each other. Keep letting Grigoriy task you. It might seem counterintuitive, but Italy needs you to do some work for the Russians."

CHAPTER TWENTY-SEVEN

Victor stepped out of the elevator of La Minerve hotel and ascended a small flight of stairs to the rooftop. The summer sun would soon pass to fall, and he saw Francesco Restani lounging on a shady couch under a sail-like cover, sipping a glass of prosecco. The bottle was nestled in a bucket of ice next to him. The enormous concrete dome of the Pantheon rose just beyond the terrace. Victor could hear the din of the tourists below, lining up to enter the nearly two-thousand-year-old building.

"It's good to see you," Francesco said, as he poured a glass of prosecco for Victor and motioned for him to sit down on the couch across from him. An assortment of olives, cheeses, and salami was spread on the table in-between.

"I'm sure you prefer Vanessa's company," Victor said, taking the glass from Francesco.

"I'm sure you do too."

They clinked their glasses together.

"I wanted to run something by you," Victor said. He needed to introduce the QDCHESHIRE operation carefully. He had been running an Italian citizen as an asset for several weeks. Pissing off the host country was generally a bad idea, especially when the host country was considered a close ally. "I've come across an interesting gentleman, an academic here in Rome. I think he might be in a good position to provide information on the Russian community. I've met with him a few times." Francesco raised his eyebrows. Victor continued, "I wanted to get a feel for what he might be able to report on. There was no need to waste your time, until I knew he really was well-positioned." Francesco smiled. Another fig leaf floated along the air. "Now that I know he's worth my time, *our* time, I'd like to share with you what I've learned and discuss where this might go."

Francesco appreciated Victor's attempt to be diplomatic. He understood perfectly that Victor had met with this asset several times, hiding it from the Italian government, the very government that allowed him to reside in Italy as a guest with diplomatic immunity. It was business as usual. "Who is this academic?" he asked.

"His name is Massimiliano Brevi. He works for—"

"The MussoRusso Cultural Association," Francesco cut him off. "I know of him. We've been watching him. We've seen him meet several times with Grigoriy Stepanov from the Russian embassy." Francesco popped an olive in his mouth. "You will be pleased to know we did not see him meeting with you."

Victor held back a smile. It seemed he was doing his job right.

"*Cazzo*," Francesco swore, looking down. He had spilled oil from the olive on his pants. A waiter rushed over with a spray can and brush. He reached over to spray Francesco's lap. He and Francesco locked eyes for a moment. Victor watched in fascination. Was the waiter really going to brush clean Francesco's crotch? The two held each other's stare for several seconds, the waiter poised with the spray can aimed at Francesco's lap and the brush grasped in his left hand. The waiter blinked and handed over the spray can and brush. Francesco cleaned himself up then returned the implements to the waiter, who had politely diverted his gaze.

Francesco turned back to Victor. "It's very kind of you to spare us time by checking out this potential asset for us. What do you make of his meetings with Stepanov?"

"Stepanov is his Russian handler."

"We've reached the same conclusion."

"I told him to keep seeing Stepanov and playing along, so we can learn the Russians' modus operandi."

"You've made him a double agent?"

"Effectively, yes. But he is a nationalist through and through. That's why having you aboard is a priority for us. He wants to know he is working for Italy."

Francesco leaned forward. Victor did the same.

"This is, of course, an operation of interest to my government," Francesco said. "As you know, however, that government is very likely to change in the coming weeks. Some of those politicians might be less enthusiastic."

Victor knew he meant Luca Callieri.

"Like the situation you and Vanessa now find yourselves in, I fear things in Italy's intelligence services might get . . ." Francesco thought for a moment.

"Awkward?"

"Indeed. Awkward."

"That's why I'm coming to you directly. Wilcox is aware, of course, but we thought it would be best to keep this on the working level, just between you and me. We'll need strict compartmenting of information on both sides. The fewer people who know, the better."

"I can do that," Francesco said. He looked thoughtful. "Although I am not allowed, in my official capacity, to support any political party over another, let us hope that Da Italia and Luca Callieri do not meet with the same success as your President Redd."

Victor and Francesco clinked glasses again and each took a big gulp of prosecco.

CHAPTER TWENTY-EIGHT

Several weeks later, Victor was back on the road. He stopped in Perugia, where he bought chocolates for Oliver, then circled back south to Assisi. He arrived on the day of Italy's election. He visited the Basilica of Saint Francis—San Francesco—parts of which had been demolished in a recent earthquake, and said a small prayer to the patron saint of the Italian official in whose hands much of QDCHESHIRE's security now rested. He arrived at the Giotto Hotel, tucked into a tiny alley on the city's edge, and checked in to his room. He arranged the chairs around a table under a fig tree on the little garden terrace off the room and, as usual, placed a bottle of sparkling water on the table. The church bell clanged, marking 8:00 pm. He heard a faint rap on the door.

Victor opened it and welcomed Max in. He looked tired and anxious. "No results yet," Max said, as he dropped his bag near the table. He checked his watch. He poured some water from the bottle on the table and took a long sip. He checked his watch again. "When will the election results be in?" He kept fidgeting but finally sat down. "Grigoriy gave me a new task." He reached for his bag.

Victor sat down across from him. "Stop. Slow down. Let's go over some basic security protocols." Victor had seen assets like this before, so caught up in an immediate situation that they forgot the bigger picture. Important details, like what to say if they ran into someone they knew, needed to be reviewed constantly. Even if he was agitated, Max needed to be able to explain without hesitation why he was where he was. Victor talked him through a number of security steps. It helped focus Max and calm his nerves. Only then did Victor return to the subject of Grigoriy Stepanov and his tasking for Max.

"He wants me to help spot new talent for New Russia News," Max said. "He wants me to find me, but in France or in Germany. And he wants me to go back to Moscow." Max stood up. He paced around the garden. He spotted a bottle of vodka Victor had left on a sideboard. He picked it up and looked at Victor. Victor nodded. Max returned to the table and poured a glass for Victor and one for himself. The two drank in silence for a moment. "It's for the World Family Values Congress. Dudnik will be there again, and probably many representatives from the traditionalist parties and organizations. Grigoriy hopes I might find some suitable counterparts at the conference and convince them to go on NRN, or to write articles for think tanks, or whatever. I suppose it's also a bit of indoctrination. I listen to the speakers and then know what messages and talking points I should be publicly supporting once I come back here." He shot down the rest of the vodka in his glass.

"So, you go back to Moscow." Victor refilled Max's glass.

Max took another sip of vodka, holding it in his mouth for a moment before swallowing. "It's all pretend, isn't it? I pretend to do what Grigoriy wants. Grigoriy pretends I am helping Italy. You pretend you can keep me safe and you can help Italy." A leaf fell off the fig tree and floated to the ground.

"I can keep you safe, and I can help you help Italy. Grigoriy works for Vlastov. Vlastov might break the European Union, but he won't stop there. He wants to see autocracy everywhere. Democracy in any country is a threat to him. Italy is no exception."

"I will go to Moscow."

"Be careful with the Adrianas."

"I will be careful with the Adrianas." Max smiled for the first time. "And I will avoid the USB ports." He held up the bottle of vodka. "You have good taste."

Max's phone chirped from inside the hotel suite. He got up. When he returned a minute later, he was pale.

"They've announced the election results. Da Italia has come in first, but not with enough votes to run everything outright. I guess they didn't get quite enough money from Russia. They will need to form a coalition."

"And Callieri?"

He looked down at the message on his phone. "He's been named head of the Ministry of Interior, with his consiglieri Aldo Conti." He looked up at Victor. "And me."

As head of the Interior Ministry, Callieri would oversee all of Italy's security services, including those looking for moles, which, now that he had been named an advisor to the new interior minister, Max was.

Victor had been working to protect QDCHESHIRE from Russian intelligence, as well as from the Director of his own CYA bureaucracy, not to mention the president of the United States, who people were openly saying was probably a Russian asset. Now, with the victory of Luca Callieri and a single text, he also had to protect Max from the new Italian government and Max's own boss. They were surrounded by powerful people who had good reason to want to shut Max up.

CHAPTER TWENTY-NINE

Victor was nearly alone in the bullpen when he heard the office doorbell ring and the familiar click as someone in the front office buzzed it open. Ness appeared at his desk. She did not look happy. "We have a problem." She commandeered Victor's computer mouse and pulled up a video of Kip Lawson from Facts News. The motto, "Truth, the Right Way," was displayed in bright red and blue letters on the side of the screen. The graphic on the bottom read, "FBI Spied on Redd." She clicked play.

"Harrowing news today," Kip Lawson said, "as we learn that the FBI, in the months before the election, was spying on President Richard Redd's campaign. Facts News has learned that an officer of the FBI spied on Ashley-Anne Wynscott, President Redd's campaign advisor. The officer sat outside Ms. Wynscott's home, hoping to catch her. Doing what? I don't know. Doing anything Redd's opponents could twist to their political advantage. This is truly a Deep State cabal. An actual FBI officer, who should be here to protect all Americans, who should be here to protect the Constitution, instead participated in a sickening political act in an effort to cast a negative light on President Redd and his campaign. I cannot stress enough how dangerous this is for our democracy."

Victor looked at Vanessa. She was pale. "I wasn't spying on the Redd campaign. I was surveilling a Russian intelligence officer. I was following Diana Abramovich, not Ashley-Anne Wynscott. They're totally twisting the facts."

Victor led her to his broken chair in the corner. It teetered as she sat on it and he quickly led her instead to Patrick's empty chair. He was about to say something to help ease her anxiety when his green line rang. He held up a finger to Vanessa. "One second," he said. He picked up the phone.

"Double check all your communication plans and go over all emergency protocols for QDCHESHIRE." It was Habibi. He was calm but direct. "We've got a little bit of time before the news goes public, but we need to be prepared."

Victor's throat tightened. "What news?"

"A Georgian national living in the United Kingdom who had informed on arms deals involving a group of Russian military intelligence officers was poisoned. He's dead. You won't see this part in the news, but they think the Kremlin signed off on it. Keep your boy safe. Vlastov isn't fucking around."

Victor put the phone down. Running Max as an asset was already risky, given the counterintelligence aspects involving three separate countries—the one Max worked for, the one he was providing intelligence on, and the one he was providing it to. All three leaders, Callieri, Vlastov, and Redd, had a stake in the intelligence never being collected in the first place. Now, Vlastov had made it clear he was prepared to carry out assassinations of non-Russians in Europe. This wasn't an opponent slipping off a balcony in Moscow. It wasn't even the murder of a former Russian intelligence officer who had defected to the West. Those were really bad, but in a way, it was still within the family. But now, Vlastov had struck a non-Russian individual in the middle of London, one of the biggest, busiest cities in the world, where surveillance cameras were ubiquitous. He clearly felt a sense of impunity to take such a risky action. Was Max at risk of assassination?

Victor looked back at Vanessa. She was turning green. Redd and his supporters were attacking the FBI directly. Soon enough, they might go after Vanessa specifically. She had been doing her job, but she had had the misfortune to surveil the wrong Russian intelligence officer, the one who was meeting with Redd's campaign manager.

What would Callieri or Vlastov or Redd be willing to do to protect themselves? How far would they go to stop Max, Vanessa, and Victor? The stakes for each of them had just gotten higher.

CHAPTER THIRTY

"Do I have to wear a tie?" Victor stood in front of the mirror in a white dress shirt, looking miserable as he tugged at a red-and-green tie. He wasn't wearing any pants.

Vanessa, in a red shift dress, was touching up her makeup. "Women contort their feet to wear heels. Men suffer by wearing ties. I don't make the fashion rules."

Oliver walked in. "Mom, Dad's not wearing pants again."

"It will be your burden to bear, Oliver," Vanessa said. "Once he retires, he'll never wear pants again. I'm his wife; I can't judge him. You'll have to decide if you'll be willing to be seen in public with him."

"Go pants-less with me," Victor said to his son. "We'll go to the early bird special, sans pants."

"I did not choose my parents well," Oliver said. He threw himself down on their bed. "You guys are lucky. You get Christmas cookies." For a teenage boy, food was a constant reference point.

"Yeah, but I have to wear a tie," Victor said.

"And pants," added Vanessa.

Victor rolled his eyes. Oliver laughed. Victor slid on his navy-blue dress pants. "They better be good cookies."

"I'll steal some to bring back for you," Ness said to Oliver.

Victor and Vanessa went out and started the short walk to the ambassador's residence.

"I feel like I'm walking into the enemy's lair," Vanessa said. She was still recovering from the Kip Lawson attack accusing her of spying on Redd's campaign. Lawson had not named her, but she figured it was only a matter of time before someone would. In the meantime, she had to remain silent, unable to defend herself, which she loathed.

"We have to make an appearance. Let's concentrate on the free booze." Victor grabbed her hand.

"Merry Christmas!" Erin Leonhart greeted them at the entrance to the ambassador's residence. She was the Community Liaison Officer, or CLO, in charge of organizing events for the embassy community. In essence, she was the cruise director for employees' families. "This way through security." She continued herding the crowd through the security line to enter the residence's gardens. "We're so happy to welcome everyone! This way. Keep moving."

Victor and Ness squeezed through the crowd and made their way deeper into the gardens of the ambassador's residence. Villa Taverna, its official name, had been built in the fifteenth century. A sprawling estate, it featured a swimming pool, a small cinema, and a Baroque fountain. The gardens were curated in symmetric, geometric shapes, with cypress trees trimmed into pointy pyramids and hedgerows cut into sharp cubes. The grand house, most of which was off limits for the party and reserved, rather, for the ambassador and his family, had, according to rumor, one of the best wine cellars in Italy. They entered the large foyer, which was decorated with strands of garland and red bows. Bowls full of mandarins were placed throughout the room. A Christmas tree was set up in the corner. It was as tall as the ceiling. A fire roared in the fireplace.

"When can I take off my—?"

"Don't say pants."

"Tie. When can I take off my tie?" He made a choking sound and tried to loosen it.

Someone handed them a Christmas decoration in the shape of the villa and painted to look like the American flag. Vanessa handed it to Victor. "We can decorate our tree with freedom."

"Dear Santa, please bring me democracy." Victor glanced at the back of the decoration and turned it to Vanessa. "What does that say?"

She squinted. "Made in China."

Victor set it on a windowsill and the two of them made their way to one of the many bars set up throughout the property. They ordered two glasses of prosecco. They took their drinks and stood a little on the side, awkwardly, watching the crowd, knowing they should circulate, but dreading being social.

"I can't believe you're willing to be seen in public with him, Vanessa." Patrick came up and gave her a kiss on either cheek. "You left your helmet at home, I see," he said to Victor.

Ness's phone pinged. Oliver had sent her a video. She turned the volume down and clicked it.

"Oh my god," she said with a cringe. She held her phone out for Victor and Patrick to see. It was a compilation of dozens of people, young and old, lighting their farts on fire. "It's to show support

for the RosAlleman pipeline. Look at the hashtag: FreedomGas."
Her phone pinged again.

"I know it's Russian propaganda, but it's hilarious," Oliver texted.

"I don't even know what to do with this," Ness said.

"At least you guys are educating him on disinformation," said
Patrick. "Have you had a chance to meet the new ambassador yet?"
He pointed to a short, fit man, wearing a black suit without a tie.

"How come he doesn't have to wear a tie?" Victor said. "How
much do you know about him?"

Ness said, "Ambassador Ken Grandy. He just arrived. Redd
appointed him a few weeks ago, and the Senate confirmed him
last week. He's been a bundler for Redd and the GOP for years."

"A bundler?" Victor asked.

"Bundling money. He collects donations from everyone to help
Redd and the GOP run their campaigns."

"How much are we talking?" Patrick asked.

"I don't know, but to get ambassador to Rome? I'm guessing hun-
dreds of millions. He's a real estate guy. He owns the Kosmopolitan
Hotel in Washington, and he builds strip malls all over the world.
He's been trying to build one in Moscow for years."

"Why does everything lead back to Russia with these people?"
Victor asked.

Giuseppe di Lorenzo, a local Italian who worked at the embassy,
approached them. "Everyone having a good time?"

"It's great, Giuseppe," Ness said. "The staff did a wonderful job."

Giuseppe gave a sideways glance at Ambassador Grandy. "Have
you guys met the new arrival yet?" They all shook their heads.
Giuseppe leaned in closer, in a conspiratorial way. "I understand
the daughter brought her pony from California."

Victor, Ness, and Patrick all looked at each other. The local staff, who helped handle the administration for the Americans who arrived in Italy, were the best source of gossip.

"And the wife," Giuseppe continued.

"I didn't even know there was a wife," Ness said, encouraging Giuseppe.

"Oh my god, the wife!" he said. He took a sip of red wine. "The wife brought the *trainer* of the pony with her." He winked and put his finger to his lips, to indicate this was a big secret. "She has an antique shop in California. She's only been here a week, but she already used an official shipment to send antiques from here to the United States to sell. This is causing the local staff quite a headache." Another Italian who worked at the embassy called out to him. "I must circulate now. Enjoy the party! Ciao ciao!"

Victor, Ness, and Patrick watched him go.

"Sounds like Grandy is as unethical as his boss," Ness said.

"But profamily values. Just ask the horse trainer," Patrick said.

"I suppose we're all supposed to circulate," said Ness.

"Do we have to?" asked Victor.

"I'm going to get food and pretend to circulate," Patrick said, peeling off from the group.

Victor and Ness circled around the foyer to another bar for a refill.

"Does that count as circulating?" Victor asked, as they stood on the side of another part of the room, looking at the crowd. "Going to a different bar?"

"It does when it gives us a good vantage point," Ness said. "Look."

A short distance away, Ambassador Ken Grandy was shaking hands with Luca Callieri. "Welcome, minister. We are honored to host you as we celebrate the holiest of days," Grandy said. Next to Callieri was Aldo Conti, the new interior minister's consigliere and the boss of QDCHESHIRE.

"Let's see who they chat with," Victor said. He and Ness sipped their drinks, pretending they were surveying the crowd as a couple.

Conti shook hands with another man, who was wearing a dark blue suit without a tie and who had a dark goatee. Callieri saw the man and let out a loud, "Ciao, Stefano!" while clapping him on the shoulder and shaking his hand. Callieri proceeded to introduce the man to Ambassador Grandy, who smiled and laughed.

"Who's the glad-hander in the blue suit? How come he doesn't have to wear a tie either?" Victor asked.

"The suit's too tight. Are they glad-handing or sniffing each other's butts?" Ness asked.

"You get the feeling they already sniffed each other's butts and are ready to do business."

"Standing off on the side and avoiding people does not make you look very social, my friends." Francesco Restani approached them. "Thank you for the invitation, Vanessa." He held up his glass of prosecco and clinked it against hers. He followed their gaze. Ambassador Grandy was playfully punching Callieri in the arm.

"Not that kind of football." Grandy said. "Real football! The kind you play with your hands."

"Then why do you call it football and not handball? I will never understand this!" Callieri joked.

"They are having a grand time," Francesco said.

"Do you know the guy in the blue suit?" Ness asked.

Francesco glanced at the group again. "That is Stefano Valenti. He is chairman of GasItalia. It is a little awkward that the prosecutor in Torino has recently launched an investigation of him."

Victor listened intently. Max had mentioned that Callieri and Conti had met with a GasItalia official named Stefano while they were all in Moscow. He had said that Stefano was the conduit for the money coming from Russia into Callieri's coffers. Victor had told all of this to Francesco when he informed him about the QDCHESHIRE operation. He turned to Francesco and gave him a look, asking him telepathically if this was the Stefano QDCHESHIRE had seen in Moscow.

Francesco looked at Victor and said out loud, "To answer your question, Victor, probably. The prosecutor in Torino is trying to get a more detailed answer to that."

"It can't be easy to investigate, given the political realities," Victor said, gesturing toward Callieri's group.

"It is not. However, unlike in your country, our prosecutors are very independent. Even Callieri, as interior minister, cannot stop the investigation."

Victor glanced over at the group again. Grandy was now huddling with Stefano Valenti. They were whispering to each other. Was Vlastov planning to carry out the same scheme with Redd, with Grandy, the money bundler, offering an assist?

"Maybe that's what we need in the United States," Vanessa said. Victor looked at her quizzically. "An independent prosecutor," she said to him. "A trusted, apolitical investigator to examine all the intelligence and evidence, free from politics."

"Is that possible anymore in the United States?" Victor asked.

"We have to try something," said Ness.

"I'm afraid I have more I need to discuss with you both," Francesco said. "My apologies to bring up business during what is a very lovely party. However, on my way here, I received some bad news, and I wanted to share it with you both right away. There has been a murder in Rome."

Victor and Vanessa glanced at each other.

Francesco continued, looking directly at Victor. "The deceased worked as an informant for a Western intelligence service. He was found in the park with a suicide note."

"A suicide note? You said he was murdered," Ness said.

"A suicide note and eight gunshots to his back. Forensics tell us the killer used a silencer and held the weapon directly against the victim's skin. We have identified a Russian intelligence officer we believe is the likely killer. We have footage of him leaving the scene of the crime on an electric scooter."

"That's so millennial," Ness said.

Francesco looked confused. "The battery ran low shortly after, and he discarded the scooter in the river."

"Can I ask the nationality of the deceased?" Ness said.

"Polish. We believe he was providing a specific Western intelligence service with information on Russia. The suspect was in London at the same time as a hit there, on a Georgian arms dealer."

Victor recalled his conversation with Habibi about the murder in London. Francesco was sharing information about a possible Russian assassination operation on Italian soil, while standing a few feet away from the interior minister—his boss—who was likely receiving illegal financial kickbacks from those very same Russians. Victor thought about QDCHESHIRE, on his way to

Moscow at the behest of his Russian handler for a conference on family values. Meanwhile, Russian intelligence officers were running around Europe assassinating people who were giving information about Russia to Western intelligence agencies, people just like Max.

Victor, Vanessa, and Francesco glanced over at Callieri and his group, possibly plotting to implement the same illegal scheme in the United States they had just pulled off in Italy, while the mobsters on the other end of that deal were moving freely about Europe, murdering people. Victor took a long sip of his drink. Would they be able protect America's integrity? And would he be able to keep Max safe?

CHAPTER THIRTY-ONE

-

Max once again walked into the grand Russian Bear Hotel in Moscow. One glimpse of the exquisite stained-glass dome and he felt at peace. His wonderment and love for Russia still filled him with emotion. He loved the culture. He loved the history. But he didn't love what President Vlastov was doing with it. Nor did he wish for Vlastov's personal ambitions to guide Italy. Now that he had come to terms with this reality, he felt more prepared to make it through the next two days.

Grigoriy Stepanov had sent him back to Moscow, this time for the World Family Values Congress. The gathering, also hosted by Konstantin Dudnik, was meant to be a two-day orgy of conservative ideological fornication among those who believed in traditional families and missionary-position sex. Max had worked closely with Victor to develop means to please Stepanov and continue letting him believe he was handling Max, without Max losing his soul. Max had agreed to several appearances on NRN to discuss Callieri and his anti-Europe agenda. Although Stepanov had recently started pushing Max to include pro-Russia statements, as well, Max had managed to keep the focus of his ire on Brussels and its bureaucrats.

Stepanov had told Max he hoped the occasion of the World Family Values Congress would be a chance to expand Callieri's movement and gain more worldwide supporters. Max understood, even before Victor confirmed it, that what Stepanov really meant was he wanted Max to find other like-minded individuals and groups who could push Vlastov's antidemocratic agenda. "Remember, Vlastov cares about Vlastov. He does not care about Russia. And he certainly does not care about Italy," Victor had said.

Max checked in to the hotel. Adriana was again standing behind the welcome table for the conference. She wore a tight black dress that ended where her legs began. As she leaned over to find Max's name on the list of attendees, her dress raised slightly to expose a titillating amount of ass cheek and her bosom heaved forward onto the table. She gave Max his badge on a lanyard that said, in Russian, "Family First." She said, "My name is Oksana, if you need anything, including me. I am here for your pleasure as we celebrate family values." She handed him a schedule for the conference.

Max blinked at her and rolled his suitcase toward the elevator, while he digested the fact that Dudnik had hired prostitutes to keep attendees of a family values conference happy. He enjoyed that she had mixed it up a little, at least, by changing her name from Adriana to Oksana this time around. He glanced at the conference schedule. Tomorrow, American Denny Craig would discuss legislative approaches to blocking the gay agenda. He was a former Republican speaker of the House of Representatives who, during his tenure, had fought hard to strike down gay marriage legislation in the United States. He had had to resign several years ago, after he was caught soliciting sex from an underage boy in an airport bathroom, but he had since attended a religious program, sponsored by Dudnik, during which he had managed to pray away his sins and rediscover the Lord. His conference session was titled, "Cockblocking the Rainbow." The speaker the following day, Max noted, was Jeremy Flacken, the head of a megachurch who had been photographed in Paris wearing a maid's outfit and participating in an orgy. His wife had forgiven him and that had been that. His session was titled, "Jesus is in My Wife's Vagina." Most intriguing on the conference schedule was tonight's welcoming remarks with Freedom Hos for Jesus, whose motto, according to the conference description, was, "Keeping the men straight, the race pure, and the religion Christian."

Max went to his room to drop off his bag. Taking no chances, he used an external charger for his phone. He turned on the television while he freshened up. An episode of "Our Great President" was on, showing a behind-the-scenes look at the Bolshoi Ballet rehearsing for an upcoming performance of a ballet that symbolized the struggle and glory of Mother Russia, choreographed by President Vlastov. "President Vlastov was very sensual as he worked with me," said the lead ballerina, as the screen showed Vlastov caressing her on stage. "As Russians, we are lucky he is committed to the country. As a single woman," she licked her red lips, "I would be happy to pas de deux with him anytime."

Max changed the channel to All Russia News, another state-run news organization like New Russia News.

"A citizen of the country of Georgia has died in London," the presenter said. "The man died several weeks ago, but the government of the United Kingdom, fearing that it would appear incompetent, is only now releasing details. The individual keeled over after taking high tea at a posh London hotel. Perhaps even with all of its health codes, developed through an allegedly transparent democratic process, rancid tea was still able to make its way into the supply chain. The incident is proof, once again, that a democratic government is incapable of protecting its residents. Perhaps all Georgian nationals, and nationals from other states that have a natural affinity for an alliance with Russia due to our cultural brotherhood, should think carefully before placing themselves in the dangerous environment that London has clearly become. Also in European news, a Polish man committed suicide in a park in Rome."

"What?" said Max out loud, leaning in closer to the television.

"This sad episode demonstrates the desperation many in Europe are feeling. Unable to fit in and make a proper life for himself in the ruthless workplace, the man saw death as his only escape from the corruption surrounding him in the so-called democratic country. Up next," the announcer continued, changing his tone, "our guy President Redd in the United States is fighting off a deep state plan to oust him from office. Redd said again today that America's Federal Bureau of Investigation had been spying on his administration. The president discussed how the FBI had put surveillance on his campaign advisor, Ashley-Anne Wynscott, in the months before the presidential election in the United States. Redd said a group of deep state agents embedded in the federal bureaucracy had made up the Russophobic allegations of foreign influence to delegitimize him and noted that he has been very harsh with Russia and President Vlastov." The announcer tried to swallow a laugh but failed. He quickly gathered his wits again and continued, "Congressman Matt Donovan, who recently visited Moscow and who serves as the head of the House Intelligence Committee, has said he has evidence US spies were working to oust Redd by falsely linking him to Russia. He plans to release the evidence in the coming days."

Max swallowed hard. Was the president of the United States going to learn his identity? Reveal it? Victor had assured him he had limited the number of people who knew about his existence and his assistance, but how could he keep information from the president of the United States, the most powerful man in the world, if the president asked for it? "He doesn't know you exist, and we're going to keep it that way," Victor had told him. "You're not reporting on Russia, you're reporting on Italy. Redd doesn't care about that. Plus, the information is compartmented. I have your back. You have my word."

Still, Max remained aware of the risk he was taking. The news about the Georgian national drinking rancid tea also set the hair on the back of his neck tingling. And a suicide in Rome? That was odd news. He didn't know why, but he knew not to ignore the sensation. He splashed cold water on his face and took a deep breath. He returned to the lobby.

Several women in short black dresses were circulating among the crowd. Max overheard one of them introduce herself as Oksana to a man wearing a crucifix necklace as he wiped drool off his mouth. Across the lobby, he saw Svetlana Zharkova, whom he knew from the Russian Cultural Center in Rome. She was wearing a black lace bustier and not much else, except for her "Family Values" lanyard. She was in a group of people laughing with a short, puffy, American man, who had a stubby arm around her waist. Max recognized him as America's Senator Kyle Lewis. "I'm chafed here now," the senator said, rubbing his inner thighs with his free hand. "I never thought riding a bear would cause so much friction!" The whole group was loudly amused by the story.

Max wondered if Senator Lewis had been warned not to use USB plugs and to check for hidden cameras in his hotel room. He thought about the news item he had just seen, about Florida Congressman Matt Donovan, who had recently visited Moscow and was now prepared to release evidence showing Russian interference was a hoax perpetrated by an American Deep State, something Max knew, for a fact, was not true, since he was participating in a similar operation in Italy on behalf of Russia. Up on the mezzanine stood Konstantin Dudnik, who had organized the conference. Like Zeus looking down at mere mortals, he observed the behavior of the people in the lobby, likely keeping a mental note of who spoke to whom.

Max heard a tap on a microphone. Everyone in the lobby turned to a young woman standing on a makeshift stage. She wore a skin tight, red pleather mini dress with diamond-encrusted stilettos. On her naked shoulder was a tattoo of Mary Magdalene. She tapped the microphone again.

"Welcome, everyone, to this year's World Family Values Congress," she said to the crowd. "I'm here to kick off what is going to be a fun and pure couple of days!" Everyone applauded. Max noticed one of the Oksanas looking bored and adjusting her boobs. "For those of you who don't know me, I'm Candy, the founder of Freedom Hos for Jesus." The crowd applauded again. Candy blushed. "Thank you. I turn every day for strength to our

Founding Mother, Mary Magdalene," she touched her shoulder tattoo, "who understood the burden of servicing Jesus for the greater good. I recently found myself servicing the member of a staffer of US President Richard Redd. He said to me, 'I work for the most powerful man in the world.' And I thought, wow, even in the service of America he continues to work for Jesus. My jaw was sore, but I felt so privileged to serve America in such an impactful way, knowing I was contributing to keeping the men straight, the race pure, and the religion Christian." The lobby erupted in applause.

It was going to be a long weekend, Max realized. Now that Vlastov's true intentions had become so clear, he saw all this pomp and circumstance as just that, a means to keep the crowds entertained while Vlastov used them to further his agenda, while convincing them it was for their own good. He knew he needed to play along. He reminded himself about Callieri, now running the interior ministry, and Redd speaking casually about intelligence sources. His own life was on the line. He longed to be eating plums in Ventotene. Instead, he applauded enthusiastically as Candy wrapped up, "It has been the honor of a lifetime to suck cock for President Redd and Jesus."

The crowd dispersed as Candy stepped off the dais and greeted her enthusiastic supporters. Jeremy Flacken, the mega-church pastor, embraced her in a friendly hug before pulling her closer and grinding against her a little. She planted a wet kiss on his cheek and he said, "The Lord loves you," while squeezing her more and letting one hand slide down to her ass.

Max ordered a glass of vodka at the bar and noticed Julien Duclos sitting at a nearby table. Julien worked at an organization similar to the MussoRusso Cultural Association in Paris. The two had often found themselves at conferences in Europe for conservative political parties and had become friendly. He was sitting with another man Max did not recognize. Max joined them.

"Let me introduce you to Will Garrett," Julien said. "He works with President Redd, is that right?"

"Well, I work *for* him, I'd say," the man said. "I'm his personal lawyer." He was dressed in an ill-fitting suit. His glasses kept sliding down his nose, and he would shove them back up with his middle finger. "He turns to me for a lot of different types of work. And yes, sometimes he asks for my advice on politics and policies. Messaging, in particular. I sometimes help him set the tone and the narrative."

"You Americans are so good at that," said Julien. "We've been studying your methods. Your use of social media to control the narrative is masterful. Redd is very good at never admitting a mistake, even when he is caught in a complete lie."

"He never lies," said Will. "Never. He might massage the truth, but he never lies."

"That! That right there!" said Julien, excited. "He massages the truth. That is beautiful how you did that."

"You guys are learning, though. I like that," said Will. "In France, Julien, your France Forward party has adopted many of our techniques. In Italy, Da Italia. I know Luca Callieri quite well, in fact. I've been working on some natural gas investments. He was kind enough to introduce me to people at GasItalia. That's why I'm here. I mean, I'm here for the conference, too, but it's a good chance to get other business done as well."

"You do natural gas investments?" asked Max. "I thought you were Redd's personal lawyer?"

Will looked uncomfortable. "I have many clients. He's my main client. But I help others too. Sometimes they help me, and they help me help the president, who is my only client."

"Your only client or your main client?"

"That too."

Max and Julien glanced at each other, reassured to see they were both confused.

A tall man with a dark goatee approached their table. Will waved and stood up. "I'm here, Stefano." Will turned back to Julien and Max. "Nice to meet you, fellas. I see my partners are here now."

Max watched Redd's lawyer greet the man named Stefano, who led Will to a corner table where two gruff-looking Russian men were sitting. One had a scar over his right eye. When the other turned his head for a moment, Max caught a glance of a butterfly tattoo behind his ear. They were the same men Callieri had met with to discuss using the RosAlleman pipeline to send illegal payments into the coffers of Callieri's Da Italia party. A Stefano had also been mentioned during those conversations. Was Will Garrett, President Redd's personal lawyer, meeting the same people who had illegally financed Da Italia? Were they running the same scheme for Redd? If so, what were the Russians getting in return?

Max felt the situation was dicey. He carried on talking with Julien, repeating all the proper arguments about how to remake France and Italy into the traditional nations they once were, but he knew he was only going through the motions. He felt anxious. He had to be able to report to Stepanov he had at least made an effort to find like-minded thinkers who could also go on New

Russia News. The more machinations he saw, the less confident he was he could keep up the charade.

He now understood much better what a charade it was. He thought about the news report he had watched while washing up. "Our guy President Redd," the news announcer had said. And here was Redd's personal representative meeting the same people who had made Luca Callieri *their guy* in Italy. But Max's appearances, and appearances by others like him—Stepanov, his Russian handler, had encouraged him to use this conference to find others who could make similar appearances—had helped set the narrative, helped create the doubt about who was playing whom, who was being manipulated, and who was doing the manipulating. He started to understand his own role in creating the disinformation, and worse, how others were using that disinformation to gain power over others. It was hard to know what to believe anymore.

He thought again about the other news report he had seen earlier, about the Georgian man who had died in London after drinking rancid tea and the Polish man committing suicide in Rome. Max shivered. Was there more to those stories too?

He had to get through the conference. He could not raise anyone's suspicions. He vowed to look interested when Denny Craig, the former American congressman, would lecture about Lucifer tempting him in an airport bathroom long ago, and how legislation was the only way to ensure Lucifer never tempted him or any man again. Max was determined to listen intently when Jeremy Flacken, the megachurch founder and orgy participant, lectured him and others about the resurrection of his wife's vagina.

He would thank Konstantin Dudnik, conference organizer and Vlastov whisperer, who looked down from the balcony and quietly observed—and perhaps manipulated—the intrigues between the various attendees. And when Oksana knocked on his door in the middle of the night, he simply would not answer.

CHAPTER THIRTY-TWO

Victor arrived in Urbino after a long, circuitous route through the snow-dusted Appennine Mountains. He checked in to the Hotel del Colle. It was quiet. The holidays had passed and most people had returned to their routine lives. Victor entered his suite and arranged the table and chairs near the large sliding glass doors that looked out on the fifteenth-century Palazzo Ducale, its two round towers looking like the setting for a Rapunzel saga. At precisely one o'clock, Max came in. He looked tired and anxious. He seemed relieved to let Victor direct everything once the hotel door closed.

Victor led him to the table and poured him some sparkling water. He placed a bowl of mandarins in front of Max. Max started to peel one, pulling the skin off in a single piece.

"Let's go over all the security precautions again," Victor said.

"I am already aware it is getting more dangerous by the day," Max responded. "In Moscow, the news announcers talk about Redd and your government as if they control it. Is Redd going to share information about me?"

"Only a small group of people know about you. Even if information you give us goes to Redd, he won't know who gave it to us."

"He is the president. He could ask who the source is."

Victor sighed. This was true. He and Habibi were simply hoping that would never happen, although they both felt confident that they could maneuver around it if such an order ever came down. "I need you to trust I have your best interests at heart, trust that the moment I sense this is too dangerous, I will get you to safety."

"You have my trust, Victor. Unlike Grigoriy, you have never asked me to do anything against Italy. But I do not know how much longer I can please him. It is very hard to convince him I am following his orders. He doesn't think I did enough in Moscow."

"Let's start with basic security issues first. Then we'll move on to how we handle Grigoriy and what happened in Moscow."

Max nodded and ate the mandarin. As he did at the previous meeting, Victor reiterated their cover story, what they would say if anyone came to the room, what they would say if they ran into anyone they knew while walking back to their cars, and how they would explain their travel once they were back in Rome. He went over emergency communication plans. "Max, this will be hard to hear, but our meeting is getting more and more risky for you," Victor said. "Did you hear about the Georgian man in London who was assassinated?"

Max looked terrified. "Assassinated? Russian news reported on his death. They said he drank rancid tea."

"That's one way of putting it," Victor said. "The tea was rancid because a Russian assassin laced it with poison."

"They left that part out."

Victor weighed whether to tell him the same individual was suspected of carrying out another assassination in Rome recently, but decided against it. It wouldn't make him any more aware of the danger, but would likely scare him to paralysis.

Max then recounted everything he had learned in Moscow. He reported how Stepanov had tasked him to find others like him who could speak authoritatively on NRN about Europe while simultaneously advancing Russia's agenda. He mentioned his friend Julien, whose name he had given Stepanov. Victor made a note to have one of his colleagues in France meet Julien. He assessed that Grigoriy planned to continue using Max to spread confusion and chaos in the West. The Russians had Callieri in their pocket already, so they didn't need Max pulling strings inside the Italian government. It seemed their intention was to keep him in a propaganda role. "Your Senator Kyle Lewis was there, as well, with Svetlana Zharkova. Are you familiar with her?"

"I am," Victor said, recalling photos of her posing with a gun stuck down her Spandex leggings, surrounded by conservative politicians.

"Senator Lewis rode a bear." Victor looked unimpressed. Max continued, "I saw him go upstairs with Svetlana and one of the Oksanas. I saw Oksana leaving his hotel room the following morning, when I left my room to go to breakfast."

"She spent the night with him?"

"It looked that way. He had a big smile when he came downstairs for breakfast. Did anyone warn him about the cameras in Moscow hotel rooms?"

Victor shrugged. "The FBI can warn these guys, but they make their own decisions. They're adults. Even if they often act like children."

"I also saw Will Garrett, President Redd's personal attorney while I was at the hotel. He met with the same Russians Callieri did to arrange the kickbacks from the RosAlleman pipeline. A guy named Stefano was there too. Tall guy, with a dark goatee."

Victor had suspected something like this was being cooked up when he saw a man from GasItalia named Stefano meet with Ambassador Grandy at the embassy Christmas party, but Max's information was corroboration.

He'd have to report all of this to Vanessa, which would put her in an even more precarious position inside the FBI. How would she report information that a sitting US senator had likely been compromised in Moscow and that the president of the United States and his personal attorney were possibly running a scheme to illegally funnel money to groups supporting one of the country's two main political parties?

"You think Redd is running the same scheme as Callieri?" Victor asked.

"You have it backward, Victor," Max said. "Vlastov is running the same scheme with Redd that he ran with Callieri. Vlastov is the puppet master, even if the puppets like their strings attached."

CHAPTER THIRTY-THREE

Ruslan Bebchuk knocked on the door and poked his head into the office of Russian President Darko Vlastov. "Apologies, Mr. President. Your secretary seems to be absent."

Vlastov was reclining in his high-back leather chair, his fingers clasped behind his head. His vast desk was nearly empty, save for a gold pen resting in the exact middle. A photo of him in his younger years hung on the wall behind him. The handsome twenty-four-year-old wore a military uniform, his angular jaw and sharp cheekbones offsetting his big, round, blue eyes, which bore into the camera. The president glanced down and waved his hand. His secretary scurried out from under the desk, wiping her mouth, and ran out of the office.

Vlastov took a deep breath and looked out at the garden, where a bear—his bear—was ambling about before motioning for Bebchuk to take a seat.

"Tell me what's being done today to destroy the West, my dear friend," Vlastov said.

"We've got a development involving America's Senator Kyle Lewis, the head of their foreign relations committee." Bebchuk pulled a laptop out of his bag and opened a video file. He turned the screen toward Vlastov and clicked play.

Vlastov watched the grainy footage impassively. After a few seconds, a wide, satisfied grin spread across his face. He turned his head sideways for a better view. "He is more flexible than I thought, both physically and morally. Who is the other one?"

"Oksana."

"Oksana from that Sochi trip with the—"

"No."

"The one from the yacht party in Antibes with the—"

"No, a new one. The family values conference was her first event with us."

Vlastov watched for another minute. Bebchuk stared out at the bear in the garden. Vlastov's secretary interrupted them.

"Mr. President, I just got a call from Ken Grandy's people. He's still hoping to build that strip mall here in Moscow. Shall I have Toropov handle it?"

"Toropov is busy covering up our athletic doping program and he doesn't multitask well."

"How about Zaslavsky?"

"He's running mercenaries in Central Africa and helping me secure the arctic. I don't want to stretch him too thin." He shook his head and looked at Bebchuk. "It's all so complicated and tiring." He looked back at his secretary. "I'm going to need another blow job later."

She jotted that down on her notepad.

"How about Surikov?" Bebchuk said.

"He always needs a blow job. That's why he keeps what's her name around."

"No, to talk with Grandy."

"Good idea." Vlastov looked back at his secretary. "Have Surikov deal with Grandy. Also," he pointed at the laptop, "this Oksana must be honored as a Hero of the Russian Federation. I will present the award to her personally. Make sure to arrange a private dinner for her and me, as well." The secretary scribbled on her notepad then went out. Vlastov turned again to Bebchuk. "Why can't Surikov be a normal oligarch and purchase a football team? Does he understand how difficult it is to launder money through a curling club? It goes much faster with behemoth football clubs that generate billions every year."

"We could help the Vancouver Turtles generate more revenue."

"No one would believe a Canadian curling club was moving billions of dollars annually. Work on him with the football thing, would you? He'll know what to do with Grandy."

"Yes, sir. And that?" Bebchuk pointed to the laptop.

"Let's let Senator Lewis know we are very pleased he enjoyed his stay in Moscow."

CHAPTER THIRTY-FOUR

Ness took her time strolling through Villa Borghese on her way to the office. Victor was still away at his clandestine meeting with Max, so she walked on her own, in no hurry. She stopped at a cafe and perused the news on her phone. She clicked on a video of Senator Kyle Lewis, chairman of the Foreign Relations Committee.

"I've recently returned from an eye-opening trip to Moscow," he said to the reporters surrounding him at the Capitol. "Russia is a beautiful country with beautiful people—I mean, *really* beautiful—and a strong sense of sovereignty and tradition. All this Russophobic talk in the United States is nonsense and needs to stop. Why wouldn't we want to emulate Russia? It is a great society. That's why I think it is time to move past this Russia hoax. We need to start discussing lifting sanctions on Russia. We need to start discussing how Ukraine needs to compromise to help lower the temperature in Crimea. It's time for renewed relations between the US and Russia." He walked away from the gaggle of reporters without taking any questions.

She rubbed her temples and sat in silence for a minute. What had happened to him in Moscow, she wondered? She stood up and crossed the street to the embassy. She flashed her badge then climbed the grand staircase to her office. Kelsea Greyco, the NSA analyst, was sitting on Vanessa's blue exercise ball.

"What is it with all the blue balls?" she asked, bouncing. "You and Victor. Are blue balls a married thing?"

"Hilarious, Kelsea. What can I help you with?"

"You know Nikolai Surikov?" Kelsea asked.

"Not personally."

"Now who's being hilarious? We've been collecting on him, since he's a powerful oligarch who runs FaKU and has direct ties to President Vlastov. Personally, I also have been dying to know more about his zoo and where he got his albino giraffe. Seriously, how do you transport a giraffe, let alone an albino giraffe, without anyone noticing? They're eighteen feet tall. Their necks alone are six feet. Think about that."

Vanessa looked at her, waiting.

"Sorry, focus. We've been collecting on Surikov, and we picked up this conversation yesterday." Kelsea waved a piece of paper in her hand. "Surikov was talking to someone with an Italian phone number."

"That's not for me, then. Bring it to CYA."

"The guy talking on the Italian number is an American here in Italy." She glanced around furtively. "You're not going to like it. I mean, I don't like it. It brings me no pleasure to have to report this. They discuss an American organization." Kelsea pushed the paper against her chest, as if afraid its contents would leap off the page into the open.

"Kelsea, spit it out. How bad could it be?"

"You're going to wish it was about giraffes." Kelsea shoved the paper at Vanessa.

Ness read the transcript. With each line, she shook her head more and more. They weren't doing this, were they? And they weren't moronic enough to get caught, were they? This hadn't just landed on her desk, had it? She wanted to go back in time, not to be here, holding this grenade in her hand.

Kelsea stepped backward toward the exit, without a word. Vanessa sat down, her eyes still on the transcript. Kelsea slipped out, and Vanessa read.

GRANDY: Nikolai, it's good to talk to you.

SURIKOV: Hello, Ken. How are you enjoying Rome?
The family settling in?

GRANDY: It's great here. Business is going well. I
can't seem to get my wife away from the horse
trainer, though. She takes her riding seriously.

[muffled laughter]

GRANDY: We can't get too comfortable, though. As
you know, politics is an expensive industry these
days, and the campaign never stops. President
Redd has been holding fundraisers despite his
very busy schedule serving the American people.

SURIKOV: He is an important man.

GRANDY: You and I agree there! But, well, that's
just how the system works, right? It's not easy,
always needing more, in order to keep the
right people in office. That's all this is about, of

course. You and I want to see the right people in office, right?

SURIKOV: Of course. Listen, I've got plans to invest in a small business in South Dakota. This business also has an interest in seeing the right people are in office. What is it you say in America, corporations are people?

GRANDY: You are very well-versed, sir. That is, indeed, what we say. I'd like to see that small company in South Dakota exercise its right to free political speech in the form of money. Did I mention I help bundle donations for President Redd's Dick SACPAC? Maybe that company in South Dakota would be interested in getting involved in that?

SURIKOV: I am certain that would be of interest.

GRANDY: That's great, Nikolai. We're always excited to reach out and network with new businesses that want to contribute to the political system here. Democracy demands involvement from the people, am I right? So, we really like it when we see the right, quality people energized to get involved.

SURIKOV: On a separate topic, Ken.

GRANDY: Go ahead.

SURIKOV: As you know, and I think President Redd agrees, the RosAlleman pipeline is very important to the future of Europe. We see it as a real job creator.

GRANDY: Redd loves to hear that.

SURIKOV: We are rather disappointed Ukraine has used this project and other misconceptions to build ill will toward Russia.

GRANDY: Couldn't agree with you more.

SURIKOV: I'm happy to hear that. I think President Vlastov would love to hear that.

GRANDY: To hear what?

SURIKOV: To hear President Redd state his support for the pipeline and for the right of Russians in Ukraine and Crimea to rejoin Russia. Those areas are Russia.

GRANDY: Indeed, indeed.

[sounds of man screaming, water splashing, more screaming, inaudible]

SURIKOV: Get me a clean track suit!

GRANDY: Nikolai?

SURIKOV: I'm here. I'm here. It was time to feed the piranhas.

[more water splashing]

SURIKOV: I got a little wet. As I was saying, it would thrill President Vlastov to hear these words of support from President Redd.

GRANDY: I'll see what I can do.

SURIKOV: By the way, I understand you are still trying to get a permit for your mall in Moscow.

GRANDY: Yes. I've been trying for years.

SURIKOV: Well, sometimes a little push from the right places can help things along. I'll see if I

can put in a good word for you. Thanks for passing the message to Redd. Good talking to you
Ken. Send our best to Little Dickie.

Vanessa leaned back in her chair and closed her eyes. Only one
word came to mind. "Fuck." How was she going to report that the
US ambassador to Italy, a top bundler for the president's party,
was soliciting Russian money to feed into the president's political
action committee and offering to get the president to announce
a pro-Russia policy in return? She thought about the accusations
now circulating widely that the FBI had spied on Redd's campaign,
when, in fact, she had been following a Russian spy in Washington
who was invited into the home of Ashley-Anne Wynnscott. Now,
the NSA had caught one of Redd's ambassadors and donors participating in a quid pro quo with a Russian oligarch close to President
Vlastov. Twice, that she knew of, US intelligence agencies were
legitimately surveilling Russian targets, and twice they had caught
Redd's people meeting with them. The crime was bad enough. The
consequences for a democratic system of government were worse.

CHAPTER THIRTY-FIVE

Victor paced around his hotel suite. He stared a moment at the grand palace outside his window, mindlessly peeling a mandarin. He glanced at his watch, although he already knew it was 9:04 am, since he had checked it only a few seconds before. Max was four minutes late. That had never happened. He looked at the pile of mandarins he had peeled in the previous minute, piled on the table, uneaten. He downed another espresso, cursing himself as he did so, knowing it would make him more jittery. He couldn't help himself.

Last night's meeting had ended well, hadn't it? Max had given him incredible information about what had gone down in Moscow, with Vlastov's people running schemes to help Redd stay in power. They had likely run similar schemes to help him get to power in the first place. Max had seemed relaxed at the end of the evening, relieved to have gotten the burden off his chest, ready for a good night's sleep before reconvening this morning. Right? Victor asked himself. Or was he only imagining Max's comfort level. Maybe his asset had realized the weight of the information he had shared—information that could destroy a presidency, information that could get Max killed—and he had run. It was possible. Was he dead? Had Russian hitmen worked quickly to clean up the mess? Had they discovered Max was reporting to the Americans? Had they swooped in to silence him before he said too much? Victor's mind raced through the possibilities. He looked at his watch: 9:05. Something was definitely wrong.

There was nothing to do. That was the worst part. The emergency contact plan they had worked out, and which thankfully they had reviewed last night, was built around a site in Rome. Victor could pace every square foot of the hotel suite all day and night, but if Max didn't show, he could do nothing except wait until QDCHESHIRE showed a sign of life by triggering an emergency meeting.

CHAPTER THIRTY-SIX

B y the time Victor arrived in Rome, the sun had sunk low and the sky was turning from pink to darkness. The temperature dropped, and he wrapped his scarf around his neck and pulled his coat collar up as he raced through Villa Borghese, hoping to catch Ness at her office. His phone rang. It was Francesco.

"Are you close to the embassy, Victor? I need to see you right away."

Victor's heart was in his throat, but he managed to eek out a quiet yes when Francesco said he would wait for him at a nearby cafe. He picked up his speed and soon stepped out of the park, passed under the wall that had surrounded ancient Rome, and turned down the street to meet Francesco.

The Italian intelligence officer was standing at the bar with an espresso. He asked if Victor wanted one. Victor declined. His adrenaline was already racing; a large infusion of caffeine would not help.

"The matter that we discussed at your embassy Christmas party, involving the Georgian man in London and the Polish man in Rome," Francesco said.

Victor nodded, recalling the two men who had gone against Russian interests and were now dead at the hand of a Russian assassin. He had an image of Max leaving the hotel room last night. He tried to stay calm.

Francesco continued, "It seems an associate of the man we believe is responsible for those terrible episodes is in Italy."

Victor went cold. They were on to Max. How had this happened? How could Victor have let this happen? Max's security was Victor's responsibility. His mind flashed to their conversation the evening before, Victor methodically reviewing the security protocols with Max, Max reciting the emergency communications plan. Maybe Victor hadn't done enough. A wave of guilt, anger, and rage washed over him.

"With Callieri watching over us, we don't have many resources for anything related to . . ." Francesco's voice trailed off. Victor understood. Given his own involvement with Russians, Callieri would be reluctant to approve surveillance related to Russia. Francesco continued, "We lost track of him." He could see the dread in Victor's eyes. "We'll find him, Victor."

"You don't understand," Victor said. "He didn't show up this morning."

"Who?"

"Max. We met last night. We were supposed to meet again this morning. He never showed."

"Let's try not to imagine the worst-case scenario." Francesco tried to sound calm, but his voice was trembling. "We've heard nothing about a dead body or a missing person. Victor, I am sure you are always careful with the security of your assets. Therefore, I am also sure Max has taken good security precautions. However, as you wait to hear from him—and I am confident you will hear from him—you and I should perhaps start planning for the next steps."

Victor tried to mirror Francesco's optimism as they discussed their plans, but he found it difficult. The weight of the responsibility, the guilt if something had gone wrong, was unbearable. Still, he had to keep going. Francesco was right. Until they knew for sure, they had to keep doing everything they could to ensure Max's safety going forward.

Once he and Francesco had laid out their plans, Victor left the cafe. The evening air helped clear his head as he headed down the street. By the time he entered the embassy compound, he had calmed himself enough to allow a sliver of hope that Max was fine, that his failure to show that morning had a reasonable explanation. He rushed up the grand stairway of the main chancery, hoping Vanessa was still at work. He burst through her office door. She was slumped in a chair, staring at the wall. She managed to glance at him when he entered, then went back to staring at the wall.

"I don't want it, Victor."

"You don't want what?"

"Whatever it is you're about to give me. We're in so much trouble. You. Me. The country. Democracy."

"I know. That's why we have to talk." He grabbed her hand and pulled her out of her chair. He led her to his office and was pleased to see it was mostly empty, which meant no one would bother asking him too many questions right now, but which also meant the office wasn't totally shut, requiring him to remember six different codes to get in, which he didn't think he could handle at the moment. He ushered Ness to a door in the hallway of the station and punched in a code. He pulled the door open, exposing a narrow metal staircase. At the bottom was what looked like a mini tennis pavilion, a small white bubble of a room. It was the most secure location in the entire station, and thus in the entire embassy. Victor tapped in a code on another cipher pad and the door to the bubble clicked open. He and Vanessa went in. There was nothing but a small table and four chairs. They sat down across from one another.

"You first," Victor said to Ness.

She closed her eyes a moment and took a deep breath. She told him about the transcript, about how it seemed likely Grandy was helping Redd run an illegal scheme to feed Russian money into Republican coffers, specifically into Redd's own Dick's SACPAC. In return, Vlastov—using Nikolai Surikov as his middleman—was asking Redd to state that Crimea was part of Russia, not Ukraine, and to voice his support for the RosAlleman pipeline. It was a clear-cut deal. Surikov had even hinted that, if Grandy delivered the goods, his long-desired permit to build a mall in Moscow would be approved.

"Maybe I'm interpreting it wrong?" Vanessa looked desperate. "Maybe there's an innocuous reading of the transcript?" She shook her head. "I don't see it. We know this isn't the first time Redd has accepted foreign money. He helped make it possible to accept foreign money, without it being called foreign money. Run it through an LLC. It's not corruption if you legalize it. But maybe there's another explanation?" She looked at Victor hopefully, although she already knew the answer.

Victor finally released her hand and leaned back in his chair. "There isn't. It's as bad as you think. In fact, it's worse. It looks like there was one scheme for Surikov to run money into Dick's SACPAC through Grandy's LLC in South Dakota. But Vlastov also used Surikov to funnel money from RosGaz to Da Italia, using financing for the RosAlleman pipeline, to help Callieri with elections here. It worked. They're running the same scheme for Redd. Max witnessed the deal go down in Moscow. Will Garrett was there."

"Redd's lawyer?"

"Talking to the same Russians who arranged payments for Callieri."

"Redd has his ambassador and his lawyer running illegal operations to keep him in office." She thought about Ashley-Anne Wynnscott meeting with Diana Abramovich, who sold her house for triple the average neighborhood price, to the director of New Russia News North America. "Redd's campaign manager was doing it too. How many schemes do you think they had going?" She looked up at Victor. "Or still have going?"

Victor thought a moment. She was right. It was likely that Vlastov, with help from his oligarchs and intelligence services, had at least attempted to set up multiple revenue streams to help Redd and his party. He and Vanessa now personally knew about three of those schemes. Redd and his supporters were already twisting the Ashley-Anne incident to make it seem like the FBI was spying on Redd's campaign. They hadn't named Vanessa, but he figured they would soon. Now, a second scheme—the one involving Grandy and Surikov—had landed in her lap. On top of that, Victor had a missing asset who had reported on the third illegal funding scheme, involving Redd's lawyer and Russian mobsters. This was information that could get high-level people in three countries—Russia, Italy, and the United States—in a lot of trouble if it were ever revealed.

He leaned forward and took her hands. "You could relay all this back to your boss in Washington, and he could report it to Congress. You'd have to do it in total secrecy, so Redd and his allies don't catch a whiff of it, because God knows what that vengeance would look like."

"What if people in Congress are compromised? Congressman Matt Donovan, the head of the House Intelligence Committee for Christ's sake, is threatening to release evidence about the incident involving me and Ashley-Anne."

"I think Senator Kyle Lewis is compromised too," Victor said. "He rode a bear."

"That would explain his speech to reporters last night, calling for lifting sanctions and starting a closer relationship with Russia. Svetlana knew what she was doing." Ness threw up her hands. "So, we have no faith in Congress."

"I have faith in the Constitution," Victor said. "Remember, I chose the United States. I wasn't born there. I have to have faith its people will adhere to the Constitution."

"Cue the swelling patriotic music," said Ness.

"I mean it," Victor continued. "Otherwise, what has all this been for?" he asked, gesturing around the bubble, which in that moment represented two decades of his life, their life. Two decades spent in the nearest and farthest reaches of the world in the service of a country he actively chose for its values. "You said it yourself at the Christmas party. If we can put this in the hands of a special prosecutor, you would be protected. Knowledge of the investigation would be public. It would be really hard for Redd or any of his buddies to stop it at that point. The media would also pick up the pieces and try to run down the details."

Ness looked at her husband and smiled. For once, he wasn't the cynical one. Despite everything he had seen and experienced over his twenty-year career—wars that still had not ended, dictators who managed to hold on to power, a political system corrupted more each year by dark money, a burdensome bureaucracy that required him to take a safety course before he could sit down—here he was, at the end of his career, still believing the good guys would win. "How is Max?" she asked.

He shook his head. The wave of guilt crashed over him once more. "He gave me a load of information yesterday. We were supposed to meet again this morning to finish up. He never showed. And now, Francesco told me an associate of the Russian assassin is in Italy. I don't know if Max got the jitters, if he's dead, or something else entirely."

"I'd love to tell you you're being dramatic, but . . ."

He took her hand again. "I know. It's possible." They sat like that in the bubble for a moment in silence, their minds racing. The Russian president had launched a multiprong attack on the West, using disinformation, hacking, leaking, money, political corruption, business corruption, assassinations, everything he could, to weaken it. While digging into the people carrying that out, Victor and Vanessa had come across very powerful American officials, the exact people who were supposed to protect the country—the president of the United States!—who were not only willing to allow it to happen but were actively participating in it. How would those people react if they knew they were found out? Would they come after Victor and Vanessa? Had they already come after Max?

"We're in trouble," Ness said.

Victor squeezed her hand. "I guess we shouldn't have gone after the criminals they chose to work with."

CHAPTER THIRTY-SEVEN

That evening, Victor and Vanessa walked home slowly through Villa Borghese, still holding hands. They strolled around to the back side of the Borghese gallery and went to the window. The gallery was closed but the lights were on. There was Persephone, being whisked away against her will to an unknown—but likely unpleasant—fate, by a force much larger than she was. They both took in her agony, never letting go of the other's hand.

At last, they turned away and continued toward home. Victor led Ness past several nude statues with their fig leaves and toward a bench in a far corner of the park. His pace picked up as they neared it.

"What's going on?" Ness asked.

"I know it's not likely, but I have to know. I'll be checking it every day now."

They walked toward the bench, Victor eyeing the side of it for a chalk mark, a sign of life from QDCHESHIRE.

Nothing.

Victor dropped his head and his shoulders slumped forward. They continued past the bench, Vanessa squeezing Victor's hand, encouraging him to hold on.

He barely slept that night. Images of Max poisoned in a hotel room or shot in the back, his body thrown in the bushes in a Roman park, kept popping into his head. In his twenty years with the CYA, he had never lost an asset. Had his luck run out? Worse, had he screwed up? He tossed and turned, relieved to see rays from the rising sun beginning to filter into the hallway outside his bedroom door. He slipped out of bed, happy to see Vanessa had managed to fall into a deep slumber, and dressed quietly to go to the office.

He armed himself with a double espresso at the cafe across from the embassy, then marched up the stairs to Rome Station. He sat on his ball. He took a deep breath and looked down at his neon blue bike helmet. He grabbed it, placed it on his head, and attached it, as if it were a battle helmet, then opened a map of Italy on his computer screen. He had a major problem to solve.

Several hours later, he saw Habibi was online. He picked up the green phone to call him.

"Seven in the morning and you're already there? I'll never understand Washington work hours," Victor said.

"I leave my house at five to get here. If I leave five minutes later, I don't get in until noon. Seriously, don't ever come back here. What's up?"

Victor told him what had happened with Max, then explained, "I've started working on an exfil plan, in case he shows up."

"He'll show up," Habibi reassured him. "You've never been one to take your asset's security lightly. If I know you, you drilled the protocol and the commo plan into his brain so many times, it will come naturally to him now that everything's gone tits up. What's your exfil plan?"

Victor looked at the map on his computer screen and outlined his idea for Habibi.

"It's a good plan." Habibi paused for a moment. "Shit, Ivan the commissar is coming for a visit. I have to go. You have a solid plan, Victor. Keep working out the details and we'll chat again soon." He hung up.

Victor went back to his research. He pulled up wind patterns, water currents, and weather trends. He pulled up a map of the coast and was studying it when COS Wilcox came in and looked at Victor sitting on his blue exercise ball wearing his neon blue helmet. From his look of disdain, Victor knew he was about to say something. Victor cut in first. "It's good for my back."

"No need to explain, Caro. I'm not judging."

"You're judging."

"I am judging. When did you grow a vagina?" Then he looked at Victor's computer screen. "First you take days at a time seeing the sites in order to meet your asset, and now you're planning another vacation?"

"It's an exfil plan."

Wilcox squinted at the screen. He looked thoughtful for a moment. "Is that the Mediterranean?"

Victor nodded. Wilcox wanted to contribute to the plan.

"I can call in the Sixth Fleet," he said. "We could bring in an aircraft carrier, a few destroyers, and an amphibious assault team."

"I don't think that will be necessary."

"Keep it in mind," Wilcox said. "I'll be back from Washington on Monday and we can discuss it then if you want."

"I didn't know you were heading back for consultations, chief."

"Not for consultations. I'm going back for my award ceremony." Victor looked at him, confused. "I won the gingerbread house competition! Director has a big party planned in my honor. I'm going to get a plaque . . ." he paused, encouraging Victor to guess the next part. "Made out of . . ."

"Made out of gingerbread?"

"Yes! We'll discuss your exfil when I'm back." Wilcox left the bullpen.

Victor turned his head and jumped when he realized DCOS Mary Driscoll was standing by his desk. He hadn't noticed her until she picked up an orange highlighter from a nearby table.

"I've spoken with the promotion panel, Victor. They were very pleased with your PowerPoint presentation. They said your creative use of the color purple was very insightful. It looks like you're in the running!"

Victor was about to say something when Patrick walked in behind Mary and made a gesture telling Victor to keep quiet. Mary left. Victor bounced over to Patrick's desk. "What was that?"

Patrick said, "I turned in a PowerPoint presentation on your behalf. Just purple slides with bullet points. You were so busy, and I had nothing to do since we won the war on terror. I thought I'd help you out."

"I appreciate that, Patrick. How are you on a boat?"

"I puke every time."

Victor bounced back to his work space. "Alright. No exfil for you then." He turned back to his research. "I hope Max doesn't do the same."

CHAPTER THIRTY-EIGHT

That night, Victor again walked home through Villa Borghese and passed the bench in the corner of the park behind the gallery. He was distressed to see there was still no chalk mark. A range of emotions stirred through him: fear, doubt, guilt, anger. The next morning, he passed it again, and again the following night on the way home. Each day, he felt more hopeless.

On the fourth evening, he walked home with Vanessa. Once again, they stopped by the back of the gallery to look at Persephone, then continued toward the bench. As they got closer, they both saw it: a small chalk mark on the side. They went a few more steps before Victor grabbed Vanessa and kissed her. He embraced her. Vanessa wrapped her arms tightly around him. He nearly collapsed, and she helped hold him up. She could feel him releasing pressure, finally breathing once again with the understanding of what it meant. He squeezed her back and whispered, "He's alive."

***

The following morning, Victor got up early. He put on his running gear and set out for an early morning jog. Or at least that's what anyone watching him would think. He ran through his neighborhood of Parioli and into Villa Ada, a park not far outside Rome's historic center that once belonged to the royal House of Savoy. He ran through an entrance gate and down a ramp, where stone pines and rare dawn redwood trees stood, covering him with their canopy. He felt the temperature drop in the shade. He ran along the well-trodden dirt path then turned off onto a smaller trail, which he followed up a hill and around some stables. He continued, ducking branches, until he reached a small creek. There, standing next to a boulder, was Max. He, too, was in running shorts and had a leg up on the rocks, as though he were stretching.

"You can't imagine how happy I am to see you," Victor said, holding a tree while he grabbed his right foot behind him, stretching his thigh muscles.

"I'm happy to see you too" Max said. "I'm sorry I disappeared. That evening, when I left you, I went for a walk in Urbino. Someone was following me. I saw him again the next morning. You and I had talked so much about security. Maybe I was being paranoid, but I decided not to risk meeting you."

"You did the right thing. Do you know who was following you?"

"I don't know and I didn't want to wait to find out. You mentioned to me the Georgian man in London, who drank the tea."

"Yes."

"Russian news also talked about a strange suicide in Rome. Was there more to that death too?"

"I didn't see the point in making you more scared."

"So, it could have been a Russian assassin following me? Or maybe Callieri's people?" He bent into a lunge stretch. "I always tell you that you are being paranoid. Now listen to me. Maybe it was nothing and the guy happened to be walking around the same time and place I was."

"I don't believe in coincidences," Victor said. He thought about his last conversation with Francesco.

Max looked at him. "Grigoriy has been calling me nonstop since that night. I keep finding excuses to put off meeting him." He switched legs. "You said you could get me out if I needed. Do you think I need to?"

Max had provided excellent intelligence and had incredible access to a high-priority target. It was heart-wrenching to end it. He thought about Grigoriy, Callieri, Redd, and Vlastov, the dead men in London and Rome, the assassin's associate taking in the Italian sites. He had never lost an asset, and was not about to start now. It was time to get QDCHESHIRE out. "I'm working on a plan," said Victor. "Meet me here in forty-eight hours. Go to work. Act normal."

"What is normal behavior for someone at risk of assassination?"

"Two days. I'll have it set up."

"Two days, my friend. Please, no more." Max ran off.

Victor splashed water from the creek over his face. He had spent the last several days pulling the pieces together. Now, he had forty-eight hours to finalize and execute the exfiltration plan for QDCHESHIRE without anyone finding out.

CHAPTER THIRTY-NINE

A clear blue sky spread over the Mediterranean Sea. Victor double-checked the equipment then looked at his watch.

"It's one minute later than when you last checked, Dad." Oliver shook his head. "He'll be here."

"Are you ready for this?" Victor asked.

"This is going to make the coolest college application essay ever. I helped my dad exfil an asset on a sailboat so he wouldn't get assassinated by Russians."

"You can't actually write that."

"You and Mom ruin everything."

Vanessa was below deck organizing their supplies, stacking water bottles under the floorboards and shoving bottles of wine into compartments behind the bench seat cushions. Just because it was an exfil operation didn't mean it couldn't be enjoyable.

Victor saw a man wearing a warm hat and carrying a backpack walking down the quay. It was Max. He stopped and looked at the sailboat. He looked up at Victor. "I thought you meant a big boat."

Victor recounted their second encounter in Villa Ada, when he told Max the details about his plan to get him to safety. He had tried to make the voyage sound easy, so as not to worry Max. "We've got three cabins. It's huge." He held out his hand to help Max on board. Max knocked his head against the boom, the large pole holding the bottom of the main sail, then slammed his knee on the side of the cockpit. "Maybe huge isn't the right word, but it's the right size for what we're doing. This is my first mate, Oliver."

Oliver shook his hand and said hello in Russian. Max raised his eyebrows.

"Maybe now isn't the time for Russian, Oliver. Let's get Max settled and get on our way." Oliver cussed in Russian and Max laughed.

Vanessa poked her head up from down below. "This is my wife, Vanessa."

"Hand me your bag," she said to Max. "I'll put it in your cabin."

He gave her his backpack then turned to Victor. "The prosecutor in Torino announced he is expanding his investigation into Stefano Valenti. It seems someone got an audio recording of him, Aldo Conti, and Luca Callieri discussing using RosGaz and GasItalia to fund Da Italia."

"Will Callieri have to step down?" Victor asked.

"This is Italy, Victor. The prosecutor will remain independent, but until he brings charges, the people still love Callieri."

Oliver threw off the mooring lines as Victor steered the boat out of the tiny port hidden behind Fiumicino airport.

"I put your new identification documents on your bunk," Victor said. He thought about Francesco, who had managed to supply the documents for Max within days after their last conversation.

He and his team had still not managed to locate the associate of the Russian assassin.

Vanessa came up top and she and Oliver began pulling up the boat's fenders. Victor smiled watching her. She had handed over to her boss all the information they had gathered. They had learned, just the night before, that Congress would publicly announce a special prosecutor to carry out an apolitical investigation of Russia and Redd's campaign. Her boss in Washington had asked her to join the special prosecutor's team.

It was welcome news. As corrupt as Congress' members had become, as dirty as the politics were, there were still people ready to do the right thing and embody the country's values. She would be working with the special prosecutor that would try to unearth the full nature of President Vlastov and President Redd's relationship. She would continue doing her part to serve the country she and Victor loved and had dedicated their careers—hell, their lives—to. Together they had taken on terrorists, narco-trafficking dictators, and now corrupt politicians who, for their own political and financial benefit, were willing to help a corrupt, power-hungry Russian president break an international system the United States had led for seventy years.

"Let's hope the investigation in Torino leads quickly to the arrest of Callieri and his cronies and ends this nightmare for my country," Max said, looking back toward land. "And that my exile won't be long."

Victor hoped the same for all of them. They—Victor, Vanessa, Max, the United States, Italy, democracy, the West—had been in deep trouble. Hopefully, this new investigation in Washington, and the Italian one in Torino, would get them all out of it.

Victor looked at the sea opening up before them. This would likely be one of the final acts he would carry out in his career, and it seemed fitting. Liberated on a sailboat, exfiltrating an asset from the country of his birth while protecting the country he had chosen. He smiled.

Oliver began pulling up the main sail, and Victor announced, "Sixteen hours to Ventotene."

"I brought zucchini flowers," Max said. "I will make us strozzapreti for dinner."

EPILOGUE

Valeriy Chekhov sat down at his desk and slid a notepad and pen in front of him. A glint of sun reflected off his Oscar statue and onto the paper. He picked up the pen and wrote, "Talking Points, for distribution to FaKU and NRN." His phone rang. It was Ruslan Bebchuk.

"Turn on the television to Redd's press conference." Bebchuk laughed then hung up.

Chekhov switched on his television. Redd was standing behind a lectern in the Rose Garden at the White House. Several journalists were taking notes.

"Congress has announced a special counsel to look into Russian interference in our election. This is all political. These people in Congress are only doing this because they hate me and they hate you. It is all part of a deep state plot aimed at delegitimizing me. They are Russophobes. Nothing more. They don't want to see us have good relations with Russia. The main people behind this plot are two holdovers from the previous administration, CYA officer Victor Caro and FBI agent Vanessa Caro. They're married! How is that for a coincidence? Two married deep state plotters who set up this whole Russia thing to try to make me look bad. And get this. This isn't the first time they've gone after me. These two unpatriotic lovebirds went after me years ago, when I was building strong relations, the strongest relations, with the Middle East. That's how devious these two are. How deep this plot goes. For years, they've been out to get me. They even engaged their own child—get this, how sick is this—they used their own son to infiltrate Russian youth groups, innocent Russian children! For what? Some sicko plot to get the Russians to like me and get me elected so these unpatriots could then go after me and try to get me thrown out of office. I have instructed the attorney general to launch an investigation into these two and many others, because there were others. Oh yes, there were plenty of others. He will be meeting with our friends in Rome, where so much of this plot against me took place. I have authorized him to tell the Italian government the United States will withhold foreign aid helping them with their immigration problem unless they tell us what we want to hear about these Victor and Vanessa characters. They even spied on the US ambassador at the Christmas party. Can you believe that? Sickening, how they desecrated our holiest of days. I have been informed that Victor, the sneaky CYA guy, retired. The CYA actually wanted to promote him! I can assure you I put the kibosh on that. Instead, the little coward retired. But I have instructed my staff to ensure this traitor won't get any of his retirement benefits. Why should he? What has he done for this country? And that wife of his, she's a piece of work. She was illegally spying on my campaign! We're going to get rid of her too. No clearances for either of them! If they have any thoughts that they're going to come back or work for contractors

or something, no way! Not on my watch! It's a Rolex, by the way."
He held up his wrist for the camera. "We haven't figured out who
their sources were, but the attorney general will be working on
that. As soon as we know, you'll know. Also, be sure to tune in
tomorrow night to Kip Lawson's Facts News. He'll be interviewing
Senator Kyle Lewis, who will be talking about increasing business
ties with Russia. He'll be speaking from the groundbreaking of the
new Kosmopolitan Mall in Moscow, which is being built by my
friend Ken Grandy. And stick around after I leave. Ashley-Anne
Wynscott will be up here to discuss our plan to include Cold Sun
lessons in our public-school science curriculum. Any questions?"

A journalist from Facts News raised her hand. Redd pointed to
her. "Sir, how do you plan to manage the intelligence community?
It must be frustrating to have an intelligence apparatus you don't
feel you can trust."

Valeriy put his pen down and pushed the notepad aside. He
leaned back in his chair and folded his hands across his stomach.
A wide grin spread across his face. He had no need to write up
talking points. The Americans were doing his job for him.

ACKNOWLEDGMENTS

Writing a humorous book in the middle of a global pandemic while simultaneously watching the country I served and love slide toward authoritarianism was not easy. Our strange, postfactual existence was so out of whack that it was hard to write anything satirical for fear it would be seen as either too absurd or too real.

I set out to write about the challenges of running intelligence operations when the president's allegiances are being questioned and when that president does nothing to help alleviate the suspicions (and, in fact, does everything to exacerbate them). But I was also frustrated by America's fixation on itself. Public debate about election interference was consistently filtered through a political lens, with Donald Trump smack in the middle. Lost in the conversation was the fact that Russia was carrying out similar operations across a huge swath of democratic countries. Vladimir Putin's goal was never Trump-specific. His aim was (and still is) to weaken democracies everywhere. Democracy anywhere is a threat to dictators everywhere. So, I set out to highlight that these operations were taking place in many countries that are our allies, in an effort to demonstrate that our political focus on the United States and Trump was short-sighted. That's not a very funny topic to satirize, but then again, neither was the war on terror. Yet, it was all so absurd, I figured there was material there. I hope I've succeeded in passing along my message while also being entertaining.

I was happy to have a number of people to help me keep my feet on the ground, firmly fixed in empirical reality, as I wrapped my head around the propaganda and disinformation operations that helped inform the book.

A big thanks to Chuck for reading an early draft and providing feedback in the nicest way possible, and who, despite the pitfalls of the early draft, offered to read a much later draft. Seriously, no one should have to do that. But he did so voluntarily and happily, and I am forever grateful for his insights, which greatly improved the manuscript. He and Kerstin also get a special shout-out for our regular walks, which kept us all sane during lockdowns and quarantines, and for their enthusiasm to hear about my process and my progress, often over a good glass of vermut. Thank you.

Tammy is a dear friend who has read and provided feedback on so much of my writing, and she always delivers it with humor and (usually) wine. My next writer's residency may be in her wine pantry.

Humayun is also a dear friend who has encouraged my writing for years and who has provided helpful critiques to improve. He was also, quite possibly, the most entertaining guest at our wedding.

Aki has proven a steady and reliable sparring partner. He also read an early draft and provided much-needed suggestions. I thank him for his willingness to help with any and all projects and enjoy his insights and humor.

I have to thank Chris and Amanda for Candy and the Freedom Hos. What started as a backyard barbecue joke simmered over the years to reemerge at the height of the pandemic lockdown when I most needed a laugh. It broke my writer's block and set me back on the path toward finishing this book.

Thank you to Patrick and Kevin for all the happy hours and your entertaining stories.

Jeffrey Smith gave me the chance to immerse myself in all things Russia and get paid for it, and I am forever grateful.

My agent, Judy Coppage, has been a reliable sounding board, and I appreciate her efforts to keep me going and her enthusiasm in sharing my work with people.

I want to thank my parents for their constant encouragement. My son inspired a lot of Oliver's dialogue in this book. I thank him for putting up with my constant warnings about disinformation and all the evil lurking online, as well as for indulging us during our dinner table conversations about geopolitics and the state of the world. Kid, you did not choose your parents wisely, but I am the luckier for it.

Lastly, I want to thank my husband. He reads multiple drafts of everything I write and is always willing to help me work through my ideas, often over a glass of wine or during a long walk. Without him, Victor would not exist.

Did you enjoy this book? Great!
Would you mind doing me a favor?

Like all authors, I rely on online reviews to encourage future sales. Your opinion is invaluable. Would you take a few moments now to share your assessment of my book at the review site of your choice? Your opinion will help the book marketplace become more transparent and useful to all.

Thank you very much!

ABOUT THE AUTHOR

Alex Finley is a former officer of the CIA's Directorate of Operations, where she served in West Africa and Europe. Before becoming a bureaucrat living large off the system, she chased puffy white men around Washington, DC, as a member of the wild dog pack better known as the Washington media elite. Her writing has appeared in Slate, Reductress, Funny or Die, POLITICO, Vox, the Center for Public Integrity, and other publications. She has spoken to the BBC, C-SPAN's The Washington Journal, CBC's The National, Sirius XM's Yahoo! Politics, France24, the Spy Museum's SpyCast, and other media outlets.

Follow her on Twitter: @alexzfinley

alexzfinley.com